Praise for the
# MURDER MOST UNLADYLIKE
mysteries

Murder Most Unladylike mysteries:

# MURDER MOST UNLADYLIKE

# ARSENIC FOR TEA

# FIRST CLASS MURDER

# JOLLY FOUL PLAY

# MISTLETOE AND MURDER

# A SPOONFUL OF MURDER

# DEATH IN THE SPOTLIGHT

# TOP MARKS FOR MURDER

# DEATH SETS SAIL

Tuck-box-sized mysteries:

# CREAM BUNS AND CRIME

Based on an idea and characters
by Siobhan Dowd:

# THE GUGGENHEIM MYSTERY

# ONCE UPON A CRIME

A MURDER
MOST UNLADYLIKE
Collection

## ROBIN STEVENS

PUFFIN

PUFFIN BOOKS

UK | USA | Canada | Ireland | Australia
India | New Zealand | South Africa

Puffin Books is part of the Penguin Random House group of companies
whose addresses can be found at global.penguinrandomhouse.com.

www.penguin.co.uk
www.puffin.co.uk
www.ladybird.co.uk

First published 2021

001

Set in 11/16 pt ITC New Baskerville Std
Typeset by Jouve (UK), Milton Keynes
Printed and bound in Great Britain by Clays Ltd, Elcograf S.p.A.

A CIP catalogue record for this book is available from the British Library

Imported into the EEA by Penguin Random House Ireland,
Morrison Chambers, 32 Nassau Street, Dublin D02 YH68

ISBN: 978–0–241–41983–0

All correspondence to:
Puffin Books
Penguin Random House Children's
One Embassy Gardens, 8 Viaduct Gardens, London SW11 7BW

Penguin Random House is committed to a
sustainable future for our business, our readers
and our planet. This book is made from Forest
Stewardship Council® certified paper.

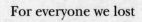

For everyone we lost

Being an account of cases old and new
from the Detective Society, the
Junior Pinkertons and May Wong.

September 1939

# CONTENTS

# THE CASE OF THE UNINVITED GUEST

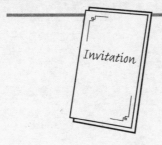

Being an account of
What Happened at Uncle Felix and
Aunt Lucy's Wedding,
an investigation by the Wells and Wong
Detective Society.

Written by Hazel Wong
(Detective Society Vice-President and Secretary),
aged 14.

Begun 3rd January 1936.

This is not the story of a murder case. It might well have been, which gives me a funny feeling when I think how close we came to disaster. But it *is* the story of a mystery, a very puzzling and dramatic one, that the Detective Society solved during a most important wedding.

The Detective Society, of course, is Daisy Wells and me, Hazel Wong. We are fourth formers at Deepdean School for Girls – though lately we have felt much more like detectives than schoolgirls, for only two days ago we were still in Cambridge, where we solved our fifth murder.

The wedding was Daisy's uncle Felix's, and it took place on New Year's Day 1936, in London, at the St Pancras Registry Office. It was the first English wedding I had ever been to, and I was rather surprised at how different it was from the weddings I have read about in books. Story weddings have clouds of tulle and yards of satin, bridesmaids with posies and Kate Greenaway

3

dresses, and the voices of angelic choirs echoing off vaulted church ceilings. Uncle Felix and Miss Livedon's wedding turned out to be nothing like that at all.

Daisy's great-aunt, Aunt Eustacia, was shocked when Uncle Felix and Miss Livedon came to visit us at St Lucy's College in Cambridge and told us their plans. 'What are you thinking?' she said to Miss Livedon. 'A wedding without a white dress! With hardly any guests! On a simply ridiculous day of the year! If that nephew of mine is forcing you into this—'

'He certainly is not,' said Miss Livedon cheerfully. 'We've discussed it thoroughly. Neither of us are interested in making a fuss. We simply want to be married, and New Year's Day is the perfect day for a quiet ceremony. No one is paying attention. And as for the dress, I spend my life wearing the most ridiculous costumes, so it's perfectly reasonable for me to want to look sensible and like myself on my wedding day. I will wear my blue skirt suit, and Daisy and Hazel can tie blue ribbons round dresses that they already have. We shall all match nicely.'

Aunt Eustacia huffed furiously and stalked off back down the chilly college corridor to her office.

'I don't know what she's so upset about,' said Daisy. 'It isn't as though *she's* ever been married! She's perfectly no-nonsense and unconventional usually.'

I wondered if that was part of the reason. I was also scretly rather pleased that Daisy and I had escaped being dressed up like dolls. Daisy is a vision in lace, but I simply look as though I'm pretending.

There was only one thing I was worried about. 'But what about the cake?' I asked Daisy on our last night in Cambridge as we pulled our white dresses from our cases and laid them out for the St Lucy's maid to iron. The cake is a very important part of English book weddings, and I quite desperately wanted to taste one in real life.

'Of course there will be cake,' said Daisy. 'It simply isn't a wedding without cake, Hazel.'

We drove down to London on New Year's Day, bowling through the countryside in Uncle Felix's silver rocket car. It was so cold that breathing gave me a tingle in my throat and I had to tuck my hands into my warm winter coat. We left Cambridge when all the light in the sky was still an orange and blue glow at the very far horizon, and we drove through the sunrise, light sparkling off the snow on the soft hills around us.

Daisy was snuggled down next to me, her nose in the fur of her coat, and Aunt Eustacia was crammed in beside her. Miss Livedon sat in the front, with Daisy's brother Bertie next to her, and Uncle Felix drove. As we came into London the winter sun was on my face and I could hear church bells ringing out. I felt myself smiling.

As the car stopped outside the registry office, Aunt Eustacia and Miss Livedon got out and made their way towards the building, with Bertie following behind them. But as we began to climb out of the car, Uncle Felix turned to us.

'Daisy, Hazel,' he said. 'One moment, please. I have a job for you.'

'Collecting a bouquet, I suppose,' said Daisy witheringly. 'You know Miss Livedon doesn't have one? Really, Uncle Felix, you haven't put any thought into this wedding at *all*.'

'The maid of honour is bringing the bouquet with her shortly, Daisy,' said Uncle Felix. 'And don't be so impertinent, otherwise I shan't give you this special job at all.' His voice had dropped, and he was leaning towards us seriously. I realized with a jump that this might be detective business.

'Don't you threaten us like that!' cried Daisy. 'Hazel, tell him that we're up to it!'

'Please, we're listening,' I said rather awkwardly to Uncle Felix. He is so very blond and grand that I am always a little nervous about speaking familiarly to him. 'Er, what do you want us to do?'

'I need you to look out for someone,' said Uncle Felix.

I could feel Daisy's ears perk up.

'Or rather, I want to you ensure that a *particular person* is not allowed to come anywhere near the registry office. They must not enter the building, and they must certainly

6

not come into the room where the ceremony is being held. If they do, there will be terrible consequences.'

'What consequences?' breathed Daisy.

'None of your business, nosy niece,' said Uncle Felix, grinning.

'What do they look like?' I asked. I was imagining a shadowy figure, a man in a bowler hat and suit.

'A woman,' said Uncle Felix. My shadowy man evaporated. 'About fifty – that is, older than me, younger than Aunt E.'

'*Everyone's* younger than Aunt E,' said Daisy.

'Rude,' said Uncle Felix. 'Don't let her hear you say that. Anyway, this woman is tall, grey-haired and big-nosed. She will most likely be carrying a large handbag. If you see her, you must come and find me immediately, do you understand?'

'No!' said Daisy at once. 'I don't understand at all. Who is this woman? Why don't you want her about? Is she a spy? What if she's in disguise?'

'You don't need to know any of that to do the job,' said Uncle Felix, screwing his monocle tighter into his eye to stop himself smiling. 'And I trust you to see through any disguise. Do you accept?'

'Of course we do!' cried Daisy.

She seized my arm and dragged me out of the car so that the sleeve of my coat twisted. 'Ouch!' I cried.

'Hazel, be quiet. We are going to be detectives!' hissed Daisy.

I sighed.

The registry office was a handsome yellow-stone building with a set of steps leading to a wide stone archway. The steps were dusted with snow and scattered freshly with white petals.

'That's from the last wedding,' said Daisy to me knowledgeably. 'Registry offices have lots every day. Oh, who's that woman?'

She was glaring over my shoulder at someone coming down the street towards us. I turned and looked. It was a woman – but I did not think it could be the person we were supposed to warn Uncle Felix about. She was younger than fifty, almost the same age as Miss Livedon (though I am never sure what age I think Miss Livedon is exactly; she can look older or younger depending on how she is dressed), and she was of medium height, with a thin face and a long thin nose holding up a pair of black spectacles. She was wearing a smart pink skirt suit and a little hat and holding a bouquet of red roses and yellow lilies, and she waved enthusiastically.

'Lucy!' she cried. 'Hallo!'

Miss Livedon, standing halfway up the steps brushing dust from her own skirt suit, which was a beautiful bright blue with a red silk blouse underneath, threw up her hands and gave a most un-Miss Livedonish cry of delight.

'Ethel!' she shouted. 'Ethel!' And she leaped towards the woman, her smart red high heels striking the stone steps. The two embraced, laughing. 'You haven't changed a bit!' cried Miss Livedon.

'Of course I have,' said the woman called Ethel. 'So have you. But – oh, I should still know you anywhere!'

'Felix, everyone – this is Ethel Baker,' said Miss Livedon, turning to us with her arm round Ethel's waist. 'We met at school, *years* ago. Oh, dear old Headington Grammar!'

'School friends!' said Daisy.

'Yes, don't be so suspicious, Daisy,' said Uncle Felix. 'Ethel is Lucy's maid of honour. I should think you'd have guessed that from the flowers.'

Daisy turned red. She hates to be out-detected by anyone.

I was staring at Ethel and Miss Livedon with a very odd feeling in my stomach. *School friends* is what Daisy and I are. I cannot imagine, now that I know her, ever being without her – but might it happen, anyway, once we are old and grown up? I thought about being married then, and decided that I could not imagine Daisy ever marrying anyone.

Uncle Felix looked at his watch. 'Time to go inside,' he said. He turned away up the steps, ushering Aunt

Eustacia before him – but before he did so he looked at me and Daisy significantly through his monocle, and I knew that he meant for us to keep watch.

The columned and softly carpeted stone foyer was confusingly full of people. There was a charwoman sweeping up more petals from the earlier wedding, a woman in a smart grey skirt suit hurrying past us, clutching some documents to her chest, a clerk-like man pinning papers to a large noticeboard and another standing at the entrance of an office, looking doubtfully at us as we entered.

'Eleven o'clock, is it?' he asked. 'Mountfitchet and Livedon? I am Mr Tempest, the registrar.'

Then a figure detached itself from the shadow of a pillar and stepped towards us. It gave me rather a shock. He was an old man, round-shouldered and a little hunched, with greyish skin and a very worn brown suit. How had I missed him?

'Mountfitchet!' said the man in a voice just as grey as he was. 'Pardon me for waiting inside, but I was early.'

'Sir!' cried Uncle Felix, striding over to him and clapping him on the back. I half expected dust to float up off his jacket. 'Thank you for coming! Please meet my fiancée. Lucy, this is the Old Man.'

Daisy nudged me hard, an expression of delight on her face. Bertie rolled his eyes at us.

'That's the Old Man!' she hissed at me. 'He's famous!'

'I've never heard of him!' I whispered back.

'*Exactly!*' said Daisy. 'Only the most important people have heard of him! He works with Uncle Felix, Hazel. Or, should I say, Uncle Felix works for *him*.'

It is difficult to talk about Uncle Felix's work. *He* never does, for a start. And it does seem ridiculous to write in black and white that I think he is *a spy*. But I suppose our adventures would seem quite ridiculous to most people, and I know that they are quite real.

That was not the only surprise we were to have, though. The woman who had been sweeping the floor put down her broom against the wall and untied her apron. I saw that her dress, though not particularly well fitting, was nicer than I had first assumed, and although she looked very round and unprepossessing, her eyes were sharp and her chin had a determined set to it.

I tensed. Was *this* the woman we had been asked to watch for?

'Lucy,' she said. 'I fear I am a little early.'

'Oh!' said Miss Livedon, laughing. 'Miss Sperry! Very good!'

'I try,' said the woman, dusting her dress down efficiently. 'I noticed the Old Man ten minutes ago, though I don't think he saw me.'

The registrar, Mr Tempest, was staring at Miss Sperry and the Old Man with his mouth hanging open. Uncle

Felix turned the full force of his most charming smile on him, twinkling his blue eyes.

'As you'll see, the party is all here,' he said. 'Shall we begin?'

'I—' said Mr Tempest weakly.

Ethel handed Miss Livedon her bouquet, and she moved to stand next to Uncle Felix, her hand on his arm. They both stared at the registrar, and he wilted before them.

'If the bride and groom come into my office,' he muttered, 'we can take care of the preliminaries. I assume you have your identification documents with you? And the two witnesses? I will need you after the bride and groom.'

Uncle Felix gestured at the Old Man and Miss Sperry.

'And I believe you are going to be the best man, sir?' Mr Tempest asked Bertie.

Bertie gulped and nodded. He had been unusually quiet all morning, and I saw now how very nervous he was.

'Marvellous. Then the ceremony can begin at eleven, as scheduled. Your final guest is already waiting in the Collins Room, by the way.'

'What final guest?' asked Uncle Felix sharply. 'This is the wedding party in its entirety. The two bridesmaids, my aunt, my best man, my fiancée's school friend and her colleague, and my own colleague. We are not expecting anyone else.'

Mr Tempest had clearly had enough.

'The lady was very clear that she was here for the eleven o'clock ceremony,' he said stiffly. 'We are a public building, not a members' club, sir. We do not refuse entry to anyone. She is waiting in the Collins Room where the ceremony will be held, as I said. You may go and see her if you would like.'

'*Daisy*,' said Uncle Felix. '*Hazel.*'

We understood at once. As Uncle Felix and Miss Livedon went into the registrar's office to do whatever mysterious thing brides and grooms have to do before a wedding, and Aunt Eustacia, Bertie, the Old Man, Ethel and Miss Sperry made awkward grown-up small talk in the foyer, Daisy and I went rushing into the ceremony room.

And there, just as Mr Tempest had said, was a woman already sitting in one of the guest chairs.

Again, I had a moment of panic: *was* this the mysterious woman Uncle Felix had asked us to guard against? But a single calmer glance told me that she could not be. She was younger than fifty, younger even than Miss Livedon and Ethel – and although you might make yourself older with a disguise, you cannot look much *younger* without something giving you away. And – most importantly – her nose was small and snub, not big. I know perfectly well that no matter how good you are at disguises, you cannot make your nose significantly *shorter* than it is. This woman was not the person we were looking for.

But who *was* she?

I looked at her with my detective eyes. She had walked here – her shoes were still wet with melted snow. Her dress was well cut and expensive, but a little old. She wore no rings on her fingers, but she was holding a small reticule, clutching it close to her chest.

Daisy and I glanced at each other. She gave the tiniest of nods to me, and I knew that we were agreed: this was not our mysterious woman, but it *was* a mystery that we must solve as quickly as we could.

She stepped towards the woman, and I followed.

It is funny to see Daisy at work. When she is not being watched, she moves like a burglar. But when she wants to convince people she is not a threat she skips about like a sweet little girl, and this is how she walked now. She tripped over to the woman's chair, a vision in white and blue, and plopped down next to her with a happy sigh. I moved in on the other side, so she was pinned between us.

The woman jumped, and made a small noise of surprise.

'Goodness!' she said. 'Hello!'

'*Hello!*' said Daisy, giving a charming smile and a blue-eyed stare very similar to Uncle Felix's a few minutes before. 'What's your name?'

'I'm – I'm Miss Foster,' said the woman, blinking nervously. 'And who are—'

'Are *you* here for the wedding too?'

'Oh – yes . . .' said Miss Foster hesitantly. 'But . . .'

'Are you friends with the bride or the groom?' I asked.

'Oh, the bride,' said Miss Foster after a pause. 'School, you know. We sat next to each other in Latin. Lily was always a bookish girl. It seems so far away now!'

She glanced around nervously and tightened her fingers on her handbag. I saw Daisy watching it like a cat.

'Where is everyone?' Miss Foster burst out. 'I was sure there would be others – this is most odd!'

'Oh, they'll be on their way,' said Daisy smoothly. 'They'll be waiting for – what *is* his name? You know, old—'

'Oh, Uncle Mark!' cried Miss Foster, smiling for the first time. 'Yes, I remember, L never could *stand* how slow he is!'

'Uncle Mark,' said Daisy. 'Of course.'

I had a moment of uncertainty. The names Lily and Uncle Mark meant nothing to me – but what if this really was one of Miss Livedon's friends, who knew her under another one of her many names? What if everything was perfectly understandable? But then—

'Just think,' said Daisy. 'In half an hour she'll be quite a different person!'

'Mrs Harcourt,' sighed Miss Foster. 'Mrs Gerard Harcourt. Oh, it does seem such a long time since we were all at dear old Deepdean together!'

'But *we're* at Deepdean!' I cried.

Miss Foster lit up. 'Never!' she gasped. 'Oh, has it changed? Is Miss Lappet still there?'

Daisy launched into a swift, easy conversation about lessons and mistresses and House and bunbreak – and gave me a meaningful glance while she did so. We finally had a last name – Harcourt – one that I, and clearly Daisy too, had never heard before. This woman was not here for Uncle Felix and Miss Livedon's wedding, after all. So why was she here?

Miss Foster kept talking (she missed school terribly, and it sounded that she had come down in the world since she had left Deepdean – she was now secretary to a horrid businessman who made her work at weekends and holidays). 'The Clemences were always so good to me!' she kept on saying. 'We all had such good fun in the hols! L was so wild, of course, running away and so on, but Mr and Mrs Clemence always forgave her.'

Daisy cleared her throat significantly, and I said, 'Excuse me. I must just use the—'

I hurried out of the Collins Room and back into the corridor that led to the registry office foyer. I went up to the board I had seen the clerk pinning a piece of paper to.

'Hullo, Hazel!' said Bertie, a nervous wobble in his voice – I guessed from the thought of being Uncle Felix's best man. 'Where are you off to in such a hurry?'

'Oh,' I said, trying to seem calm and ordinary. 'I'm just looking at the noticeboard. Daisy wanted me to make sure of something.'

'Hmm,' said Bertie, and I thanked everything that he was too preoccupied to really consider how odd this sounded.

I peered at the board, and saw a list of names and the date *1ˢᵗ January 1936.*

10 a.m.: Roger Thomas Bowen and Annie
    Bradley
11 a.m.: Felix Henry Charles Seldom
    Mountfitchet and Lucy Felicity Livedon
12 p.m.: Gerard Harcourt and Lily Victoria
    Clemence

It was odd. It made my fingers tingle. Was Miss Foster simply confused about the timings of the two weddings? Or was someone telling a lie?

I hurried back to the Collins Room. As I stepped through the door, Daisy said, 'But, goodness, don't you think we ought to clear out of here? The eleven o'clock wedding will take place in twelve minutes!'

Miss Foster looked bewildered. 'Of course I shall stay,' she said. 'The eleven o'clock is Lily and Gerard's wedding!'

'I'm afraid it isn't,' I said. 'I went to look just now. Their wedding is at twelve. The eleven o'clock is Felix Mountfitchet and Lucy Livedon.'

'But . . .' Miss Foster cried. 'But – oh, what a mix-up! I did wonder – but then the invitation arrived in the post, and it most *definitely* said eleven o'clock. Perhaps . . .'

Miss Foster, I thought, as I came back to where she and Daisy were sitting, seemed like the sort of person who did not finish her thoughts or sentences properly. It was most frustrating – or, I wondered suddenly, perhaps it was deliberate. Was she on her guard as much as we were? How did we know she was telling the truth?

'Invitation?' asked Daisy.

'Oh yes, here, look,' said Miss Foster – and at last her fingers moved on her little reticule and she clicked it open. We leaned forward. I caught a glimpse of the shadowed insides of the bag, with powder compact and lipstick, and plenty of pencils and paper – and two other things. One was a tiny green glass bottle and the other was something that glinted in the room's electric lights. It was as long as my hand, silver and sharp. Surely it could not be . . . a knife?

But before I could lean forward further and make sure of it, Miss Foster drew a bit of card out and shut the reticule again with a snap.

'See here!' she said. 'Eleven o'clock sharp at St Pancras Registry Office.'

We both looked. Miss Foster was holding out a pretty cream invitation, handwritten in green ink. It said:

> You are invited to the wedding of
> ### Gerard Harcourt &
> ### the Honourable Lily Victoria Clemence
> at 11 o'clock sharp at the St Pancras Registry Office, London NW1
>
> Please arrive twenty minutes early
>
> celebrations to follow

'The noticeboard was wrong, of course; that's what Lily said in her letter,' Miss Foster went on distractedly. 'She told me that there had been some mix-up, but eleven o'clock was quite definitely the time— Oh, I don't understand it!'

'The noticeboard was wrong?' asked Daisy, giving her best kind look.

'Yes, you see, I saw it last week. I came in to run an errand for Mr Thompson – his office is only a few minutes away, and he needed me to work all the way up to Christmas this year – and I just happened to glance over at the board in the foyer. And Lily's name *leaped* out at me. I enquired and they gave me her London address – lucky, or I should have written to her in Scotland, you know. I wrote to her asking if I might be allowed to come. She wrote back – so thoughtful; I haven't seen her for years – and enclosed this invitation. And here I am. But I simply don't understand it! Perhaps— Oh, I don't understand *at all*!'

'Excuse us for a moment,' said Daisy smoothly. 'Hazel and I will go and see if we can discover what has happened. You stay there.'

'Thank you!' said Miss Foster gratefully, clinging to her handbag. Her lip wobbled a little, I saw – she really was nervous. But again I wondered. Could we believe her story? Or was there more to this than there seemed?

We slipped out of the Collins Room and huddled in the corridor.

'Emergency Detective Society meeting!' hissed Daisy. 'We have less than ten minutes to solve this case. So, quickly, *talk*. Can we believe her?'

'I don't know, Daisy. But I saw inside her bag, and I think she had a knife!' I said.

'It did look like one, didn't it?' agreed Daisy. 'And that bottle – could it be poison . . . or ink? That invitation is interesting, isn't it? Handwritten, which is very suggestive.'

'Why?' I asked. 'Oh! Because—'

'Because there's no way of knowing how many other people were sent the invitation, or even whether it's real,' said Daisy. 'You might handwrite invitations to a hundred people, or one. Which suggests four possibilities. Watson, list them.'

'Either she was sent an invitation with the wrong time by mistake,' I said, 'or she was sent the invitation with the wrong time on purpose. Or, she wrote out the invitation herself and made a mistake with the time, or she wrote the wrong time on purpose.'

'If the first,' said Daisy, nodding, 'then there is nothing to worry about. If the second, third or fourth, then we most certainly do need to worry. All right. Say it's *the second* – which, I have to say, seems a distinct possibility. After all, she said Lily claimed that the noticeboard at the registry office – the one that says this other wedding's meant to start to twelve – was wrong, when we know it isn't. So, who might want to send Miss Foster the wrong invitation, and why?'

'Well, the bride – like you've just said, she told Miss Foster in her letter that the wedding was definitely at eleven. You might write the time down wrong just once, if you weren't concentrating, but she did it twice, and that has to have been on purpose. Or perhaps it was the groom, pretending to be his fiancée – or another guest – wanting Miss Foster to miss the wedding!' I said. As soon as I did, I knew that was wrong. 'But it can't be.

She's here already, so all she needs to do is wait until twelve. Why would anyone want her to arrive at the wedding *early*?'

'If she wrote it herself, that might make rather more sense,' said Daisy. 'It gives her a reason to arrive at the registry office before the rest of the wedding party. And – well. You saw inside her handbag. Once we are all in the Collins Room for Uncle Felix and Miss Livedon's ceremony, she'd be quite free to wander about the rest of the registry office alone. What if she wants to lie in wait for the bride or groom, and use the knife or the bottle on them?'

'It's possible,' I said. 'We don't *know* she's the bride's friend, do we? We only have her word for it. We don't know anything about her at all!'

'No we don't,' said Daisy. 'She might be anyone. She might be a – a jilted lover! She might be this Gerard person's secret wife! She might be blackmailing them!'

Daisy, I thought, was stretching probability – but I did agree with her that we could not simply believe Miss Foster's story.

'We need to find out who these Gerard and Lily people are,' said Daisy determinedly.

'What are you doing?' asked a voice. We looked round. It was Ethel, Miss Livedon's friend. She was clutching Miss Livedon's bouquet of flowers, and there was a worried look on her face.

'There's a woman in there who shouldn't be,' I said, nodding at the door to the Collins Room. Daisy made a clicking noise with her teeth, and I knew what she was thinking: we did not know Ethel, not really. Miss Livedon knew her, and Miss Livedon (for all her secrecy) was a friend of the Detective Society – but was that enough? We have learned again and again, and sometimes quite horribly, that knowing someone does not mean you know everything they are capable of.

Ethel gasped. 'Fifty-ish?' she asked. 'Tall? Big nose?'

'No!' said Daisy, and now she was looking at Ethel appraisingly. So she knew about that woman too.

Ethel breathed out in relief, and somehow that convinced me.

'This is a younger woman,' I told her. 'She's here for the wedding after ours, but she's got her timings wrong. She thinks the wedding at eleven is between Gerard Harcourt and Lily Clemence.'

'The *Honourable* Lily Clemence,' said Daisy. 'Have you heard of either of them?'

Ethel looked puzzled. 'Clemence,' she said. 'Why do I know that name . . .? Oh, of course! John Clemence, MP for East Lothian. Yes, I think he does have daughters.'

'I know Harcourt,' said a deep, dusty voice in the corridor. We all jumped, and I backed against Daisy. Somehow, although it ought to have been impossible, the Old Man was leaning against the closed door to our left, his suit perfectly blending into the shadowed wood. 'He has troubled us before.'

'Who—' said Daisy.

'Gerard Harcourt is a bounder,' said the Old Man, and then he coughed rather apologetically. 'Excuse my language. From a perfectly respectable family, which I suppose is the problem. Given the world on a plate, which often I've found leads to boredom. Sometimes it is the good kind of boredom –' his eyes raked across us, and I wriggled – 'and sometimes it is the bad. Gerard Harcourt has the bad kind. Burned through his father's money after his death and then tried to turn to con-artistry, quite unsuccessfully. But companies got wise to him, with a little help from our organization – they won't accept any kind of credit note in his name these days – so, last I'd heard, he was trying to make money the old-fashioned way again.'

'Working?' asked Ethel, who was clearly just as interested as we were.

'Marriage,' said the Old Man. 'But, of course, any self-respecting parent wouldn't admit him into their home. I did hear he was trying to court the older Clemence girl – she stands to inherit a sizeable fortune on her marriage – but her father wouldn't give consent. I see that his disapproval had the usual effect. Pity, I thought the girl had more sense than that. She always seemed a thoughtful, rather bookish creature, quite unlike – well.

People do change, and there is nothing more romantic than being told you mayn't have someone.'

I looked at my wristwatch. The time was five minutes to eleven. I got a funny feeling then. We had a wicked man marrying a woman he had been forbidden to. We had a guest who had arrived for that wedding at the wrong time. The two things felt somehow connected, and important, and – dangerous. I turned to Daisy, and saw that she was wearing her most thoughtful expression.

'Lucy and Mr Mountfitchet will be ready in a moment,' said Ethel to us. 'Will you go and remove that lady? She oughtn't to be in our ceremony. I know Lucy won't be pleased.' She looked back at the foyer, where Bertie was pacing about, muttering to himself and fiddling with his buttonhole, while Aunt Eustacia tried to calm him.

'We ought to go and attend to the bride and groom,' said the Old Man. 'I trust the two of you can deal with this small problem?'

'I don't like this,' Daisy said, once Ethel and the Old Man had gone.

'There's something *wrong*!' I burst out. 'I can feel it!'

'The question is, what can we do about it? We're almost out of time,' said Daisy.

'Something dreadful is going to happen,' I said. I could feel it in all of my detective senses. 'We *have* to make her leave.'

'I've just thought of something,' said Daisy. 'The Old Man said that Mr Harcourt has been trying to get married for a while. What if Miss Foster is one of the women who he tried with? What if she's in love with him, but when he found out she doesn't have enough money he jilted her – and she's angry that he's marrying her school friend instead? What if she's here for *revenge*?'

I thought of the bottle and the knife.

'Or – wait! What if he *did* marry her, and then threw her over! You saw her dress, Hazel – expensive, but from at least three seasons ago. Perhaps that's why she's poor and has to be someone's secretary. What if Mr Harcourt is about to commit bigamy, and she's here to stop him?'

'Perhaps, Daisy,' I said. 'But it doesn't quite explain the invitation, does it?'

'Hmm,' said Daisy, frowning. 'Oh, let's go and talk to her one more time. We may uncover something crucial!'

We burst back into the Collins Room. Miss Foster, still sitting alone in her chair, started.

'Is everyone on their way?' she cried.

'Miss Foster,' said Daisy, 'there really has been a mix-up. Lily's wedding is definitely at twelve, not eleven o'clock.'

Miss Foster's face crumpled. 'I don't understand how I could have been so silly about that invitation!' she said. 'I ought to have known – the notice did say twelve!'

I realized I believed Miss Foster's story. She truly had nothing to do with the incorrect invitation. Someone else *had* sent it to her. But – *why*?

'I do hope that John and Emmeline and Isabelle will be here,' Miss Foster was saying. 'Even if it is to be a quiet affair. Why, I haven't seen them since—'

Ethel popped her head round the door.

'Three minutes!' she hissed. 'Hurry up! Daisy, Hazel, Lucy needs you with her.'

'You have to go, Miss Foster!' said Daisy.

'Please,' I said, 'please will you leave? Can't you go home?'

Miss Foster stared at me.

'Certainly not!' she said. 'I came especially. Besides, Lily wants me here!'

'Does she?' asked Daisy. 'Because – what if she put the wrong time on purpose to embarrass you?'

'Lily is my friend!' said Miss Foster, flushing. 'She would never be so cruel. I've known her for years, since we were all girls together. You are horrid children!' She leaped up and rushed out of the room, clutching her reticule to her like a shield.

'We are not children!' muttered Daisy.

I wanted to shout just like Miss Foster. It was utterly frustrating – I ought to be excited about the wedding, but all I could think of was the mystery.

'Why does real life always get in the way of detection?' Daisy hissed at me as we hurried towards the door and stood on either side of it.

Aunt Eustacia, Miss Sperry and the Old Man walked past us to take their places on two of the waiting seats. Ethel gave me and Daisy yellow lily stems to hold. (I got rather a shock at that – we seemed not to be able to escape lilies today.) Daisy adjusted the blue ribbon on my dress. I found that my heart was pounding.

And then there was Bertie with another lily in his buttonhole, trembling in his morning suit and squeezing something in his right hand.

'Easy, old boy,' said Uncle Felix, clapping him soothingly on the back. 'Don't crush the rings before you hand them over.'

Uncle Felix looked just as smooth and golden as ever, I thought – but then I saw that his hand on Bertie's shoulder was shaking, and he was screwing in his monocle again and again like an automaton and wiping at his eyes.

They walked by us, Uncle Felix turning and giving Daisy a smile so nervous that my own stomach clenched. His face had gone curiously red. Mr Tempest followed, his black wedding register under his arm and a sheaf of papers in his hand.

Then a side door opened into the corridor behind us, and out came Miss Livedon and Ethel.

I have always thought that stories about brides on their wedding day – that love makes them radiant and more beautiful than they have ever been – were nonsense. But, looking at Miss Livedon, I suddenly understood. Miss Livedon, just like Uncle Felix, still looked like she always had, square-jawed and brown-haired, and although her blue suit was beautifully cut, it was really quite ordinary. But somehow her entire face shone, her eyes bright with not crying, and when Ethel gasped, 'Lucy! You look so lovely!' I entirely agreed.

'I wish my hands would stop shaking,' said Miss Livedon. 'What if something goes wrong?'

'That's what the bouquet is for, I think,' said Ethel. 'Nothing will go wrong, dear. It's all quite all right.'

'Bridesmaids, are you ready?' asked Miss Livedon.

Daisy curtseyed beautifully and I nodded – and Miss Livedon proceeded inside the Collins Room, with Ethel just behind her, and Daisy and I following. But just before the door closed behind us, I turned and saw Miss Foster disappearing into a side room with a woman in a grey suit who looked familiar to me. I had seen her before today – but where?

I could not think – and then it was too late. We were walking up the aisle, and a gramophone was playing the wedding march, and Miss Livedon was laughing and sobbing, moving towards a beaming Uncle Felix at such a pace that Daisy and I could barely keep up with her.

Then they were both standing in front of Mr Tempest the registrar, clasping hands and staring into each other's eyes so intently that they seemed to forget that any of the rest of us were there.

'Fancy!' whispered Daisy to me. 'I think they really *are* in love!'

The wedding service began, and both Ethel and Miss Sperry got out their handkerchiefs. The Old Man snuffled into his sleeve. Mr Tempest said some solemn words about love and duty that I do not really think Miss Livedon and Uncle Felix heard, as they were so busy smiling at each other. My mind drifted too, to the mystery. I still did not understand why someone would ask a guest to come to a wedding *early*. It did not make sense!

'Felix Henry Charles Seldom Mountfitchet,' said Mr Tempest, and next to me Daisy snickered. 'Do you take Lucy Felicity Livedon . . .?'

We had known Miss Livedon by so many names, I thought, but somehow we had never heard her real, full name until today. I had sometimes wondered if Miss Livedon was even her name at all – but it must be, otherwise she would not be able to be married with it. Somehow that started a train of thought in my mind. Registry office weddings all seemed so – anonymous. You could do it with only two witnesses who you did not even have to know, wearing quite ordinary clothes, and it would still be perfectly legal.

What if – what if you were *not* yourself? I wondered. No, that would not do. We had heard people talking about both Lily Clemence and Gerard Harcourt. They were real people, and of course they would have to produce official documents, just as Miss Livedon and Uncle Felix had. But they had clearly wanted a secret marriage, in a place far away from Lily's family – and then Miss Foster had happened to walk by and see the notice with their names on it.

My detective senses twitched at that, although I did not know why. I tried to shake myself out of my mood. I looked around at the room – at everyone gathered together. *Everyone.*

My heart began to beat faster.

'And if anyone knows why these two people may not be joined together in matrimony,' said Mr Tempest.

And I had it.

I opened my mouth – but the voice that shouted out 'Oh! Stop! Something dreadful is about to happen!' was not mine.

It was Daisy.

'Stop, stop!' she gabbled. 'Someone is about to be *murdered*!'

'Pardon me?' asked Mr Tempest.

'Daisy!' said Miss Livedon. 'What on earth?'

'What do you mean?' asked Uncle Felix sharply.

'I haven't time to explain! Just follow me quickly! You can get married afterwards!' cried Daisy, gesturing – and quite suddenly the whole wedding party was surging after Daisy, bursting out of the Collins Room and into the corridor in a scatter of yellow petals. 'This is highly irregular!' Mr Tempest cried as he rushed hopelessly after us.

'In there!' I cried, pointing to the room I had seen Miss Foster entering. Daisy pushed open the door with her little blue slipper – and revealed Miss Foster sitting at a table with the woman we had all seen when we first arrived at the registry office and thought was an official, the one who had been walking past us in her grey suit clutching a sheaf of documents to her chest. There was a pot of tea beside them, and the woman was just pouring out the first cup of it.

'What's going on?' cried Miss Foster.

'Explain, Daisy!' cried Uncle Felix.

'Miss Foster is about to be poisoned!' shouted Daisy.

'She most certainly is *not*,' said Mr Tempest, face red. 'She is taking tea with the bride from today's twelve o'clock service, Miss Lily Clemence.'

'That's the bride, but that isn't Lily Clemence,' I said – and the look that flashed across the woman's face told me that I was right. 'She's only pretending to be. That's her sister, Isabelle.'

'What nonsense!' the woman cried. 'How dare you!'

She surged to her feet, her face twisted with fury, and launched herself at Daisy and me – but before we could move Miss Sperry and the Old Man stepped forward and caught her very neatly between them. With her spare hand Miss Sperry reached out and slid the cup of tea away from Miss Foster, who was staring at us, pale-faced.

'I don't understand!' she whispered. 'But – this is L, not Lily!'

'EXPLAIN,' said all the grown-ups at once. Uncle Felix, Aunt Eustacia and Bertie were all glaring at us with identical expressions, and I realized how formidable Daisy's family truly is.

'Don't listen to her!' cried the woman in the grey suit, but she was ignored.

'Well!' said Daisy. 'It all started with something we heard Miss Livedon say – that this was the best time of year to be married if you wanted a quiet wedding.

'When we met Miss Foster, she told us that she was Lily Clemence's school friend and she had been given an invitation for the wedding after this one – the twelve o'clock ceremony – but with the earlier time of eleven o'clock on it, and a note to say the registry office noticeboard was wrong. Miss Foster said that she had only seen the noticeboard in the first place because she happened to be here running an errand, and she was then only given the invitation after she wrote to Lily to congratulate her. We *did* think that Miss Foster might

33

have been lying to gain admittance to the wedding – but why would she? Yes, she had some suspicious items in her handbag – a knife and a bottle of ink, or poison – but was this proof that she wanted to do harm to someone in the wedding party?'

'Yes!' cried the woman in the grey suit. 'That's it! She was trying to do me harm!'

'A knife and a bottle of poison!' gasped Miss Foster, who was looking more and more distraught. 'My letter opener and my smelling salts, if you please! What are you *saying*, L?'

'Ethel and the Old Man told us about Lily Clemence and Gerard Harcourt,' I carried on. 'Gerard was the one who *seemed* more dangerous – he had run through his family's money and was now trying to marry to get more. He had to, because he couldn't have any more credit with shops in his own name. And Lily Clemence was a wealthy heiress whose father had forbidden her to marry Gerard. So it made sense that they might try to marry in secret, away from her family.'

'Except!' burst in Daisy. 'Except that something was wrong. Miss Foster was *surprised* at what Lily was doing, and so was the Old Man. To them this wedding seemed out of character for Lily, who was always bookish and responsible. Of course, love does silly things to lots of people, and Miss Foster did mention "L" running away as a child, and being naughty. We thought "L" meant

Lily, and it was just a nickname. But what if there was another explanation? When Ethel spoke about the Clemences, she said Mr Clemence had *daughters*. And finally Miss Foster said something very telling: she wondered whether *John and Emmeline and Isabelle* would be there. Two of those names would be Lily's parents. But who is the third? There was really only one conclusion to be drawn: the second Clemence daughter, Isabelle, must be known as *Elle*. Miss Foster isn't saying the letter "L", she's saying *Elle*, and she's talking about Isabelle, Lily's wild younger sister.'

'But – I – of course!' gasped Miss Foster. 'I never meant to confuse you!'

'Well, you did. All right, then, what if Isabelle and Gerard fell in love, while he was courting Lily? What if they decided that they wanted to marry – but they wanted Lily's inheritance too? The obvious answer would be for Isabelle to steal Lily's identity. The best person in the world to assume your identity is your own sister, after all. She could steal your identification papers quite easily, and she would look enough like you for the information in your passport to seem correct.'

'It seems an utterly stupid idea,' said Aunt Eustacia sceptically.

'But it isn't!' said Daisy. 'Lily had to be married in order to come into her inheritance. Isabelle knew she needed a marriage certificate to show to all the stores and banks in London to convince them to give her money and credit – and the marriage certificate had to show that it was *Lily* who was married to Gerard Harcourt. Imagine – the newly married "Lily Harcourt" would have been able to simply walk into jewellery stores and walk out again with extremely nice emeralds and diamonds and rubies. By the time the real Lily found out, Isabelle and Gerard would probably have already sold them on. They might even have been planning to leave the country once they'd got enough money! But something went wrong.'

Isabelle – Elle – sniffed and glared furiously at Miss Foster. She seemed to have finally run out of excuses.

'Miss Foster saw the announcement!' I said. 'She wrote to Lily to congratulate her – only Lily never got the letter. Isabelle received it, at her London address – the address she would have given to the registry office, and so the one the registry office passed on to Miss Foster – and realized that she and Gerard had a problem. Even if Miss Foster wasn't invited to the wedding, she might show up to say congratulations on the day – and she would know immediately that Isabelle wasn't Lily. You don't forget the face of your best childhood friend, just like Ethel didn't forget Miss Livedon. So Isabelle and Gerard had to make sure that she never got to the ceremony.'

'And the best way to do that was to get her to come *early*!' cried Daisy. 'She'd be guaranteed to be there, and guaranteed to be out in the corridor while everyone else was in the Collins Room for the eleven o'clock wedding. Then Isabelle could greet her, lure her into a side room to have some tea – all she'd have to say is that Lily was on her way and would be there soon – and poison her with it. Miss Livedon is getting married in a skirt suit, and Isabelle was wearing the same sort of thing. She'd look perfectly ordinary and not bride-like at all, so Miss Foster wouldn't suspect a thing. In fact, we saw her when we first arrived at the office, but we simply thought she was another clerk. We were very idiotic – but luckily Hazel and I both worked it out in the nick of time.'

'Hah!' cried Elle, getting back some steam again. 'You have no proof! Gerard will sue!'

'There certainly *is* proof, and I can't imagine that Gerard has the money,' said Uncle Felix. 'The pot of tea will be tested, and – well, sir, we ought to arrange for officers to be here when Harcourt arrives, don't you think? He should be along shortly, after all.'

'Certainly,' said the Old Man, nodding, as Elle burst into noisy tears. 'I shall do that. But first, Felix – don't you have a wedding to get to?'

'Indeed,' said Miss Sperry. 'Lucy, Mr Mountfitchet, you ought to get back.'

'Quite true,' said Uncle Felix, glancing at Miss Livedon. 'Shall we go? I suppose it is our fault for choosing Daisy and Hazel to be our bridesmaids.'

'Sorry, Uncle Felix,' said Daisy.

'The problem with you, Daisy,' said Uncle Felix, 'is that you aren't sorry at all.'

The rest of the ceremony, when we got back into the Collins Room, was a bright-coloured blur. Mr Tempest never quite recovered from the shock of what had happened halfway through, and Uncle Felix and Miss Livedon did not help matters.

'Love, honour and obey,' he said to Miss Livedon.

'Oh, just love and honour, if you will,' said Miss Livedon cheerfully.

'*I* shall obey,' put in Uncle Felix. They both shouted with laughter, and Mr Tempest dropped a page of his notes and looked as though he wanted to cry.

'I-now-pronounce-you-man-and-wife-you-may-kiss-the-bride,' he finished in a great rush, and, as we all cheered, Uncle Felix and Miss Livedon put their arms round each other and kissed so enthusiastically that I blushed.

Then we were all rushing out of the arched registry office doorway into the sharp winter sunshine, clutching dried petals that Miss Sperry had efficiently produced from her handbag. Miss Livedon – no, Aunt Lucy – and Uncle Felix appeared, laughing and holding hands, gorgeous in their blue, red and yellow, and we showered them with petals. Aunt Lucy threw her hands up and her bouquet spun into the air. Daisy caught it and handed it to me. I dropped it.

Aunt Eustacia was smiling and clapping, her objections to the wedding clearly quite forgotten, and Bertie was looking far more cheerful. He put an arm round Daisy, and she pretended to shake him off, making a face, but I could tell how happy they both were.

'Now,' said Aunt Lucy, 'after all that excitement I think the only fitting celebration for both ourselves and Daisy and Hazel is the very nice lunch we have laid on at the hotel.'

'Is there cake?' I asked.

'There is a most *enormous* cake, Hazel,' said Aunt Lucy. 'Follow me!'

But there was one more thing on my mind. I turned to Uncle Felix, and whispered in his ear, 'What about that other woman?'

'Never mind her!' said Uncle Felix brusquely.

'Don't be silly!' said Daisy. 'I want to know too. Who was she?'

'Oh, you bothersome niece!' said Uncle Felix. 'All right, if you promise not to tell.'

We both nodded.

'She is Lucy's mother. Lucy has – trouble with her family, and she and her mother especially do not get on. If she had turned up today, it would have spoiled things utterly for Lucy. That was partly why we arranged the wedding for today – so that she would not know to attend. She lives in Oxfordshire, and does not come to London often. I knew that this time of year was quite safe, but all the same, I worried. So I asked you to be on the lookout.'

'Oh!' I said.

'Oh!' said Daisy. 'I suppose—'

'We do indeed understand about difficult people in this family,' said Uncle Felix, and for a moment he looked tired. 'But today, Daisy Wells, I would like to celebrate with the people I love, and that, for all that you vex me, is you, your brother and your great-aunt.'

'And your wife!' said Daisy.

'And my wife,' said Uncle Felix, a look of utter wonder on his face. 'I have a wife.'

As though she had heard him, Aunt Lucy turned round and waved, her face bright with happiness.

'Hurry up!' she shouted. 'You'll miss the cake!'

And that is really all, except for one thing: I have eaten wedding cake, and in real life it turns out to be simply Christmas cake with another name. I have decided that although I like weddings very much, I much prefer other forms of bunbreak.

# THE CASE OF THE MISSING TREASURE

Being an account of

The Case of the Cursed Mummy.
Written by Daisy Wells,
Detective Society President, aged 15.

Begun 30th May 1936, concerning
exciting events that took place on
Saturday 9th May 1936.

My Secretary and Vice-President, Hazel, is busy writing the story of our seventh murder case. It is taking her a long time, because it was such an excellent mystery. We have faced plenty of dastardly murderers in our careers to date, but I believe we have seldom come up against such a cunning crime.

Hazel tells me that I always say that. Perhaps I do. Or perhaps the criminals we meet are becoming cleverer. Nevertheless, we are better detectives with every new case. It is now almost impossible to outwit us – or at least no one has managed it yet.

So, while Hazel is writing away, I, the Honourable Daisy Wells, have decided to give an account of another mystery we faced in recent weeks. It was very exciting, and very heroic, and I was very brilliant and brave (Hazel and our friends George and Alexander helped too). We caught criminals, and recovered treasure, and really everyone in England should be grateful to us.

Although I do not think I need any more introduction, Hazel insists upon it. So: I am Daisy Wells, and my best friend Hazel Wong and I are the two most important members of the Detective Society, an organization which is famous on at least two continents. One day we will own the world's finest consulting detective agency, although at the moment we are still forced to struggle through our schooldays as though we were ordinary children.

We are currently on our way back to Deepdean School for Girls, although (very pleasingly) we have not been there much this year. For reasons that I shall let Hazel's other casebooks tell you about, we have spent this spring first in Hong Kong, and then in London. In London we were staying with my Uncle Felix and his new wife, whom we have been told to call Aunt Lucy.

Because of his utterly secret and extremely important job, Uncle Felix is not exactly a *usual* sort of uncle, nor is Aunt Lucy an ordinary aunt, and so living in their flat is fascinating. There are mysteries everywhere, and we encountered our first only a few days after our arrival in London.

We were sitting round the breakfast table on Wednesday morning, and Bridget had just brought in the morning papers. Bridget is supposed to be Aunt Lucy and Uncle

Felix's maid, but, like every other part of Uncle Felix and Aunt Lucy's life, she is rather unusual. She can read coded messages as quickly as I can read English, and when she answers the telephone I have heard her speak at least six different languages. I suppose it is clever of Uncle Felix to use her for other purposes, for who really pays attention to a maid?

'There's been another one, Mr M,' Bridget said to Uncle Felix, dropping the pile of newspapers on the table next to the butter dish. 'Sir John Soane's Museum this time!'

'Another what?' I asked, on the alert. I could see that Hazel was sitting up too. I peered at the paper on the top of the pile:

### Sneak Thief Strikes Again

Yesterday morning the curators at Sir John Soane's Museum were horrified to discover the theft of several of their most precious Greek and Roman artefacts. A window was smashed, the cases themselves lay open and the items, including a small bust and a gold necklace, were missing. This is the tenth such theft in the last month, but only the second to leave behind such destruction. In many of the others, the thief arrived and left without disturbing anything. To date, many of London's most prestigious museums have been the targets of this puzzling night-time terror. The police admit to being stumped.

How long will these attacks last? And who can stop them?

Next to the article was a small and blurry picture of the outside of a building, its window smashed, and glass scattered all over the pavement below its railings.

'Golly!' I said. 'How exciting! Someone ought to look into it.'

'Someone certainly ought,' said Uncle Felix, scraping butter onto his toast.

'Most certainly,' agreed Aunt Lucy, sipping her tea. 'Felix dear, pass the crossword.'

By which I understood that Uncle Felix and Aunt Lucy knew far more about the thefts than they were telling us. In fact, I suspected that they were probably engaged in investigating them. I felt rather annoyed, and very jealous.

But my detective mind was at work, and it had noticed that there was something distinctly fishy about the article's picture. I looked over at Hazel to signal this to her with my eyes. But Hazel didn't look at me. She was staring at something poking out beneath the newspaper – a rather grubby-looking white envelope with some familiar writing on it.

'Alexander's written!' said Hazel, and glowed.

Alexander Arcady is a boy that Hazel and I met during the course of one of our investigations. He and his best friend, George Mukherjee, are members of the Junior Pinkertons, a rival detective society. They are not as good at solving crimes as us, but I suppose they're not bad.

But that is my opinion of Alexander, not Hazel's. I will never understand why a boy who is awkward and far too friendly and can never dress himself properly should always make Hazel look as if she has swallowed a light bulb. He only makes me feel annoyed.

'It's the Exeat this weekend, and so he's coming up to London with George. They're staying with George's parents,' said Hazel, reading through the letter and blushing furiously all the way down her neck.

I saw Uncle Felix and Aunt Lucy look up from the crossword they had begun to work on together and exchange a glance – a very married one. Then Uncle Felix said, 'I suppose they're coming to visit us?'

'No,' said Hazel, redder than ever. 'Well—'

As I have said, I think Hazel's obsession perfectly foolish. But she is my best friend, and so I said, 'Yes please, Uncle Felix.'

'Well then, write to the boys and invite them for Saturday,' said Uncle Felix, his monocle glinting as he screwed it into place over his eye. 'I shall have to think up some entertainment. You haven't had a birthday party yet, have you, Daisy?'

I ignored him. After what happened when I turned fourteen, I am quite cured of birthday parties. I am surprised that Uncle Felix isn't as well. And besides, I am fifteen years old, only five years away from twenty – far too old for birthday parties. I was more interested in what was wrong with that picture in the newspaper.

Whenever I wasn't busy with lessons that week, I drew up a list of all the museums that had been stolen from, and what had been taken. Meanwhile, Hazel spent several days practically beside herself at the thought of Alexander coming to visit, and pretending she was not. She was making a very bad job of it, as Hazel always does with her emotions.

'Come now, Hazel,' I said to her on Saturday morning, to distract her. 'Let us consider these robberies. The things the thief has stolen so far have all been jewellery and small figurines and so on. No paintings, and nothing that's difficult to carry. All the museums were attacked at night, and all were broken into with hardly any fuss. And look at the ones that have been stolen from! Practically the only one that hasn't reported a theft yet is the British Mus—'

Just then we heard a car draw up and pull away again, and then the doorbell rang. Bridget hurried to answer it. Hazel leaped up as though she had been electrified.

'I do wish you'd get over this obsession with him,' I said, scrumpling up my page of notes crossly.

'I have! I don't think of Alexander like that any more,' said Hazel thickly. 'We're only friends.'

'Rot,' I said, and pinched her in a friendly way. 'Don't be too dreadful about it today, will you? It's bad enough that Uncle Felix keeps going on about this birthday party idea!'

Bridget came back in then, leading George and Alexander. Alexander glanced at me and turned a silly shade of red, and then looked anywhere but at me. I ignored him. George simply winked at me. I do like George.

We all said hello, and then we had that idiotic polite moment where no one is sure whether they should say what they truly want to or simply order tea. Luckily, at that point Uncle Felix poked his head round the door.

'Hello, boys,' he said. 'Nice to see you again. Do you know, I thought I'd never meet children capable of giving Daisy a run for her money, but I think the two of you – and Hazel – almost manage it. Now, I promised my niece that I would give her a birthday party.'

'*No thank you!*' I said. 'Why can't you leave it alone? I told you, I'm not a child any more!'

'Don't look at me like that!' said Uncle Felix. 'This isn't an ordinary birthday party. I know the four of you

51

love clues and puzzles. So, how would you like to solve a mystery?'

'Yes please!' said Alexander.

My heart jumped. Could he possibly mean . . . what if Uncle Felix was letting us in on what he knew about the museum thefts? I *am* fifteen now, after all. Perhaps he had finally realized that I was a brilliant detective who had solved six murder mysteries (with help from Hazel), and could be trusted.

'What's the mystery?' I asked.

'It's a treasure hunt,' said Uncle Felix. 'A series of clues that should lead you to one answer: the present I have for you. Are you game?'

I felt sick. *A treasure hunt.* I had been wrong. Uncle Felix *did* still think that I was just a child. Hazel put her hand on mine, and I realized I was clenching my fists.

'Yes please, sir,' said George politely – but I could tell that he was rather unimpressed. George is *almost* as clever as I am, and nothing but proper mysteries will do for him.

'All right,' I said, for there was nothing else to say. Uncle Felix was *dreadful*, I thought.

'I don't think you'll be disappointed,' said Uncle Felix cheerfully. 'I have the first clue all ready for you. And now for the exciting part: Lucy and I have spoken, and we have agreed that you four are to be allowed to go out on your own today, to wherever the clues take you. You are fifteen now, after all.'

He put a folded bit of paper into my hand, winked at me and ducked out of the room like a jack-in-the-box.

'Well!' I said. '*Well!*'

I couldn't say anything else. I was so furious that I was almost speechless, which is unusual for me.

'We're allowed out on our own!' said Hazel encouragingly. 'And perhaps the treasure hunt will be more exciting than you think?'

'You're a good person, Hazel Wong,' said George, and I knew then that he was feeling sorry for me. I was deeply ashamed of my uncle.

'Hey, it's all right,' said Alexander. 'Like Hazel says, this might be fun . . .'

I looked at last at what I had been given. It was a handwritten note in Uncle Felix's dreadful scrawl.

*The world's knowledge under Britannia's rule*
*visit Clio or you'll look a fool*
_ _ _ . / _ _ / _ _ _ _ / _ _ / ...

And on the back of it was a single letter: V.

'What dreadful doggerel,' I said, rolling my eyes. 'Really, Uncle Felix could have done better.'

'But what does it mean?' asked Alexander. 'Who's Clio? Did he spell Cleopatra wrong?'

At Deepdean I would have sighed and looked at my nails and pretended to have no idea at all, but out of the corner of my eye I could see that George was about to open his mouth, and no matter how much I like him, I refuse to be beaten by George Mukherjee.

'She's the Muse of History,' I said, a fraction of a second before George. 'And Britannia is the woman on all our coins, on the opposite side to the King. Her name is just a silly way of saying Britain.'

'So Britain and History,' said Alexander. 'Which means—'

'The British Museum!' I cried, once again just a fraction ahead of George, who nodded at me, grinning. 'That was easy. Honestly, Uncle Felix had better make the next clues harder. All right, I suppose we might as well get this over with. Let's go!'

I whirled out of the room to fetch our coats and hats. I do find that other people are usually so *slow*. It makes me want to grind my teeth and bite my tongue. I thrust Hazel's coat at her (the days were still blustery and fresh, and it would never do to go out in London incorrectly dressed), but she seemed half in a dream.

'Daisy,' she said, frowning. 'What about the Morse code part of the clue?'

'It hardly matters, Hazel,' I said to her. 'Come on! We already know what the clue means – we must get to the British Museum!'

We all four galloped out of Uncle Felix and Aunt Lucy's flat – they live in a lovely red-brick building in Bloomsbury – and rushed through the streets of London. The wind dashed after us, and pigeons scattered through the air, and a red motor car swished past and nearly blew off my hat. London moves almost as quickly as I do, and I love it. When I am grown up, I will always live in London, and wear the very latest fashions, and there will be a brass plaque on the door of our detective agency that says: HERE LIVES THE HONOURABLE DAISY WELLS, GENIUS OF DETECTION (AND HAZEL WONG TOO).

We ran through Russell Square, the leaves on all the trees new. Up ahead was the British Museum. I made to turn left, towards Great Russell Street, but Hazel stopped short.

'No, not that way,' she said.

'Of course that way!' I cried. 'Britannia! She's on that triangle on the museum roof!'

'*No*,' said Hazel insistently. She really has become so bold since our Hong Kong adventure. I scarcely know what to do with her sometimes.

'Hear her out,' said Alexander. Hazel went pink and I could have stamped my foot.

'The Morse code part of the clue,' said Hazel. 'I worked it out, and it spells LIONS. Uncle Felix wants us to go round to the other entrance, where the lions are.'

The most bothersome thing about Hazel is that when she is right, she is right.

'Oh!' I said, rather wishing that I had been the one to work it out, even though I can never sit still long enough for codebreaking. 'Off we go, then.'

And there, at the Montague Place entrance, flanked by two enormous lions, was Aunt Lucy.

'Bravo!' she said when she saw us. 'You cracked the first code.'

'*Hazel* cracked the code,' said George, and smiled at her.

'It was easy,' I said to Aunt Lucy, giving her a chilly glare to show that I was not to be babied.

'They do become more difficult,' said Aunt Lucy. 'Now, are you ready for your second clue?'

'Yes,' I said.

'Please,' said Hazel.

'Doesn't Hazel have lovely manners?' said Aunt Lucy. She handed Hazel another folded piece of paper. 'Felix will be waiting for you at the end of the clues, in one hour,' she said. 'Hurry along.'

We all crowded round Hazel as she unfolded the piece of paper. The clue was in Uncle Felix's handwriting again, and was (I rolled my eyes) another one of his dreadful poems.

*seek ye first the ancient key*
*A Frenchman was the first to see*
*Three in one or one in three*
*...* / _ / _ _ _ / _ . / .

And on the other side we found another bold single letter: *C.*

We stepped back and stared at one another.

'Well,' said Alexander. 'Um. Are we looking for a . . . Continental lock? Something religious? God is supposed to be three people in one, isn't he?'

'Your god is ridiculous,' said George. 'But no, I don't think that's right. Since we're at the British Museum, it must be one of the objects.'

Hazel cleared her throat.

'What is it?' I asked.

'Well,' said Hazel, 'a *key* isn't just something that goes into a lock. It's another word for cypher – the thing that lets you break a code. And the Morse code part says STONE.'

'Oh!' said George.

'Exactly!' said Hazel.

'All right, no need to get excited, I know what it is,' I said, because I *did*. I had in fact thought of it first, and knew where we ought to go.

I led us into the museum, through the white-and-black marble entrance, up shallow marble steps and into the dusty halls of the museum itself. Lots of clever-looking grown-ups moved past us purposefully, and there was a scholarly hush to the air. I stuck my chin out, trying to look twenty, and marched through the rooms into the Egyptian sculpture gallery, making sure as I did so to keep an eye out for any suspicious clues or people.

In general, I find museums dull. I do not much care for pots and pans and small jewels. But the series of mysterious thefts had made me more interested in them – and I was also quite pleased to be in one of the Egyptian rooms. The Egyptians are how all people from history should be, huge and fierce, and their sculptures make me feel like a queen.

'Aren't the British government ever ashamed of how much they steal?' asked George, staring around at the red and yellow and black statues. 'The British Museum has thousands more objects than it can ever display, all stored away underground, but the collectors still keep on bringing back more.'

'Shhh!' said Hazel, blushing. '*You're* British!'

'It's *not* stealing, it's finders keepers,' I said. 'Anyway, we look after them properly.'

'It's *absolutely* stealing, no matter how people look after the things they steal,' said George, raising an eyebrow. 'But I suppose we're here to inspect the Rosetta Stone, not argue.'

'Of course we are,' I said. You see, the Rosetta Stone is a huge piece of rock with three kinds of writing on it: Greek and two sorts of Egyptian. A Frenchman called Mr Champollion was the first person to realize that each bit of writing said the same thing, which meant that it could be used as a key to finally read the kind of picture writing called hieroglyphs. The stone is black and rather triangular, and sticks up like an enormous tooth in the centre of the sculpture gallery.

We all began to hunt about for the next clue. I peered at all sides of the stone, and the floor around it (a gentleman in a tweed suit said, 'Hold hard, miss!' as I pushed past him), and then began to examine the brass railing.

I was getting rather frustrated when I heard George say, 'I've got it!' I looked up and saw him peeling something from the underside of the stone's information plaque.

'No, *I've* got it!' cried Alexander a moment later. He had moved away from us and was pulling something out from between the slats of a grate at the side of the room.

Hazel and I looked from Alexander to George.

'You can't *both* have it,' I said. 'Someone must have got the wrong bit of paper.'

George frowned. 'Mine's another of those poems,' he said. 'And then there's something beneath it – I think they're hieroglyphs.'

He held up his piece of paper, and we all looked at it. It certainly matched the other two – although Uncle Felix's poem-writing had got sillier than ever.

Three for a girl, four for a boy, Five and six for a dragon's toy. Something to be hoarded, something to enjoy ...

And on the other side was the letter *D*.

It did look like the next clue.

'All right, what do *you* have?' I asked Alexander.

'It isn't the same as the others at all,' he said, sounding puzzled. 'I think I must have picked up ... a tourist's note, or something. Look!'

Beware the mummy! The old nemesis is great! Hear the awful tale, the end nigh!

And on the other side were strings of numbers:

1897,0401.95
1897,0316.1
1898,1201.20

I got a chill all up and down my spine. The hairs on my arms shivered.

'That isn't Uncle Felix's clue at all,' I said.

'It isn't,' agreed George. 'But I think it *is* a code.'

'Hey, you're right!' said Alexander. 'Just look at the first letter of each word after *Beware the mummy.*'

I looked. I have to admit that all I saw at first were words, but then I squinted and I suddenly understood.

'T – O – N – I – G – H – T – A – T – T – E – N,' I spelled out.

'Tonight at ten!' agreed George.

We all looked at each other, and I felt electric. 'We've found someone else's message,' I whispered. 'Hazel, copy it, copy it exactly! What if – *what if* this has something to do with the robberies? The papers think that they're all break-ins, but that picture I saw in the newspaper was all wrong. The glass was on the ground *outside* the museum, not on the floor inside! I think they're *inside* jobs, made to look like ordinary robberies.'

'We noticed the glass too!' said Alexander. 'That would fit!'

'If that's so, then it's not just one thief, but a group of them,' I said excitedly. 'Or the thief always has accomplices who work at the museums. What if—'

'What if the British Museum is next on the list to be robbed?' Hazel gasped. 'And this note is the thief telling his accomplice where to meet him this evening!'

'The British Museum is almost the only London museum *not* to have been attacked yet,' said George. 'It's not a bad idea, Daisy!'

'Quite true, it's a very good one,' I said. My heart was beating very fast, like a rabbit running. 'Uncle Felix may think that he's sent us to the only safe museum in London, but I think that he has in fact brought us to an extremely interesting place. We must put the message back and then follow its clue at once. Detective Society – Pinkertons – I think we have stumbled on a most important mystery!'

'We have to split up,' said George, as though he were in charge. Of course, I am the only one who could possibly be in charge, but George pretends not to know that.

'If we're going to investigate this note, we have to make sure we keep our cover,' he continued. 'Some of us must go on solving Uncle Felix's clues too, otherwise he'll work out what we've really been up to.'

'You can,' I said at once. 'You and Alexander.'

'I *don't* think so,' said George infuriatingly. 'One from each society, otherwise you two'll have all the fun.' It is sometimes a bother that George and I understand each other so well.

'You and Hazel, then,' I said. This was a careful calculation – I know that I am not nearly as good at breaking codes as Hazel, just as George has shown himself to be quicker at puzzles than Alexander. I also very much wanted to solve the real mystery, and did not care at all about Uncle Felix's childish treasure hunt.

'All right,' said George. 'Now, does anyone know how to read hieroglyphs?'

'I do,' said Hazel. We all looked at her. 'At least, a little. Aunt Lucy's been teaching me about them. I think I can manage to solve Uncle Felix's clue.'

This made me remember that if I'm not careful Hazel will know more than me, and that would never do.

Hazel squinted at the five hieroglyphs. 'That's a sort of K noise at the beginning,' she said. 'And an S at the end . . . and I think an N before that, and something that looks like an I?'

'Hold on, I know!' said George. 'The bit about dragons and hoarding. Dragons hoard treasure, and treasure is coins. *COINS!* And five and six are for silver and gold in that nursery rhyme, the one that begins with "one for sorrow . . .". We've cracked it!'

George and Hazel beamed at each other, and I thought that I had chosen very well in putting them together.

'Now, look,' said George, 'before we go off after the clues, I've got one more thing to say. I think I might know which mummy the note's talking about. You know I like unsolved mysteries?'

'Of course we do!' I said.

'All right,' said George, standing up straighter than ever. 'Listen. There's a mummy here that's called the Unlucky Mummy, because it's supposed to be *cursed*. It was first brought back from Egypt in the 1890s by four young men. Two of them *died* getting it back to England and the other two died a few months later. It was taken in by a friend of theirs, but only a few months later he brought it to the British Museum in despair. He said that it had made his daughter ill, and smashed plates in his house just like a poltergeist.'

'That's not true!' I said, seeing Hazel gulping. Hazel hates ghost stories.

'It *probably* isn't!' said George, shrugging expressively. 'It's in lots of books, though. Anyway, the next part of the story is as follows: in 1912 the British Museum tried to send it to America for an exhibition. But guess which ship they put it on?'

'The *Titanic*!' cried Alexander.

'Exactly!' said George.

'This is absolutely *not true at all*!' I protested. 'If it was, it would be at the bottom of the sea, not in the mummy room.'

'Of course that part isn't true!' said George. 'But it's a brilliant story, and lots of people believe it. They're always saying that they feel an odd presence in the mummy room. Mediums even do seances in there, to see if they can contact the Unlucky Mummy's evil spirit. It's bunkum, but there's one thing that *is* a fact: most people are afraid of the mummy room in general and the Unlucky Mummy in particular, which makes the mummy room the perfect place to hold a secret meeting – especially at night! Even the guards don't like to go in there.'

*Trust George,* I thought, *to somehow bring even the silliest of stories to a very sensible conclusion.*

'Very useful,' I said graciously. 'Now, will you go away to the coin room and solve the treasure hunt before we run out of time?'

'All right, all right,' said George, clapping me on the shoulder. 'Come on, Hazel, upstairs to the coin room!'

As Hazel hurried out of the Egyptian gallery with George, she looked back at Alexander and blushed. It really does infuriate me that, around Alexander, Hazel turns back into the shy little girl I first met at Deepdean years ago, and not the downright fearsome detective she has become. He is no good for her *at all.* He really isn't, Hazel. I'm only saying it in your best interests.

'All right,' I said, standing like the leader of the group, which I was, then turned to Alexander. 'The important thing now is to uncover more about this clue. Come on, Wats— Alexander.' (For there is only one person in the world who is worthy of that nickname.) 'We must go and investigate this cursed mummy. And, while we do, we must also come up with a list of suspects. It's clear that the person who left the note could be any member of staff or visitor – but who could they leave it *for*? Who might be able to get into the museum at ten o'clock at night, after it's closed?'

'A visitor might hide until after closing,' offered Alexander, brushing the sandy hair back from his forehead. 'But I guess that's unlikely. OK, how about one of the museum staff? A keeper, or a guard.'

'A guard isn't a bad idea,' I said grudgingly. 'Someone who wouldn't look odd wandering around after dark. Now, where are these mummies?'

I had to admit that, even though I don't believe in ghosts, the mummy room was eerie. Cases loomed at us out of the dimness, menacingly still, and all the wrinkly professors and hungry-looking students and tired nannies dragging little children about the gallery seemed unusually subdued.

Alexander was rushing around, disturbing the dust and all the other visitors as he peered excitedly at the labels next to the mummy cases.

I tried to look as though I didn't know who he was, but he rather ruined this by shouting, 'Hey, Daisy, it's this one!' and waving his arm at me in its too-short shirtsleeve.

'Shush!' I said. 'You'll make people suspicious!'

'Not me,' said Alexander, grinning infuriatingly. 'I'm just an American kid who likes mummies. What's suspicious about that? Come and look! It's spooky.'

As I said, I don't believe in ghosts. That is all Hazel. But . . . looking up into the fixed, flat-eyed glare of the Unlucky Mummy made the back of my neck feel distinctly uncomfortable. Her face was very blank and calm, and her hands were crossed over her patterned and painted breast. There were winged figures all down her body, and they looked unpleasant.

'Just think!' said Alexander. 'This case used to hold a *real* dead body.'

'And this room is full of them!' I said. 'I wonder if any of them were murdered.'

Then I scowled, because I had caught myself agreeing with Alexander about something, and that would never do.

'We must search this room for further clues,' I announced. 'We have to solve the mystery of those strings of numbers, after all.'

'I thought they might be locations,' said Alexander. 'You know, latitudes and longitudes. But they don't look quite right.'

I refuse to say it to him, but perhaps Alexander is not the *worst* detective in the world. I was very glad, though, when it was me who solved the mystery of the numbers.

I was peering into a small case loaded with jewellery. At first my eyes were dazzled by the bright gold rings and chains, but then I looked at the scraps of paper next to each one. Each label had a description and two numbers, a short one and a longer one – and they exactly matched the pattern of our numbers.

'Oh!' I said. 'Alexander, come here!'

Once we'd made that breakthrough, it was not hard to discover what the numbers belonged to. The first was next to a thick gold signet ring; the second was next to a slender gold and garnet necklace; and the last was next to a grey scarab beetle, engraved with the image of a hawk.

'So, what does it mean?' asked Alexander.

'Well, *obviously*,' I said, not exactly knowing what I was going to say next, 'obviously . . . they're . . .' And then I knew. 'It's a list!' I cried. 'A shopping list, like Bridget or our housekeeper Mrs Doherty would make, only disguised. They're the things the thief has asked for from his contact here.'

'Of course!' said Alexander enthusiastically. 'That must be it! But – hey, they're only little things, just like the ones stolen from the other museums. Don't you think that's weird? I mean, if you were breaking into the British Museum, wouldn't you steal more important objects?'

'I expect they're extremely valuable,' I said – but really I had to admit that Alexander was right. They did seem awfully little things to break into a museum for. Was there more to this mystery than we had yet deduced?

Hazel and George came running in then, breathless and very pleased with themselves.

'We solved them all!' said Hazel triumphantly.

'Hazel solved most of them,' said George. 'I just watched.'

'Coin room, then chessmen, then Elgin Marbles, then Assyrian lions,' said Hazel, ticking them off on her fingers. 'And the letters: V, C, D, Q, I, O. They must spell out something, but we don't know what yet.'

I blinked. 'I know what they mean,' I said, and I got a funny twinge, because perhaps I shouldn't have been so rude about Uncle Felix's birthday present. 'Now, where is Uncle Felix waiting for us?'

'There you are!' I said, marching over with the other three behind me.

Uncle Felix turned in mock surprise from where he was posing next to one of the statues in the Greek room, his long, smooth face fitting in perfectly with the senator he was in front of.

'Not bad,' he said, screwing in his monocle and looking down at me (less far down than he used to – I have grown so much that now I nearly reach his shoulder). 'Forty-five minutes to solve the clues. Now, I have a present for you. I assume you know what it is?'

'Vidocq,' I said, scowling as hard as I could so as not to show how pleased I was. 'The French policeman who invented being a detective. You can't have bought me him, since he's dead and it's not polite to buy people anyway, so I suppose you've got me the book he wrote.'

'The first English edition,' said Uncle Felix. 'I thought it was fitting for my detective niece. Here you are.'

I do not hug Uncle Felix often – he is not a hugging sort of person, and neither am I – but I hugged him then.

'Now, I thought the four of you might like to go and have some tea,' said Uncle Felix. 'I have to— Well, something has come up at work.'

'Oh, is it the museum thief?' asked Alexander eagerly. George poked him, but it was too late.

'None of your business,' said Uncle Felix firmly, taking a step back and glaring at us. 'Do you want tea or not?'

Suddenly I found myself feeling cross with him all over again. It was not fair that Uncle Felix should call me a detective with one breath and then tell me I wasn't old enough to detect with the next. If I had been unsure about discussing the message we had found with Uncle Felix, or about following the clue ourselves, I wasn't any more.

I looked around the Greek gallery – at the old lady wrapped up in a great grey scarf, the little boy pointing at all the rude bits of the statues while his nanny tried to drag him away, and the guard standing to attention beside the door. None of them *seemed* very suspicious, but I have learned that you cannot count on people's appearances at all. Was the thief's accomplice hiding in plain sight?

'Here,' said Uncle Felix, holding out his hand and interrupting my thoughts. 'For your tea.' It was a ten-shilling note.

'Thank you, Uncle,' I said coolly, taking the note between my fingers as though it were a dead mouse. 'We shall go and get some ices.'

'Uncle Felix is treating us like children!' I said bitterly as we walked out of the museum, past a cleaning woman mopping the floor, then a tweedy lady making notes in a book, and finally past a policeman pacing to and fro on the steps. When I saw him, I knew that the police *must* be worried about a break-in here soon.

'We *are* children,' said George. 'Technically, at least.'

'We are *detectives*!' I said. 'And I know that he's been working on this mystery. It's simply not fair of him to keep us in the dark. It'll serve him right if we are the ones who solve it. Oh, come on, I'll tell you my plan over tea.'

There was an old woman feeding the pigeons on the museum steps, her hair down around her shoulders. Alexander gave her tuppence, and Hazel glowed up at him most infuriatingly.

'Really, why does everyone have to be obsessed with *love*? It's a dreadful distraction,' I muttered to George while the other two walked ahead.

'I look forward to you falling in love,' said George. 'I only hope I shall be there to see it.'

'*I never shall*,' I said, and I meant it then. Love is a silly emotion, and does not help a detective do their job. I know that Hazel sometimes has wondered whether I am in love with George, but of course she is quite wrong. He's all right as far as boys go, very tall and clean, but I have discovered that when I look at boys I cannot see what Hazel does.

'So, what are we going to do?' asked Alexander once we were all sitting around the tea-room table with our ices in front of us. The sun was shining outside, and in any other circumstances it would have been a lovely birthday treat. But I was so excited and upset that I could hardly eat mine, although I knew this went quite against the Detective Society rule of never saying no to tea.

'We're going to break into the British Museum this evening and discover who the thief is,' I said. 'What else could we possibly do?'

'It's awfully dangerous, though!' said Hazel.

'The only things worth doing are dangerous ones, Hazel. Don't you know that by now?' I asked. Anyone would think that Hazel was new to the Detective Society.

Hazel blushed and said, 'I don't mean we shouldn't do it! Only – we ought to be sure it's worth it.'

'Of course it is, and of course we should do it,' said George. 'It's a brilliant adventure, and Alex and I haven't had many of those lately. Alex, what do you say?'

'Daisy's right,' said Alexander. 'And – look, we don't have to actually surprise the thief, do we? Just watch and find out who he is. So it's not *really* dangerous. We can tell the police once we know his identity.'

'And the identity of the person in the British Museum helping him,' agreed Hazel. 'A keeper could unlock the displays, and a guard would have keys and a reason to be about late at night. It must be one of them – it has to be an inside job!'

'Quite right,' I said.

'Detectives, I've had an idea,' said George, eyes widening. 'I know where we can hide for the meeting – somewhere we'll never be discovered.'

'No,' said Hazel, very forcefully for her. 'No! I know what you're going to say, and – absolutely not!'

'Where?' I asked suspiciously.

'Inside the mummy cases,' said Hazel. 'That's what you were going to say, isn't it, George?'

It was an absolutely brilliant idea, and I was furious that I hadn't thought of it first.

'But they've got bodies in them!' cried Alexander, looking disgusted and delighted all at once.

'Hazel's quite right. And no, most of them haven't any more,' said George. 'Grave robbers took them out years before they ever arrived in London. If we get into the cases, no one will notice we're there!'

'This is the most horrid idea I have ever heard,' I said. 'We absolutely *must* do it. Well *done*, George!'

Hazel looked rather ill, and so did Alexander. They are both much too tender-hearted. But George's eyes were sparkling, and I could feel myself beaming back at him. 'All right,' I said. 'Now, how do we go about breaking into the museum?'

'There must be floorplans in the Reading Room,' said George. 'You girls go home—'

'You are *not* to have adventures without us!' I cried. 'This is *our* mystery!'

'You girls go home,' continued George, 'and see if you can have a look at your uncle's files.' He raised his eyebrows at me. 'You think he's been working on the case. Well then, see if he's found out anything that might be useful to us. *We'll* look at the plans. Then we'll go back to my house, pretend to go to bed as normal and meet you at nine p.m. at the edge of Russell Square.'

'Oh,' I said. 'I suppose that isn't a *bad* idea.'

In fact, I could feel myself becoming enthusiastic. This sounded like a proper spy mission.

'All right,' said George, nodding. 'Now, go home and pretend to be ordinary.'

'I am never ordinary,' I said, drawing myself up to my full height. 'But I shall be ordinarily brilliant.'

The rest of that day was dreadfully dull, but at the same time rather lovely, like Christmas Eve, when you know you have really splendid presents waiting for you the next morning.

Hazel distracted Bridget by asking her to make tea, and then we quickly rifled through Uncle Felix's desk, in case he had left any interesting information about the case. We didn't find much – but there was enough to show that he definitely was investigating. I found an official-looking letter that read:

Dear M: London black market flooded with valuable artefacts. Most can be matched to those reported stolen, but there are additional items of such fine quality that they must come from another museum collection, perhaps several. Are the thieves able to steal without raising the alarm? Are we dealing with a larger gang than we assumed? Please investigate. Check persons of interest at the museums – we cannot rule out guards and curators as suspects.

And there was one other thing: a scribbled note that said:

> You'll never get your things back.
> Give up now!!

It seemed to have been marked up by a handwriting expert: *Over-confident Y. Aggressive G. Clearly male*. There was also a note in Uncle Felix's writing that said:

> An unpleasant adversary. This man will attempt the next robbery soon.

'Look!' said Hazel. 'That first note – the writing matches the one we found!'

She took her bit of paper with the copy of the message we had discovered in the British Museum out of her pocket and put it next to the one on Uncle Felix's desk. 'See?'

It did indeed, and I felt jumpy all over with excitement. We really were on the right track. I remembered what Alexander had said – that it was odd to break into the British Museum for such small objects. Perhaps that was the key to solving this mystery. Had the thief been using his contact inside the museum to steal smaller items without anyone noticing? But – why *had* no one noticed things missing from their cases?

Then Bridget called that the tea was ready, and we had to hurry away.

After dinner was cleared, Hazel and I went into our room and pretended to be getting ready for bed. Really, of course, we were changing out of our day things into the dark tunics and trousers that Hazel had brought back for us from Hong Kong. Her maid, Ping, had tried to alter mine to fit me, and it almost works, although it's still short in the arms and legs.

We took out our pyjamas, wrapped them around the bolsters from our beds, and then hid them in the wardrobe, to be used later to imitate our sleeping forms in case anyone looked into our room while we were gone. We were lying down under our covers perfectly sweetly when Aunt Lucy came in to turn out the lights.

'Goodnight, girls,' she said as she closed the door. 'Well done on your detecting today.'

I knew that Hazel would be feeling rather guilty at that.

'Quick,' I said as soon as Aunt Lucy's footsteps had died away. 'Put your bolster in your bed and let's go!'

We climbed out of the bedroom window and balanced on the low balcony that runs round the building. The flats are usefully corniced and pillared, and it really was easy work to creep down the side. Of course, Hazel made heavy weather of it – but in the end we both managed it with not much more than scraped knees.

We were lucky. A lovely yellowish London fog was curling around us, smothering the street lights and muffling our breath and our footsteps. It was cold and soft where it touched my skin, just like walking through velvet.

We hared off, and it was a good thing that I had set myself to memorize London's streets, for the fog made everything strange. Once a blue-coated policeman came swinging by, and I had to pull Hazel into the shelter of an archway so he would not see us. Nice little girls do not go out at night. It was rather exhilarating to be free of being nice and little for a while.

Then the black railings of Russell Square Gardens loomed up in front of us. We followed them round until we turned a corner and heard a voice say, 'Hello? Who goes there?'

'It's us, you chump,' I said, for I recognized Alexander's voice at once. A moment later, he appeared. 'And it's no good asking *Who goes there?* What would you have done if it had been someone else?'

'We can look after ourselves,' said George, his figure swimming out of the fog to stand next to us. 'We're tall, dark strangers, after all.'

'You're boys in unsuitable clothes,' I said, for both he and Alexander were wearing their light spring coats and hats. I could see Alexander shivering. 'Now, shall we get on? Have you discovered how to break into the British Museum?'

'Of course we have,' said George. 'There's a gate on Montague Place. You'll see.'

'And what if we run into a guard?' I asked.

'We thought of that,' said George coolly. 'We came early so we could hang about outside the gate. There's a guard station just inside it – we can hear someone doing their rounds. Footsteps arrive and go away again every twenty minutes, but there's no talking, and no sound of dogs. We think he's alone.'

'Very good,' I said reluctantly. 'And once we're inside?'

'There's an easy route,' said George. 'Alex has it mapped out.'

'The place is huge!' said Alexander. 'I had no idea it was so big. There really are gigantic storerooms in the cellar for all the objects they can't show upstairs. All those treasures, and nobody ever sees them! There are offices too, but I've worked out a way for us to get to the passage that leads up to the mummy room without going past very many of them. If we're caught—'

'If we're caught, we're the nieces and nephews of some of the keepers, and their friends,' I said. 'Now, lead on to the gate.'

\*

When we got to the Montague Place gate, I stopped short.

'You didn't research this properly!' I cried. 'This isn't a gate! It's a door!'

It was true. The gate was tall and black, and set snugly into the side of the museum. There was no way over it, not if you were any bigger than a mouse.

'It's quite all right,' said George calmly. 'If you get up onto the top of that wall to our left, there, we'll show you how we can get in.'

The house to the left of the museum had white pillars on each side of its door, and a tall brick wall to its right. By shinning up the pillars and stretching, we managed to reach the top of the wall. (Hazel had to be pushed a little by George.) I crouched low and peered into the darkness.

'*There*,' whispered George. 'Look ahead. The museum may have a secure gate, but the back garden of this house shares a wall with it, and we can get over that. Beyond the wall is an alleyway, and on the other side of the alley is the museum itself. There's a door that opens straight into it. I told you it was all right. We should have ten minutes before the guard comes back here. Come on!'

Along the wall we moved, treading as carefully as cats over loose and missing bricks, and when we came to the end, we jumped down onto a little tarmacked path. In front of us was the great side of the museum – and in that side was a small door.

'Here,' whispered Alexander. 'See?'

While the others waited, I took a pin out of my hair to pick the lock (I've had practice). But it transpired that I didn't need to – the door swung open under my hand.

'Oh!' whispered Alexander. 'Of course – the accomplice! The door must have been left open for the thief!'

The idea that the thief might be on his way gave me the most wonderful thrill of excitement, but I saw Hazel start with horror. I patted her comfortingly, and pushed her through.

I followed – and there we were, inside the British Museum. In front of us was a long, shadowed corridor. Pipes trailed overhead, boxes were piled all the way down it and there was a smell in the air of very old dust.

'It *smells* like a mummy,' whispered Hazel.

'How do you know what a mummy smells like?' I asked her. But, as we crept along, stepping round boxes and crates, I privately agreed.

At the end of the corridor we turned right, then right again, and found ourselves at the bottom of a set of stairs. Up those we went, and came out onto the museum's ground floor.

'Hey! There's a guard!' hissed George, and we all flattened ourselves against an overhanging wall while footsteps swung past, and cheerful whistling grew loud in our ears and then faint again.

It was all the best fun, and made my heart race excitingly in my chest. I don't know how anyone can bear to be ordinary, and live a dull life, when they could be creeping through dark buildings at night on crucial secret missions.

I was quite giddy by the time we slipped into the mummy gallery, although I could tell that Hazel was having rather a bad time of it. She kept giving little shudders and drawing close to me. I patted her on the arm to tell her to buck up, and she nodded back at me, her face set.

Alexander whispered, 'Creepy!'

'Shh!' George and I both said at once.

It was true that the room was more eerie than ever now that the museum was dark and silent. The mummies loomed all around us, their painted faces just visible and looking extremely stern. I almost thought that I saw one breathing – but of course that was the most Hazel-ish nonsense. I told myself not to be silly.

'Where do we hide?' asked Alexander.

George pointed. 'I know that one's empty, and that one, and that one – and, of course, the Unlucky Mummy too.'

Hazel let out a very small noise.

'Oh, for heaven's sake, I'll take that one,' I said. 'There isn't any curse, Hazel. You know that!'

But, as I slipped behind the mummy's bird-painted front into the empty space behind it, I got a most unaccustomed feeling – of dread.

Perhaps it was because it was so unpleasantly easy to do, or perhaps it was because it moved just a little as I did so, making a soft little creak that somehow sounded rather like a small scream.

But I gritted my teeth and ignored the noise. I knew it was no good giving in to silliness. Good detectives never allow themselves to become so het up that they cannot properly observe the scene. I peeped round into the gallery, reminding myself to breathe slowly and calmly. I saw Hazel climbing into her case with a most imploring look in my direction, and George slipping into his with delight all over his face.

The mummy gallery was absolutely silent. And then—

'Daisy,' said Hazel very clearly.

'Shhhh!' we all said.

'Daisy, I don't have the message. It's not in my pocket. I think I left it on Uncle Felix's desk. DAISY!'

'Not now! Quiet!' I hissed urgently. 'Someone's coming!'

And they were. My heart hammered like a rabbit caught in a trap as the footsteps approached, and someone walke into the gallery.

I looked – and for a moment I thought there had been some kind of mistake. The person who had appeared was short and very stout, wearing a pinny and a kerchief, and wheeling a mop and bucket. She was, unmistakably, a cleaning woman. I had a vision of jumping out to warn her of the peril she was in, at the probable expense of my own life (I would make a lovely corpse, and it would be for a noble cause), but I paused, and then was glad I did.

A minute later, another woman came in after her. She was thinner and taller, wearing dark clothing and carrying a rucksack on her back. She looked every inch a thief. And I wondered why on earth we had all been so sure that the person behind so many robberies was a man.

'Evening,' said the plump cleaning woman calmly. 'How are you, my love?'

'Very well, Beryl,' said the thin woman. 'Now, do you have the objects I asked for?'

The cleaning woman reached into her bucket and pulled out a bundle wrapped in newspaper. 'Here you are – all three – though I couldn't quite match the ring. I found something near enough, I hope. Take a look.'

The thin woman made a small annoyed noise. 'Humph!' she said. 'Well, I suppose you tried. Now, hand them over, and I'll give you your payment.'

The case fell into place in my head. I thought of Bridget, and the way she can be clever without anyone noticing. I thought of how the list of objects had reminded me of one of Mrs Doherty's shopping lists. We had suspected a keeper or a guard, but of course cleaners knew the museum too, and its objects. A cleaning woman could be here at night, and leave a door open for the thief – the *female* thief. Girls can be detectives, just as much as boys. So why shouldn't a girl become a master criminal?

I remembered what George and Alexander had said too: that there were huge rooms below the museum, full of objects that the galleries couldn't display. What if the requests were not for the objects in the cases, but for objects *like* them from those packed away downstairs? *They* would never be missed.

I knew I had the answer. But something else was happening. Beryl, the cleaning woman, had brought in an air of dust around her, and it added to the dust of the room and the corridors. And, although I am usually perfectly in control of myself, in this particular instance my nose acted independently of me in the most traitorous way.

I hardly like to write it, but the fact is that at that moment – I sneezed.

It was a very loud sneeze, and it echoed about the room, and Beryl yelled and dropped the packet she was holding out. It fell to the floor, clinking, and out of it rolled a golden ring and a little stone scarab, and something else that I didn't have the chance to see before the black-clad woman rushed across the room and pulled me out from behind the mummy case – which was turning out to be very unlucky indeed.

I kicked out with all my might, and she yelled but did not drop me.

Then I heard several voices at once.

'Put her DOWN!' screamed Hazel, shoving her mummy case open with a bang.

'Drop her! Drop her!' shouted George and Alexander, leaping out of theirs.

'You little rats!' screamed the criminal mastermind, and she took me by the neck and shook me so hard and so ferociously that her face blurred in front of me. My throat was hurting dreadfully, and I was furious with her, and with myself. I clawed at her cheeks. She yelled, and shook me even harder, and then there was a very loud noise, and all at once I was falling to the floor and the woman's hands were no longer around my neck.

Although my mind is brilliant, I had been quite shaken by my adventure, and so it took me a moment to realize that the loud noise had been someone shouting. It took me another moment to make sure that I had not been hurt – and then I sat up quickly, my neck aching like anything, and looked about.

The two women were crouching on the floor with their hands up. Hazel, looking extremely warlike, was standing between me and them, and behind her was Uncle Felix and a whole group of very menacing-looking policemen.

'Uncle Felix!' I croaked.

'Daisy!' gasped Hazel. 'You're all right!' She knelt down and threw her arms about me. That hurt.

'Do stop it,' I said, through my very sore throat. 'Haven't I told you that heroines never die?'

'Daisy Wells,' said Uncle Felix in his coldest voice, 'you are in more trouble than you can possibly imagine. Now, the police will be taking these two women outside to their Black Maria, and I will be helping them, and while I do so the four of you will follow me in absolute silence. Do you understand?'

'Yes, Uncle Felix,' I said. 'But, if you *do* need help, you should tell us.'

'George and I can tie excellent knots . . .' began Alexander – and withered under Uncle Felix's glare.

The four of us followed Uncle Felix and the policemen as they led the two women out of the museum in handcuffs. We were in the most terrible trouble, some of the worst we had ever been in, but—

'We *did* catch the thieves,' I whispered.

'And how!' George whispered back. 'Pinkertons and Detective Society for ever!'

We all beamed at each other, very secretly.

When we got back to the flat, Uncle Felix's wrath was terrible. I was almost impressed. He shouted at us for quite ten minutes about being impertinent idiots who thought we were detectives.

'We *are* detectives!' I said, again and again. 'We caught the criminals, and I wouldn't really have died – anyway, *you* were there. We left the incriminating note for you on purpose.'

We had not, but Uncle Felix did not need to know that.

'Doesn't it prove that we are good at solving crime?' I asked.

'YOU ALMOST GOT YOURSELVES KILLED!' bellowed Uncle Felix.

'And *you* almost got yourself killed twice last month,' said Aunt Lucy, who was watching the argument from a chair in the living room. 'Felix dear, do calm down. You've caught the thief you were looking for, and it *was* an inside job, just as you thought. That woman had worked at a whole string of museums under various different aliases, and I suppose she recruited her accomplices from her old friends. A gang of criminal charwomen, how clever!'

Uncle Felix sighed hugely. 'Well,' he said, 'I suppose I did. And it was clever of you.'

'It was!' I cried.

'BUT,' he went on, 'you must stop putting yourself in danger. You know I have to at least *appear* to look after you, tiresome child.'

'We *both* do,' said Aunt Lucy. 'Now, Felix, do let the children explain their side of the story. I'm dying to know. Bridget has called George's father, and he should be here in half an hour. I shall look after Daisy's injuries while they tell us all about it.'

Aunt Lucy smeared arnica on my bruises, and we told her how the treasure hunt had led us to uncover a real criminal plot. It sounded even more thrilling now that it was over.

'I must say,' Uncle Felix said rather grudgingly when we had finished, 'one day you might be rather good spies.'

'We're good spies *now*!' I said. 'In fact, we're quite brilliant.'

'Indeed,' he said drily. 'All the same, I would prefer you to work up to it more slowly. Boys, you will be safely back at school by Monday, but – let's see – we need to find something to occupy Hazel and Daisy; something not remotely criminal. It's a good thing you'll be with them, Lucy. Make sure they're bored this week, will you?'

I rolled my eyes. Aunt Lucy smiled.

But that is really the funniest part of this whole story. Because our utterly boring week ... turned out to be not so boring, after all. In fact, it turned out to lead us straight to the Rue Theatre and our seventh murder mystery.

# THE CASE OF THE DROWNED PEARL

Being an account of
The Body at the Seaside,
an investigation by the Wells and
Wong Detective Society, with assistance
from the Junior Pinkertons.

Written by Daisy Wells
(Detective Society President), aged 15,
and Hazel Wong
(Detective Society Vice-President and Secretary),
aged very nearly 15.

Wednesday 29th July 1936.

# HAZEL

My name is Hazel Wong, and I never expected a murder on my summer holiday – but then nothing about the English seaside was as I'd imagined it.

Two and a half years ago I was sent from my home in Hong Kong to Deepdean School for Girls, a very English boarding school. Before I arrived, I hoped I might have polite English boarding-school adventures, with midnight feasts and jolly pranks, and a best friend who looked like a character from an English children's book. And I *did* – but somehow the midnight feasts and the pranks became the least exciting parts of my life in England. For my best friend Daisy Wells and I have been caught up in several real-life murder mysteries during the last few years, and we are now seasoned detectives, with horrid murders, kidnappings and midnight chases as ordinary to us as Geography lessons.

I am not the girl I was when I first arrived in England – but all the same she is still there, underneath everything that has happened, and some things never change. No matter how hard I try to understand the English, I never quite succeed. And this trip was no exception.

When Daisy and I were invited to the seaside by Daisy's mysterious Uncle Felix and Aunt Lucy, and instructed to bring our friends (and rival detectives) Alexander and George, I was delighted. A beach to me is a soft, smooth stretch of sand between pure blue sea and high green mountains. The water, when you dip your toe into it, is as warm as a bath, and the sun beats down beautifully hot.

I know now that I ought to have been prepared. I have suffered through two chilblainy English winters, three blustery springs and three drizzly summers, but somehow I still saw that soft white beach in my mind.

And then we stepped off the train at Saltings yesterday, and a seaweed-strong gust of wind slapped my face and rain spattered against my cheeks, and Daisy took in a huge breath and said, 'Oh, heaven!'

I stared at her in shock. My teeth were chattering and my bare legs were goosepimpled. This was not the beach holiday of my imagination. This was hardly a holiday at all. This was torture.

George burst out laughing at the look on my face, and I glared at him.

'Hurry up, all of you!' said Aunt Lucy briskly, leaning into the wind. 'The hotel's just down this street.'

She had on a very sensible tweed suit, and looked as dull and respectable as anything. She fitted in perfectly with the other cheerful English holidaymakers piling off the train, clutching buckets and spades and chattering – but I had the feeling that whatever mission she and Felix were on was not respectable in the slightest.

That, of course, was why the four of us were here: to pretend to be ordinary children on holiday while they carried out an important and secret errand for the government. Uncle Felix wiped drops of rain from his monocle, and winked at me.

'It ought to clear up soon,' he said.

But it did not.

Saltings was small, bare and white, the houses as flat and featureless as the sky. We arrived at our hotel in another terrific gust of rain. The sea was just behind us, beyond a long, lonely front. It was deserted apart from a rather harassed-looking young woman walking a dog, and a policeman proceeding slowly along, his blank face as blue with cold as his uniform.

I had been hoping for grandeur, something rather like the Peninsula Hotel in Hong Kong. But our hotel was only a white, four-storey house at the end of a terrace of identical white houses, all a little worn, although they did have rather fancy filigree railings and handsome stone pillars round their doorways). The plaque next to the door read THE LAST RESORT, which made Aunt Lucy and Uncle Felix laugh.

'Won't we have a lovely holiday here?' said Uncle Felix.

'A *holiday*,' said Daisy, raising her eyebrow at him. 'Yes, of course, *won't* we?'

Uncle Felix raised his eyebrow back at her, and for a moment they looked intensely like each other, both so tall and golden and blue.

'Do be a good girl, Daisy,' he told her. '*You* are here to run about on the beach, eating ices. Who Lucy and I happen to meet while we're here ... well, that is no one's business but our own. Do you understand?'

Daisy rolled her eyes, and the rest of us nodded. I have seen hints of Felix and Lucy's secret life – the coded messages they get at all hours of the night; the times they rushed out of their London flat carrying nothing but their hats, and then stayed away for days before coming back in disguise. It is all quite classified, I know, and I try not to be too curious, but it makes Daisy hungry to discover more.

We went inside, into a foyer with worn leather chairs and a rather chipped chandelier, and windswept guests murmuring politely about the weather. The hotel restaurant and bar were on our right, and the lounge was to our left – I could hear the chink of cups and saucers, the rustle of newspapers, the hum of voices. A chambermaid hurried by, fresh folded towels in her arms, and vanished through a doorway behind the front desk. A sign at shoulder-height read: THIS WAY TO ROOMS. GROUND FLOOR: 1–4. FIRST FLOOR: 5–12. SECOND FLOOR: 13–20. THIRD FLOOR: 21–28.

The desk itself was staffed by a round-faced man in a smart green and silver-buttoned suit who introduced himself as the hotel manager, Mr Geck. He was passing out our keys (Daisy and I were in Room 3 on the ground floor, while the boys' room was number 6 on the first floor, where Aunt Lucy and Uncle Felix, in Room 7, could keep a respectable, chaperoning eye on them) and calling for the porter to take our cases, when there was a commotion in the Last Resort.

All our detective work has taught me to notice everything, even if it does not seem important, so I had already been half listening to two women who were speaking together in low tones in the lounge. Then I turned as a small, slight woman came through the front door of the hotel, staggering under the weight of an enormous, battered suitcase. I felt rather delighted because I saw that she had skin as dark as George's. It is always a little gift not to feel quite so alone among people who look like Daisy.

At the same moment, a tall, muscular man with a moustache came through the doorway to the rooms, a towel under his arm. He caught sight of the woman with the suitcase, and then looked beyond her at the women in the lounge – and I saw his handsome face change and redden.

'Now, Toni, we AGREED!' he shouted, and he went storming past us into the lounge.

The two women stopped speaking. One of them – I saw she was holding a notepad and a pen – had an eager look on her face, while the other folded her arms and set her jaw. This woman was pale-skinned, tall and broad-shouldered, and her hair was cut short, just brushing her earlobes. The woman carrying the suitcase went rushing forward in concern, but the tall woman brushed her aside.

'It's all right, Karam. Now, what's up this time, Reggie?' she asked the moustachioed man. The journalist – for I was sure this was what she was – began to write again, scribbling and blinking up at the man in great excitement.

'Oooh, Watson, I recognize that journalist!' Daisy breathed in my ear. She was watching the action too, of course. 'She's quite a famous one – Miss Mottson, from *The Times of London*. And that lady – why, I know who she's talking to! Antonia Braithwaite, the swimmer! She's *the* woman of the moment – she swam the Channel last year, and she's been preparing for the Olympics next week!'

I noticed Mr Geck looking suddenly nervous as he watched the scene, his knuckles white on his desk.

'Didn't we agree, no press?' shouted the man Reggie at Antonia Braithwaite. 'It's hardly fair! You can't spend a day out of the papers!'

'We didn't agree any such thing,' she said coolly. 'I recall you bellowing that at me at the meet in Great Sandmouth earlier this year, but you never gave me a chance to respond. And, if you had, I'd have told you to go away. Why shouldn't I give interviews? The Games are in a few days, and I've a real shot at a medal.'

'Because – because – look here, why don't you want to interview *me*?' said the man, putting his hand rather roughly on Miss Mottson's arm.

'I haven't heard *you* spoken about as a medal hope, Mr Victor,' she said, jerking away from him. 'You haven't won a race in months.'

Reggie Victor turned red. 'See here! I've got just as much chance as she – and, besides, how am I to win sponsorships if I don't get any press? Toni's taken the Fry's sponsorship, and the Guinness too – how's a fellow to live?'

'Reggie, *do* go away,' said Miss Braithwaite irritably. 'Karam, for heaven's sake, put that case down and show him out, will you? Or get Sam to do it. Sam! I must finish this interview.'

At that, Mr Geck jumped into action. He strode forward, put his hand on Karam's shoulder and whispered in her ear. He was not formal with her as he had been with us, and Karam bent towards him and nodded – they seemed to know each other well. I was fascinated.

'Here, what are you two muttering about?' asked Reggie Victor.

Mr Geck, ignoring him, went hurrying to the front door to wave into the street. Beyond him I saw the policeman, still proceeding slowly along, take notice and begin to move rather more quickly towards the Last Resort.

'Sir,' said Mr Geck to Mr Victor, stepping back inside. 'I've just called Constable Neaves over. Now, don't you think it'd be wise for you to leave the ladies alone, before he arrives?'

Mr Victor wilted. He gave Miss Braithwaite, Mr Geck and Karam one more glare, turned on his heel and stormed back the way he had come. Miss Mottson stared after him, making frantic notes on her pad.

'Please do ignore him, Miss Mottson,' said Miss Braithwaite. 'And Sam – call off Neaves, will you?'

'If you're sure, Toni?' said Mr Geck. 'You don't think Reggie will come back and make more trouble?'

'Of course I am!' Miss Braithwaite snapped. 'Oh – I can't stand it. He never leaves me alone!' Her face had gone pale with rage.

'Well, all right,' said Mr Geck, sighing and waving Constable Neaves away.

The women took their seats again, and Mr Geck came back over to us. Everyone tried to behave as though they had not noticed any argument.

'Is that lady . . . local?' asked Aunt Lucy, nodding at Antonia Braithwaite.

'She's my half-sister,' said Mr Geck proudly, suddenly smiling. 'Miss Antonia Braithwaite, the Pearl of Saltings! She was born and bred here, like me. She's a very famous swimmer now, but she still remembers where she came from. And Miss Singh is her assistant – we all went to school together, so she's family too, really.' He pulled a wry face. 'Antonia's always been a personality, and Karam was always a timid little mouse – if you ask me, Toni takes advantage of her, but then it seems to work. Now, Evans will show you to your rooms.'

Daisy nudged me as we left the foyer, the porter walking ahead with our suitcases. 'Fascinating, Watson!' she hissed. 'A celebrity swimmer, her jealous rival – and her down-trodden assistant. Could be the makings of an interesting case, don't you think?'

It rained all that afternoon, so heavily that even Daisy could not persuade us to go outside. She fidgeted and grumbled, kneeling up against the tall windows of our room, itching to get out into the wet garden behind the Last Resort. As soon as it began to ease, she wriggled straight out of the window and clattered onto the iron fire escape that snaked up the back of the hotel to pound on the boys' window and declare that she was taking a walk *at once.* I was forced to follow her, even though Daisy knows I don't enjoy heights, a fact which has caused trouble during several of our cases in the past.

'I'll come!' said Alexander, once he had recovered from his shock at seeing us. He opened the window so we could scramble inside.

'We'll all go,' said George. 'And, honestly, you could have come up the ordinary way.'

Daisy scoffed. Daisy Wells never does anything *the ordinary way* if she can help it.

And then we were out of the hotel and walking down to the front, in a landscape that was entirely water. There was water in the sky and under our damp feet, and there to the left of us was a grey sea pressing itself up against a grey beach that stretched out as flat as the palm of a hand and then gathered itself up into lumpy, pebbly hills. It was broken up by long wooden walls that began up by the front and vanished into the sea. They looked rather like ribs, as though the beach had a skeleton. Gulls dived out of the dull sky above us, shrieking, their orange feet and beaks the only bright things I could see. A few families played on the beach, children running screaming in and out of the waves. I clenched my fists inside the pockets of my thin summer mac and tried not to shiver.

'Isn't it lovely?' sighed Daisy, turning her face up to the drizzle. 'Ugh, you're all dreadful. Making me stay cooped up inside when it's like *this*! *I'm* going for a paddle.'

She pulled off her shoes, tucked her socks into them and went scampering away down the beach towards the sea.

'What's a paddle?' I whispered to George – for sometimes I still do not understand English expressions.

'It's when it's too cold to swim, so you just stand in the sea,' George explained.

'Oh!' said Alexander, who is half American, and often as surprised at English things as I am. 'Nothing to do with boats, then?'

'You're all WET!' Daisy shouted up at us. She was in the sea up to her knees, her skirt in a knot.

'CORRECT!' George shouted back, holding out his arms and shaking water droplets off himself. I couldn't help it – I laughed. Alexander did too, and grinned at me, and I felt myself light up.

'Come back, Daisy!' I called. 'I'm freezing.'

'You're BORING!' Daisy shouted – but she came pattering back up the beach, leaving perfect prints in the shingle. 'I've brought my bathing costume, and I mean to swim, whatever you say.'

'We could go swimming tomorrow morning!' said Alexander eagerly.

'Early-morning swimming!' said George. '*Spiffing*, eh?' And he winked at me.

'I'll come if everyone else is,' I said, through gritted teeth.

'Oh, you'll love it!' Daisy said to me blissfully. 'It's the most marvellous feeling.'

I absolutely knew that was a lie.

# DAISY

Now it is my turn to write, for this time Hazel shan't have all the fun. Ignore what she has said. *This* account is the true story of the quickest murder mystery the Detective Society has ever solved (and I suppose the boys of our rival agency, the Junior Pinkertons, were also there).

I have looked over the pages that Hazel has already written and I find them lacking, primarily because Hazel, for all that I have taught her well, still does not understand the true joy of the seaside. First of all, it is quite frankly indecent to expect sun when one goes to an English beach. The rain is part of the fun of it. The pebbles should prickle your toes and the water should shock your skin. You should feel braced, and electrified, and above all *surprised*. Hazel wants the sea to behave like a bathtub because she has *no* sense of adventure.

That was why I wanted us to go for a bathe before breakfast was served on Wednesday, the morning after we arrived in Saltings: to have an adventure. But, I must admit, I was not expecting the kind of adventure we had.

I was first of the four of us outside, of course, because no one else moves fast enough. It was 7:01 by my wristwatch, and the rain had just stopped. Hazel was grumbling about food, just as I knew she would be, but who wants to wait until after breakfast to go for a bathe? Anyway, Uncle Felix and Aunt Lucy had already left on their mission, whatever it was, so *they* weren't bothering with breakfast.

The day had begun misty, and gulls went sweeping above my head, screaming. They were the only things that moved in the stillness apart from me, and I ran and ran, across the road, over the front and onto the beach, as fast as I could to make the world wake up.

I went rattling down the pebbles towards the sand and the sea, wriggling out of my good clothes (my bathing suit was on underneath, of course – a lady never leaves the hotel in just her bathing suit, and we would need to be dressed nicely again for breakfast). The tide was going out, lapping gently away from the silver sand. The others were following behind me (too slow!) and that was why I was the first to see the thing huddled on the shore.

This *thing* was lying on the stones just above the high-tide mark, next to a clump of seaweed stretched out like a hand. I looked at it, all lumpy and discarded in the mist, and I thought to myself immediately: *That's a dead body*. I assumed I was being hopeful and romantic, but I ought to have learned to listen to myself by now. My instincts are always brilliant, and so they were this time.

'What's that?' said George sharply from behind me.

'A seal,' said Alexander. I *cannot* understand how Alexander's mind works. Whoever heard of a seal wearing clothes?

'It's not a seal,' said Hazel. 'Look, oh, look, it's a bathing suit – no, it's *in* a bathing suit.'

'It's a body,' I said, quite certain at this point.

'Quickly!' cried Hazel. 'They might be hurt!'

She and Alexander hared over to it, kneeling down on the pebbles to shake its shoulders and pat its cheeks.

'It's a woman – the swimmer from yesterday!' gasped Hazel. 'Oh, poor thing – she's so cold!'

I turned to look at George. I hate to admit it, but our minds work in similar ways sometimes, and I saw that this was one of them. His face was set and frowning.

'She's dead, isn't she?' he asked me.

I nodded.

'Daisy!' Hazel called. Her voice wobbled. 'Daisy, she's – she's—'

'And, um,' said Alexander, sitting back on his heels, 'there's something I think you should— George, come here, will you? She – she doesn't smell right.'

'What d'you mean?' I cried, and I went rushing over and knelt down over the body.

Hazel hates describing dead bodies, and that is why I am writing this part. But *I* don't mind saying that when I looked into her face – she had a strong jaw and wide cheekbones – I realized that this was indeed Miss Antonia Braithwaite, the Pearl of Saltings, who had crossed the Channel last year and was one of our hopes for a medal at the Berlin Olympics the following week. She has been in all the papers. Her bathing costume, I noted, was a Jantzen, suitable for long swims. Her hair was brown, and escaping from under her bathing cap, which had not been put on properly. Her face was not at all nice to look at – but I have seen plenty of dead bodies by now, and I felt reasonably certain from the clues it gave me that she had drowned.

I said this to the others, and they all looked rather horrified.

'Imagine,' said Hazel in a small voice. 'Just yesterday she was alive. We *saw* her. She was full of plans, and – and *life*, and now that's all gone. It's awful!'

I tried not to roll my eyes and remind her that this was exactly how murder worked.

'Yes, but *smell* her, come on!' said Alexander. 'She smells – I can't explain it – all *wrong*!'

I leaned down to the body and sniffed. I hated to admit it, but Alexander was perfectly correct. I ought to have smelled nothing but the sea, salty and sharp, but instead I got a whiff of something else extremely familiar.

She smelled clean, soft and fresh – it was the scent of Pears soap.

'She's taken a bath,' I said. 'And she hasn't been in the sea since, or it would have been washed off.'

'But why would she take a bath and then go to the beach?' asked George.

'Exactly,' said Hazel. 'Why not just stay in the tub where it's warm?'

I glared at her. Hazel is so bold these days, even when faced with dead bodies. 'Antonia Braithwaite is a great athlete,' I said coldly. 'Great athletes do not have time to think about things like *staying warm.* But it is odd.'

I was still kneeling to peer at Miss Braithwaite, and I noticed she had flecks of something on her shoulder, and more on her arm. I thought at first that they were hairs from her head, but they were the wrong colour – a much darker, richer brown – and far too short. I pointed them out to Hazel, and she carefully folded some into her handkerchief.

My heart was beating fast. We had a dead body, a strange smell and some unknown hairs. This felt very much like the beginning of an excellent murder investigation.

And that was when a man came running at us out of the mist.

# HAZEL

I gasped, and Daisy shouted, 'STAY BACK!'

The man stumbled backwards, startled. 'I'm just out for a run,' he said. He was pale and broad-chested, with black hair and a rather gorgeous moustache – I realized that we had also seen him yesterday afternoon: Reggie Victor.

'What are you doing here, lurking on the beach like this? And what's wrong with your friend?' He gestured to the body.

'She's not our friend, she's Miss Braithwaite. And she's dead!' I choked out.

Mr Victor stared at the body. His face went absolutely grey.

'What do you mean *dead*?' he cried. 'Nonsense – but— What did you— How—?'

'We found her like this,' said Daisy smoothly, pinching my arm. She was telling me to be on my guard,

112

to watch his reaction. I gave myself a little shake and pulled myself together. 'Do you know her?'

'She – Antonia's a swimmer. Like me. I'm a – and she's rather a – I mean – we – yes, we knew each other,' Mr Victor finished weakly. It was clear that he did not realize we were the people who had overheard their argument yesterday. He was stumbling over his words, gasping, mopping his brow again and again. My detective senses tingled. This man, I thought, was highly suspicious. He knew – and disliked – the victim. He was on the spot. He must be our first suspect.

'But surely we know who you are!' said Daisy, fluttering her eyelashes encouragingly.

Mr Victor took the bait.

'You may well,' he said, drawing himself up. '*I* am Reggie Victor. I won the Templeton Baths Meet this year, and – well – I'm currently in my final week of training for the Olympic Games.'

'Oooh!' said Daisy, and only I could hear the mockery in her tone.

'Do you live in Saltings, sir?' asked George.

'I'm staying at a hotel,' said Mr Victor. 'You know, the Last Resort.'

'But that's where we are!' cried Alexander. He sounded so eager and innocent – but then I saw the determined set of his jaw and I knew it was all an act. The Pinkertons were as focused on detection as Daisy and I were. 'See here, shouldn't someone go and get the police?'

'You all ought to go,' said Mr Victor, trying to look heroic. I found this even more suspicious than his manner before. 'I'll stay here. You're kids – you don't need to see this.'

'Oh, sir, we can't just leave you!' said George. 'I'll stay too. Alex, you take the girls.'

I saw the angry spark in Daisy's eye, and I knew that leaving the body – and with the Junior Pinkertons, who, as much as they were our friends, would always be our detecting rivals in Daisy's mind – was the last thing she wanted to do. Now that George had suggested it, she had to play along, but she would do it on her own terms.

'Oh no, Alex must stay as well!' she said. 'We'll be quite all right on our own, won't we, Hazel? This is really *too* horrid – we're better off waiting in the hotel while you brave boys stay here to guard the body until that *excellent* policeman arrives.'

She and George stared at each other for a moment, and then George nodded and said, 'All right, Daisy.'

Only I could see the tremble of her lips as she tried not to laugh. I realized what she had done. She had freed us up to investigate clues at the hotel, while the Junior Pinkertons were stuck with a body we had already looked at.

We stepped away up the beach together, Daisy quickly pulling on her clothes again, leaving George, Alexander and Mr Victor standing over Miss Braithwaite's huddled body. The mist was still thick, and Daisy had to catch my arm several times as I stumbled over the stones.

'Do you think they'll be all right with him?' I whispered to her as soon as we had moved out of earshot. 'What if he – what if he *did it*?'

'He's not likely to hurt them either way,' Daisy said, shrugging. 'He has no idea we're anything more than a group of silly schoolchildren. But, Hazel, that's not important. What *is* important is that, before that clodhopper Neaves arrives to ruin everything, we must get into the dead woman's room, and Mr Victor's, and find out all we can about them both!'

# DAISY

I thought we should never get away from the Junior Pinkertons to begin our investigation in earnest. Hazel is so obsessed with that boy Alexander – although he is not *half* as clever as she is, and his arms are *too long*, still she pines after him. Dull.

But at last we escaped, and I was free to run and run and run all the way back to the hotel – but I did not lead Hazel through the front door once she had caught up. That would have been a terrible error. No, I paused and told her about my excellent plan.

'We must go to the front desk together,' I said. 'I shall inform whoever's there in my prettiest voice that there is a dead body on the beach. They will panic and, while they're busy running about and fetching that bumbling Neaves man, we can scan the visitors' book for Miss Braithwaite's and Mr Victor's names at our leisure. Then we shall have the time it takes *him* to arrive and mess

116

about with interviews – I estimate at least twenty minutes – to detect unhindered. The chambermaids won't go in to tidy the rooms until everyone is at breakfast, after all, and it's still only twenty-five past seven.'

'But how are we going to get into the rooms?' asked Hazel. 'Oh, wait, I know! We can get out of our bedroom window like we did yesterday, go up the fire escape and see if any of the other windows are open.'

I felt . . . well, not resentful, for Hazel is my best friend and I am perfectly aware by this point that she sometimes has ideas almost as excellent as mine. But certainly I was . . . taken aback somewhat. It had been exactly what I was about to say, but I had not quite got round to saying it yet.

'I *was* going to say that there are other ways to get into a room,' I said at last. 'We may not need to use the fire escape.'

'You were *not* going to say that,' said Hazel. 'You just invented it because I said your idea.'

'Silence, Watson,' I said, sticking out my tongue at her crossly. 'It's true. I've heard of an excellent way to get into a hotel room using only a teaspoon. Now, before we begin, do we have any more facts that could be of use? Did either of us hear anything or see anything that might be relevant?'

'Apart from that argument yesterday?' asked Hazel. 'I've been trying to think, but nothing particularly – we

117

went to bed at ten last night, we woke up at a quarter to seven, and we went out for a bathe. *Before* breakfast!'

'Hmm,' I said. 'Yes, but there is one thing. I remember half waking up in the night and hearing a bath running.'

Hazel gazed at me. 'You don't think – no!' she said, sickened. 'You don't think you heard the murder?'

'I don't know,' I said slowly. 'But it may be important. It was at eleven p.m. by my wristwatch. Bear it in mind as you search the room – not all of them have bathrooms, so we may be able to work out which one it was. Now, are you ready? As soon as we've announced Miss Braithwaite's death, we shall only have a few minutes in which to work.'

Hazel set her chin and nodded.

'All right. Let us begin the case in earnest!'

# HAZEL

This sort of detective work always leaves me feeling unsettled.

Mr Geck, as smartly dressed as yesterday and sorting through the morning papers at the front desk, seemed appalled when we told him what we had discovered on the beach. His rather round, friendly face turned absolutely white, and he could only stammer in shock. He looked about frantically, gasping and absolutely forgetting to order anyone to take his place or to telephone the police station. That bought us more time, of course, but I could not feel glad about it, for we had just informed him that his sister had died.

We watched him stumble out of the front door towards the beach. I was thinking about my own little sisters. Daisy gave me a sharp poke in the ribs. 'Buck up, Watson! He's a suspect too, since he was the victim's half-brother. Come on – we must act quickly.'

We waited as an old guest in a lacy wrap picked up a newspaper and shuffled into the lounge, and then we were free to slip behind the front desk to look at the visitors' book.

Antonia Braithwaite was in Room 1, and Reggie Victor in Room 4, both on the ground floor, just as we were. That was an odd thought – that the players in this mystery had been so close to us, *and* to each other.

'Yes, indeed,' said Daisy, catching my thoughts. 'Interesting, isn't it? Well, I know at least one thing: this will make it terrifically easy for us to detect. We don't even need to climb the fire escape again! Isn't that useful for you, Hazel?'

I glared at her.

'I shall take Miss Braithwaite's room, of course,' said Daisy, who always gives herself the plum jobs, 'and you can look at Mr Victor's. Agreed?'

'Agreed,' I said with a sigh.

'Excellent,' said Daisy. 'And now, Hazel, I shall have to put my teaspoon plan into practice. How useful that breakfast has already been laid out. I trust I do not need to explain to you how to search a room?'

Daisy, for all we have solved eight murder mysteries together, still has very little faith in anyone who is not herself.

*

Daisy and I crouched together at Reggie Victor's door. Daisy had unscrewed its handle, and she was wriggling a breakfast teaspoon around in the hole where it ought to sit. She gave it one last determined prod, and then, just as I was convinced we would have to give up, the door creaked open.

'There!' said Daisy. 'See?'

I stood up, sighing, and stepped inside, while she went on to Room 1.

I got a surprise when I saw the room, for I had expected it to be the image of ours – all pale blue chintz and potted plants and fringed lamps. But this room was rather more masculine, red papered walls covered with sporting scenes and a large iron-framed bed, its sheets tumbled back restlessly. The air smelled of cologne, and there was a ewer and basin with shaving things next to the bed – this was not one of the rooms with a bath. I felt rather intimidated.

But nevertheless I went to work – and, as I did so, my suspicions about Mr Victor hardened. I was very glad he had decided to go for a run on the beach. He had left all his things behind, not bothering to lock them away in the hotel safe: his passport, a hopelessly unbalanced chequebook (he was several hundred pounds in debt, which made me feel rather queasy), and a pile of letters from sponsors withdrawing their support following poor performances (so there was no money coming in, either). On the side there were pots of pills and potions and muscle creams that promised renewed vigour. The story was clear: Reggie Victor was no longer a swimmer at the top of his game and, since he was not winning races or being sponsored any more, he was facing money troubles. Now I understood why he had been so cross with Miss Braithwaite yesterday. But could this be a motive for him to have committed murder?

I had found out what I could from this room – now I wanted to see what clues Daisy had uncovered.

# DAISY

The victim's door opened easily. I was proud of my new skills as a locksmith. I slipped inside and looked around.

The window was a touch open. *So we could have come in through the garden!* I thought. The room – with a bathroom attached, I noticed – was well ordered. I saw at once what sort of person Miss Braithwaite had been: one who was absolutely dedicated to her sport. There were pictures of her dotted about the room: Antonia swimming; Antonia with medals round her neck. There were weights for her to exercise with, and training schedules. I had a look at one, and saw dates neatly ticked off. This was a woman whose whole life had been preparing for her next competition.

I was rather impressed. It is usually Hazel who feels sad for the victims (and even the murderers. Hazel's heart is much too soft and kind, no matter how I try to teach her), but I felt ... sorry, I must admit, that this woman would never get to the Olympics. It is always nice to see someone be the best at something, as I am the best at detecting, and she was the very best swimmer England had to offer. She had crossed the Channel faster than any man has ever managed – but now she would not be around to show the world how excellent she was.

I shook myself out of this daydream and got to work. What else could I glean about Miss Braithwaite?

There was a sheet of paper on the writing desk, much scribbled over and crossed out. At the top it said *Last Will and Testament of Antonia Braithwaite* – it was not signed, and looked very much unfinished, but I scanned it quickly. All her money – quite a considerable amount – was to be left to Karam Singh and Samuel Geck, divided between them equally. This was interesting: was it a motive for Miss Singh and Mr Geck, or did it rule them out, because the will was not yet signed? And why had such a careful woman not left this in the hotel safe?

The bed was neatly made, and her clothes folded in their drawers – there, again, was the tidy person who had created all those schedules. Antonia Braithwaite did not seem much interested in fashion, or beauty. There were only two simple rings and a few necklaces in her jewellery box, and only a powder compact and a lipstick on her chest of drawers. Next to that, though, I saw something much more interesting: a tray with a bottle and two glasses, both empty. I sniffed at them and, although they seemed to have been rather badly rinsed, I smelled alcohol. But in one glass there was something else as well – something that made me stand up straighter in surprise. It was a sleeping draught, I was sure of it.

Then I ducked my head into the bathroom, and found quite a different scene. It was not tidy at all – water had been splashed about as though a whale had been bathing there. A towel had been put down to mop it up, but water was all over the floor, where a heap of damp clothes was soaking in it. A half-melted cake of Pears soap still lurked where it had slipped to the bottom of the tub, along with a slick of soapy water.

A lesser mind than mine might have struggled to make sense of the scene, but, what with this and the glasses, I was beginning to piece things together – and an unpleasant picture they made too.

I suddenly had a thought, and went darting out of the bathroom to the wardrobe. I pulled it open, and there – I had hardly dared hope, but – there was a woman's thick, luscious fur coat, in a rich brown colour. I needed to check it against the hairs Hazel had in her handkerchief, but I was convinced they would match.

I reached out and ran my fingers lightly over the fur. *And it was damp.* Damp inside and out, with a smell on the lining (I leaned forward and sniffed carefully) of clean soap and water. And, at the place where the sleeve met the body, a small tear in the lining that looked new.

I felt electrified. A damp, torn coat. Water still in the bath, and a heap of wet clothes beside it. A bottle and two glasses, one smelling of something to put you to sleep. A body lying on the beach with the scent of soap.

I heard footsteps behind me and I whirled about in triumph.

'*I know what happened to Antonia Braithwaite!*' I said.

# HAZEL

I pushed open the unlocked door and stepped into Antonia Braithwaite's room to find Daisy poised in the middle of the floor, eyes blazing and arms outstretched. She did not seem at all surprised to see me.

'Hazel, you absolutely must listen to me!' she cried. 'I know exactly what happened! Of course, I don't know the murderer's name yet, but that will come. Hazel, *I know everything.*'

'*Except* the murderer's name,' I repeated, making a face at her.

'Quiet!' hissed Daisy. '*Don't* speak. *Listen.* Now, we both inspected the body, didn't we? So we can verify that it smelled of soap, not the sea. Yes?'

'Yes,' I said.

Daisy glared at me.

'I told you, *do not speak*! Now, I have looked at the victim's room, and what have I found? There is a bathroom, and it's in *terrible* disarray. There's water all over the floor, clothes in a wet heap and soap still at the bottom of the tub. And what, added to the fact that I heard a bath running last night, does that tell you?'

I caught my breath. 'You think she drowned – in *this* bath! She was murdered *here* last night and then carried to the beach!'

Daisy narrowed her eyes. She always hates it when other people steal her denouements. 'Indeed,' she said at last. 'But that is only the beginning of my deduction. There are two glasses and one of them smells odd – I think Miss Braithwaite was drugged before she was murdered! I have been wondering why I didn't hear anything apart from the bath last night, seeing as we were so close, and that would explain it. She wasn't awake to struggle!

'Then I looked in the wardrobe and I found a brown fur coat, with fur that I believe matches the hairs we discovered – a damp coat that *also* smells of soap. And I understood how the body was moved. After she was drowned, she was undressed and then put into her swimming things – remember that ill-fitting bathing cap? Then she was wrapped in her fur coat, and carried to the beach. It was raining last night, so no one else was likely to have been out – and of course that's why the coat is still damp, and a little torn.'

'But why the coat at all?' I asked, pulling out my handkerchief and giving it to Daisy, who made a pleased

128

noise when she saw the hairs. 'Oh! You think – to make things look ordinary, in case someone *did* see them?'

'Exactly,' said Daisy, twinkling at me. 'A lady in a fur coat being helped along by a friend after a long night out is quite uninteresting. And this, along with the running bath I heard, gives us a strong idea of *when* the murder and the moving of the body took place – some time after eleven last night and before the rain stopped this morning. Then the coat was returned to the wardrobe.'

I frowned. 'But, if there was time to bring the coat back, why not clean up the scene of the crime too, instead of leaving such a mess? And why take her all the way to the beach? Was she supposed to have been swept out to sea and not found?'

'No,' said Daisy, and I saw the crease at the top of her nose deepen as she thought about it. 'No, she was left above the high-tide mark – which means the water would never come up to cover her. I noticed that at once. She couldn't have been swept away unless there was a storm – and no storm's been forecast. What if—'

But there she was brought up short, because suddenly the door to Antonia Braithwaite's room opened and Karam Singh, the small dark woman we had seen with Antonia yesterday, stepped inside.

We froze, and I heard myself gasp.

'What on earth are you doing here?' demanded Miss Singh.

# DAISY

I thought on my feet, which is something all the best detectives must be able to do.

'Ah, Miss Singh!' I said. 'Thank goodness you're here. Mr Geck's been looking for you.'

'Sam?' asked Miss Singh. 'Why?' She was frowning, distracted, and she looked around the room as though she hardly cared that we were there.

'It's because of Miss Braithwaite,' I said, and her eyes came back to mine, and went wide and frightened.

'What happened?' she asked. Now, I have been a detective for several years, and I thought that an odd question. I had not said anything other than Miss Braithwaite's name, but here was her friend, assuming the worst.

'Oh *dear*,' said Hazel, and I nudged her as hard as I could to tell her not to be wet and sorry for a suspect – for since Miss Singh was named in Antonia Braithwaite's will, I had decided that we must add her to the suspect list, along with Mr Geck, until we could detect further.

'Her bed hasn't been slept in,' said Miss Singh, pointing as she moved across the room. 'And what on earth's happened in the bathroom?'

'You – you might want to sit down. I'm afraid we have some news,' said Hazel gently. 'Miss Braithwaite— There's been an accident. I'm terribly sorry. She's – she's dead.'

Miss Singh froze.

'Nonsense,' she snapped, and her eyes snapped too, sharp and black. I suddenly saw the shadow of someone else beneath the sweet politeness, someone firm and fierce. 'Of course she's not *dead*. She's going to the Olympics next week. She can't be *dead*. Who told you she was?'

'We saw her,' said Hazel apologetically. 'We found the body.'

'Nonsense!' cried Miss Singh again, glancing at her wristwatch. 'It's five to eight – she's out for her morning swim. She'll be back at eight for breakfast, and then you'll see!'

Hazel and I exchanged a look, and I felt delighted that the same understanding still flowed between us.

'You know rather a lot about her schedule,' I said.

'Of course I do,' said Miss Singh wildly. 'Who do you think drew it up? Who do you think planned it all? Who d'you think manages the sponsorships and the journalists and the training? Why, Antonia hasn't an organized bone in her body – never has, and I've known her since we were ten years old. If I didn't lay out her life for her, she'd miss everything. I'm even drawing up her will for her – she's looking through it at the moment. She went travelling without me once and it was a disaster. *Not* that she thanks me for it, most of the time.'

I am not ordinarily cross with myself, but I was briefly cross now. It had not occurred to me that Antonia might be tidy because someone else was tidying for her – and it ought to have done. First impressions, after all, can be misleading, and a good detective should never simply accept the obvious answer.

'You must know her very well,' said Hazel, still gentle.

'She's my best friend,' said Miss Singh. 'And she can't be dead. It's nonsense, I tell you.'

'Of course it's not nonsense!' I cried. I was tired of this. 'It's absolutely true. Miss Braithwaite is dead, and you stood to profit from her death. The question is, where were *you* at eleven o'clock last night?'

# HAZEL

Sometimes I wish Daisy were not quite so . . . Daisyish. She simply leaps to conclusions and forgets how other people work. I saw the horror on Miss Singh's face, and I knew that Daisy had made a mistake.

'It's none of your business!' she gasped. 'I don't even know who you are! Get out of Toni's room! Get OUT! SAM! SAM! HELP!'

And, of course, we had to leave.

'*Daisy!*' I hissed as the door slammed behind us.

Daisy glared at me. 'What ought I to have said?' she asked. 'She was being idiotic. Grown-ups never listen! She needed to understand.'

'But – her friend died,' I said. 'You heard: best friends since they were ten, Daisy. They're just like us!'

'They are *not* like us,' grumbled Daisy. 'First of all, we didn't meet until we were eleven. And, second, neither of us will ever die. I won't allow it, Hazel.'

'*Exactly!*' I said, sharper than I meant to. 'That's it. If someone told you I'd died, you'd never believe it.'

'Do be quiet, Hazel. That is not relevant. What *is* relevant is the other information we heard in the course of our interrogation.'

'I'm not sure that was an—' I began.

'*What did we hear?*' Daisy pushed on, through gritted teeth.

'Miss Singh said Miss Braithwaite hadn't been to bed,' I said, sighing. 'She might be lying, of course, but the bed didn't look slept in – and that fits with the timing of the bath you heard. Miss Braithwaite was making a will, which would have left all her money to Miss Singh and to her brother, Sam – Mr Geck. And Miss Singh organizes everything for her, even her sponsorships. What if she thinks that Miss Braithwaite's been taking her for granted, and she wanted some of that money?'

'But there's a problem with that,' said Daisy. 'The will isn't signed – Miss Braithwaite never got the chance to. So that motive doesn't quite work. Unless – what if Miss Singh wasn't happy with just half? What if she's been squirrelling away Miss Brathwaite's money, and didn't like the idea of it being divided up between her and Mr Geck? She could have decided to take matters into her own hands.'

'Well, all right, say she did,' I said. 'Say she knocked out Miss Braithwaite with a sleeping draught – how could she have even lifted her into the bath, let alone carried her all the way to the beach? Miss Braithwaite was tall and strong, and Miss Singh's smaller than I am.'

'Easy!' said Daisy. 'I'm sure she could. I'll show you. Hazel, hold me.'

She suddenly slumped, making me catch her. I got a thumping blow from her shoulder, yelped and staggered forward. Daisy was a dead weight, astonishingly heavy, and I was shocked.

'Ow! Daisy!' I gasped. 'Stop it! Please! I can't do it!'

'Yes you can, Hazel!' said Daisy. 'Go on, go at it properly!'

Then I heard a voice say, 'Whatever are you two doing?'

# DAISY

It was George, his arms crossed. It must have begun to rain again, for his hair was slicked down with water. He looked amused. Alexander was standing just behind him.

'We are carrying out a reconstruction,' I told him with dignity. 'What are you two doing? Why aren't you still with the body? This is dreadful detective work. We gave you one job!'

'A job you didn't want!' said George. 'And Mr Victor didn't try to kill us, thank you for asking. He only ranted on about Miss Braithwaite dying. I think he's almost upset that his competition's gone – or perhaps that's just an act. Anyway, we had to leave when that Neaves man, the neighbourhood bobby, arrived. I think he's the only policeman in Saltings – and Mr Geck said he's new here, so he's hopeless. Doesn't have the first idea of what to do. He touched the body and rolled it about when he was searching it for clues! We tried to stop him, only it was no good, and we were beginning to look suspicious. We left Mr Victor arguing with him and came to find you – only we got caught by Mr Geck. He's in a terrible state – he's so upset he's *telling* us things.'

Inside I raged. I am so tired of useless, clod-hopping policemen ruining our cases! But there was nothing to be done – we simply had to reveal the real murderer, and quickly, before this Neaves person arrived at the wrong answer.

'You have to come and talk to him,' said Alexander. 'The stuff he told us sounds important.'

We all hurried out to the foyer, where we found Mr Geck slumped against the desk, his head buried in his hands. He pulled himself upright when he heard us coming.

'Oh dear!' cried Hazel. 'I'm sorry!'

I did not say anything, for I never can see the point of polite nothings. And anyway I was suspicious. How could we be sure that this grief was not simply a clever ruse to throw us off the scent?

Mr Geck gave a sob.

'*I'm* sorry – this is terribly unprofessional of me – but Toni's *gone*!' he choked out.

'But you saw something, didn't you, sir?' said Alexander encouragingly. 'You were telling us – something happened last night. In the bar.'

'Mr Geck,' George explained, 'also works at the Last Resort's bar.'

'Everyone's more than one thing here,' muttered Mr Geck. 'The postman's our chef some evenings. Antonia used to be one of the chambermaids, when I was the porter. But now she's our Pearl – I mean, she *was*.' His face twisted with sorrow. 'She travels all over – we didn't see her for a year while she was in foreign parts – but, when she's back in Saltings, she always stays here. That way we can see one another, and Karam – Miss Singh – and I can make sure reporters don't get to her without an appointment. We were *protecting* her, and now—'

He gave another sob, and Hazel and Alexander made encouraging noises. I was simply desperate to get to the story. And I could see that George was too.

'So, the bar,' he said carefully. 'Everyone was there, weren't they?'

I felt frustrated. If only *we* had been there too, instead of asleep – but, once again, we were foiled by our ages! Oh, how I long to rush forward in time and simply *become* twenty.

'Yes, Toni and Karam were at the bar with the journalist – Miss Mottson, I think – and so was that fellow Reggie Victor. He's washed up, and that's a fact. I can always tell the desperate ones. There's a certain look in their eyes, and he had it. He snarled at Toni and Karam – Toni looked flustered; she was odd all evening, kept checking her watch – and then began to flirt with Miss Mottson. I think it was really to annoy Toni, though Miss Mottson took the bait wonderfully. They left together at about half past ten, and then Toni looked at her watch again and said, "I think we should call it a night." Karam turned to go, and Toni leaned over the bar at me and whispered, "Sam, can you send a bottle of whiskey and two glasses to my room in fifteen minutes?"

'I was curious – I asked her why, but Antonia wouldn't say, just shook her head. So I knocked on her door at a quarter to eleven, and she opened it, just a crack, and took the tray from me. I couldn't see inside – she was careful about that – but I heard a voice, and I think . . . well, I think there was *a man* in her room.'

I was intrigued. I felt my hands clench, my breath short in my chest.

'Did you know the voice?' I asked.

Mr Geck shook his head, a frown on his face. 'I don't *know*,' he said, frustrated. 'I thought he sounded familiar, but I can't be sure.'

'Hmm,' I said. 'Now, detec— er, Hazel, Alexander and George, I think we need to go and have a . . . chat. Come along quickly!'

'Thank you!' Hazel called over her shoulder as I hurried the three of them away.

It was time for a Detective Society meeting.

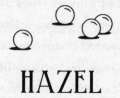

# HAZEL

Of course, this was the perfect opportunity to have breakfast, and a bunbreak. Bunbreak is an important part of our detective work. It's really the word for the biscuits we eat every morning at school, but nothing helps detection like sweet food, and so we make sure to have several bunbreaks during each of our cases, even the ones in the holidays.

We went hurrying across the foyer to the dining room and sat down at our places. The waitress (a chambermaid with an apron on over her uniform) looked at us rather askance when Daisy asked for iced buns along with the usual bacon and eggs – for it was only just after eight in the morning – but, under the circumstances, buns for breakfast felt like the only thing that would do. As we ordered, I saw Aunt Lucy and Uncle Felix walking by on the front, talking to a man wearing dark glasses, but I carefully ignored them.

*The Case of the Body at the Seaside,* I wrote down, as we all bent over my casebook. *Present: Daisy Wells, Hazel Wong, George Mukherjee and Alexander Arcady.*

We waited until our breakfasts (and extra buns) were in front of us, and then we took a deep breath and began.

'All right. What do we know?' asked Daisy.

'A woman's dead,' said George.

'Very imprecise,' said Daisy scornfully. 'The Olympic hopeful Antonia Braithwaite is dead – found drowned on Saltings beach this morning just after seven a.m. The suspects are—'

'Aren't the *clues* the important thing in this case?' asked George. 'She was found smelling of soap, not seawater. She had hairs on her bathing suit, and when you went to her room you found a fur coat that matched those hairs.'

'You're taking things out of order!' Daisy snapped. '*Suspects* first!'

George and Daisy glared at each other. They both enjoy being in charge, and do not really know what to do when challenged. Alexander and I shared a sympathetic look, and then I turned towards Daisy and said, 'All right. The suspects are Reggie Victor, Miss Braithwaite's sporting competitor; Sam Geck, her brother; and Karam Singh, Miss Braithwaite's assistant.'

'And now motives for each of them, if you please, Watson.'

I ticked them off on my fingers. 'We know Mr Victor resented Miss Braithwaite's success, and he's struggling for money at the moment. Perhaps Mr Geck was cross at being left behind, working in the family hotel, while his sister travelled the world? And Miss Singh is Miss Braithwaite's friend from school, the one who organized her life, and she might have resented Miss Braithwaite taking advantage as Mr Geck mentioned.' I frowned. 'Then there's the will. If it had been signed, then that would be an extra motive for both Mr Geck and Miss Singh – but it wasn't finished . . .' I tailed off. I wasn't quite sure what the will told us.

'Can we move on to the facts in the case *now*?' asked George.

Daisy glared at him.

'The body was on the beach, above the high-water mark. She was only wearing a bathing costume and cap – but at some point she had also been dressed in a fur coat, a coat that is back in her wardrobe this morning,' I said. 'This, and what Mr Geck says he heard, tell us that the murderer had access to her room. They were there a quarter to eleven, and Daisy heard the bath running at eleven – so the murder must have happened after that time. Daisy, you think that the murderer drugged Miss Braithwaite's drink, took her into the bathroom and drowned her in the bath.'

'I don't *think*,' said Daisy, 'I use the facts to lead me to a conclusion. It's quite different. It is also interesting that the real crime scene was not tidied away, and the murderer allowed the soap to slip into the bath and perfume the corpse – the whole crime seems so badly planned!'

'Mr Geck's story is interesting, isn't it?' asked George. 'The man's voice?'

'He might be lying,' said Daisy. 'He might have made up the whole story to seem more innocent. What if he was the person who brought the glasses to her room with one already drugged, and then killed her?'

'He might,' said George, nodding. 'That's very true. That's one possibility. If he *is* lying, he's the murderer. But if he's telling the truth—'

'Hey!' said Alexander. 'I get it! If he's telling the truth, then the murderer's a man – so it can't be Miss Singh, right?'

I suddenly remembered the dead weight of Daisy slumped against me. 'From that reconstruction Daisy and I did, we know that Miss Singh couldn't have carried Miss Braithwaite's body to the beach, either!' I put in, looking at Daisy.

She frowned. 'Hazel, you are simply weak. I don't think you were trying hard enough.'

'I *was*!' I said indignantly. 'It couldn't be done. She's too small, her voice doesn't sound deep enough – and she's too tidy, as well! This isn't the crime of a tidy person, don't you see?'

Daisy sighed. 'Oh, all right,' she said reluctantly.

'We definitely have to rule her out. That leaves us with Mr Victor and Mr Geck. But, if the murderer was Mr Victor, why would Miss Braithwaite have made an appointment to meet him in her room? She didn't like him.'

'That *is* odd,' agreed George. 'And there's something else. Why did he – or Mr Geck – take her all the way to the beach? We keep asking this, and it's important. Of course, it would have been easy to do in the rain last night – but still, why? Was it supposed to look like an accident? Her being above the high-water mark – which means the sea couldn't have washed her away – was that on purpose? Was she *supposed* to have been found so soon?'

'Here's another question we keep running up against: why murder her before the will was finished?' asked Alexander. 'If it was her brother, he's more likely to benefit if she finished and signed it, right? So maybe that points to Mr Victor.'

'Whichever of them it is, he's done a dreadful job of covering up his tracks,' said Daisy. 'The crime was so poorly cleaned up, which is odd, since the murderer had all the hours between eleven, when I heard the bath running, and ten past seven, when we found the body. It speaks to a *very* slow and lazy mind.'

'See here,' said Alexander, his face brightening. 'I've just had a thought. I can imagine a very good reason for Mr Victor to need to murder her before her will was finished, *and* a reason why she might let him into her room too.'

'Go on, Alex,' said George.

'Well, who's next of kin who isn't family?' he asked. 'Someone you're *married* to. What if – what if Mr Victor and Miss Braithwaite were secretly *married*, and only pretending to hate each other? That could explain why she let him in, why they're staying at the same hotel, and why the body *had* to be found looking as though she'd drowned. So she'd be registered as dead by misadventure, and all the money would go as quickly as possible . . . to her husband.'

'Good heavens,' said Daisy, rather faintly. 'That is . . . why, that is either arrant nonsense or rather intelligent detective work. And I did find those rings in her jewellery box . . . it would make sense. How annoying. Hazel, write all this down immediately! We have several questions we need to answer at once!'

# SUSPECT LIST

1. *Reggie Victor* — seen arguing with the victim the day before her death. An angry, violent person who is in desperate need of money. What if he is secretly married to Antonia Braithwaite, meaning he benefits from her death?

2. ~~*Karam Singh* — the victim's assistant and old schoolfriend. She manages everything for her — including the making of her will!~~ RULED OUT. She is simply too small to carry Miss Braithwaite from her room to the beach, and Mr Geck's witness statement — whether or not it is true — also shows she can't be involved.

3. *Sam Geck* — the victim's brother, and the hotel manager. What if he resents his sister for her success, and wants to kill her for her money? He says he saw the victim alive at 10:45 p.m., when he brought glasses and a bottle of whiskey to her room, just before Daisy heard the bath running. If he is lying, he is the murderer. If he is telling the truth, Reggie Victor is the murderer!

# DAISY

We jumped up from our seats at breakfast (several hotel guests tutted) and hurried back out into the foyer. I felt convinced that something was happening without me, and so it was. Mr Geck had now pulled himself together to look halfway presentable. He nodded at us.

'Constable Neaves is here,' he said dully. 'I told him everything I told you. He'll sort this out.'

I was horrified.

'Quick!' I cried. 'We must follow him before he ruins the case!'

I was not entirely sure, in the moment, what I thought might happen, but I was determined to stop it anyway. I hared past the front desk towards the rooms, Hazel, Alexander and George following. Antonia Braithwaite's door was open, and we rushed inside . . .

to find Constable Neaves standing next to her chest of drawers.

The constable was a most unattractive man, I thought at that moment – all bug-eyed and pale-faced. But, more importantly, he was reaching out for the two glasses – and he was NOT wearing gloves.

I was scandalized. What a clodhopper! Why, he was about to contaminate the crime scene! It was clear that he was in no fit state to lead this investigation.

'Stop immediately!' I cried.

'Daisy!' said Hazel. I ignored her. This was no time to be Hazel-ish and cautious.

'Stop, I say! This is an important investigation, and you're ruining it,' I snapped.

Our raised voices had been heard. Mr Geck appeared in the doorway, Reggie Victor, Miss Mottson and Karam Singh just behind him.

'See here!' said Reggie. 'You children shouldn't interfere with police business!'

'What do you mean?' Constable Neaves asked me slowly, ignoring Mr Victor. At that moment, I could have slapped him. 'Miss Braithwaite drowned. I'm merely looking through her room to confirm that it was an accident and not – well . . . you know.'

'It wasn't an accident at all! Someone drowned her!' said Alexander. Mr Geck made a noise. Constable Neaves's frown deepened.

'Have you lot been playing detective?' he asked, eyeing the four of us. 'Telling yourself stories? The poor woman drowned in the sea. It's quite clear to me.'

I clutched at Hazel's arm, gasping. It could not be! I had been prepared for him to get the wrong murderer, but not for him to assume that there was no murderer at all!

'See here, are you sure?' asked Mr Victor from the doorway, as Miss Mottson craned round him eagerly, notebook in hand. 'I know Antonia was infuriating, but I don't think – I don't think that fits. She was a good swimmer, and she knew the sea here. I don't think it was an accident.'

'Of course it wasn't!' said Mr Geck. 'Neaves, you can't be serious. My sister wouldn't drown, not at *our* beach. She's been swimming there since she was a baby! I told you I heard a man in her room, at a quarter to eleven – I've been thinking, and I'm sure now that it was Mr Victor.'

Reggie Victor jumped. 'What? NONSENSE!' he roared at Mr Geck, who looked offended.

My head was spinning, and when I looked at Hazel she seemed as puzzled as I felt. Why should both our remaining suspects insist that Antonia Braithwaite's death was murder, when we had just concluded that leaving the body on the beach was designed to make it look like an accident?

Suddenly I knew what I needed to ask.

'Why was Miss Braithwaite making a will?' I said to Miss Singh. 'Why *now*? Quickly! And *don't* say that you won't tell me because I'm too young.'

She looked puzzled and hesitant – oh, people are so frustrating! They are always three steps behind me, and it makes me itch with annoyance. 'It's important!' I said. 'If – if you tell me, I think I can tell you who killed Miss Braithwaite.'

'But— Oh, I don't see that it matters any more!' said Miss Singh, and I saw that there were tears in her eyes. Silly! 'It was because of the Olympics – the money she might win, you know. It was more money than either of us had ever – well – if she got a medal, Toni would be really quite rich suddenly. And that worried her. She kept saying she needed to make a will now because it was the only way to— Oh – well, I shouldn't say.'

'Now really, you must!' said Miss Mottson, who seemed as fascinated as we were. 'My readers will want to know!'

'Well, she didn't want *a certain person* to get any,' said Miss Singh reluctantly. 'When she went away for that year, when she travelled, she *met someone*. Those rings she always keeps in her jewellery box – they're engagement and wedding rings. She didn't want to talk about it, or tell me who he is, but . . . that's why we travel about so much. She regretted the marriage, you see. He's been following

150

her, and sending her letters, pleading with her to come back to him.'

A husband! So we were right! Miss Mottson looked quite electrified.

'You!' cried Mr Geck. He was pointing at Mr Victor. 'You – you – *you're* the husband, aren't you? That's why you followed her here! To kill her, before she could make her will!'

'Of course I'm not the HUSBAND!' shouted Mr Victor. 'I've never been married in my LIFE. That's NOT my style. If you want to know what I was doing last night, well – Miss Mottson, tell them!'

'Ah,' said Miss Mottson, and her cheeks suddenly turned pink. 'Well – I happened to have been in Mr Victor's company all evening, after we left the bar. Simply interviewing him, you know,' she added quickly. 'I certainly don't think he could have had the opportunity to be the man Mr Geck heard.'

So Mr Geck was lying, after all! But then – what about the husband?

'I – I think you ought all to calm down,' said Neaves. 'This is NOT a murder investigation. I've told you. Toni simply drowned!'

And I suddenly had a brainwave. I knew – everything. I knew who had killed Antonia Braithwaite, and why. I knew why the body had been posed so that it looked like an accident, and why the crime scene had not been tidied away. I knew why Miss Braithwaite had let her killer into her room and had a drink with him.

'Mr Victor didn't kill anyone,' I said. 'Neither did Miss Singh, or Mr Geck.'

'But then – who did?' asked Alexander.

I looked at Hazel, and she looked back at me. And, once again, understanding flowed perfectly between us.

'The person who just gave himself away by calling Antonia Braithwaite by her nickname,' she said. 'The man who arrived at the scene of the crime without ever having been called, and who has just been trying to tidy it away. Her husband. *Constable Neaves.*'

I saw the colour entirely drain from Neaves's face, and I knew that we were right.

# HAZEL

I felt the exact moment when the case clicked into place, like a door slamming shut. The window to the garden in Antonia Braithwaite's room had been open – of course, she could have let someone from Saltings in on the night of her murder. She might have arranged a meeting with her husband without telling her friend Miss Singh – some things, after all, even best friends do not talk about.

Constable Neaves was the man whose voice Mr Geck had heard. He was strong enough to carry Miss Braithwaite's body to the beach – and his uniform would have given him a perfect excuse, if anyone saw him helping a lady along late at night. He left her above the high-water mark so the sea couldn't sweep her away, and she would be discovered quickly – and, although he had quickly rinsed out the glasses, mopped at the water in the bathroom and put back the coat, he had not bothered to do anything more because he had planned to arrive on the scene before anyone went into Antonia Braithwaite's room the next morning. As the only policeman in Saltings, he would be able to call the case an accident, and tidy up loose ends at his leisure.

At least, he *would* have done – if we had not happened to be there.

This crime did not fit with Mr Victor, who Miss Braithwaite really had disliked immensely. Nor did it fit with her assistant, Miss Singh, who was too small to lift her and too precise to commit such a messy crime, or Mr Geck, who wouldn't have benefited from the unsigned will.

But it did fit with Constable Neaves.

I remembered what Mr Geck had said – that Neaves was new in town. That here, people were more than one thing. A hotel manager could be a bartender. A chambermaid could be a famous swimmer. And a policeman could be a husband, out for revenge.

I thought of what Miss Braithwaite had said the day before, when she and Mr Victor had argued, and Mr Geck had gone to fetch Neaves from outside to usher Mr Victor away: 'Oh – I can't stand it. He never leaves me alone!' We had thought she meant Mr Victor – but, of course, she meant Neaves.

I looked at him. Would he bluster, or flee? I was not sure he knew, either – but then he gasped and made a grab for the glasses on the chest of drawers. He was trying to destroy the evidence.

'STOP HIM!' shouted Daisy, and we all leaped forward. I got hold of his jacket – and it felt shocking to be laying hold of a policeman in this way. George and Alexander blocked him from touching the glasses, and Neaves gave a furious yell.

'This is ridiculous! This is madness!' Reggie Victor was shouting. Mr Geck was wringing his hands in horror. Only Miss Singh stepped forward.

'Put his cuffs on him,' she said clearly. 'Hurry up and do it. Sam, do you have a room with a lock on it? Some sort of cupboard?'

'There's an empty room on the first floor,' said Mr Geck dizzily. 'I – what—'

'Lock him up there, then,' said Miss Singh. 'Hurry! Reggie, go with him. Go on! I shall call the *real* police.'

'No, wait,' I said. 'Daisy's uncle and aunt – they're out at the moment, but they know important people in the police. They can sort all this out when they get back.'

And that was Neaves done for.

'And to think!' said Daisy that afternoon, once Uncle Felix and Aunt Lucy had returned from their mysterious meeting and called up the Commissioner. The hotel was now swarming with fingerprint experts and police photographers – and all Miss Mottson's friends from the press. 'To think that Uncle Felix and Aunt Lucy wanted to use us as cover for their mission, when *we* were the ones who had the most exciting adventure in the end!'

'I was never enough for her,' Neaves had said bitterly, as he was led away. 'I kept on hoping she'd reconsider – I spent years following her about, trying to get her to see sense. That's why I came here, and why I asked her to meet me. And she agreed, and I thought – at last! But then I saw the will on the side, and realized she was trying to cut me out of her life. I couldn't have that! So I acted.'

'What a silly sob story,' said Daisy, sniffing. 'If only he hadn't already had sleeping drugs in his pocket when he arrived at her room, we might believe it wasn't planned all along. Oh, we ought to be ashamed of ourselves that we didn't tumble to it more quickly, Watson. I've always complained about clodhopping policemen, but I never thought one of them would be a murderer!'

'But really they're only people, just like us,' I said.

'They are *not* just like us,' said Daisy with dignity. 'We are far better. And aren't we clever! We solved a murder in one morning. We *ought* to get a medal.'

'Tell Uncle Felix,' I said. 'He might give you one.'

'He won't,' said Daisy, sighing. 'He's so boring that way. And I really ought to have solved it more quickly.

This murderer was silly and lazy and, well, *clodhopping*. What an idiot!'

'We did solve it, though,' I said, smiling. 'All four of us.'

'*Two* of us!' said Daisy. 'Though I suppose the boys were there as well.'

I felt my face go scarlet.

'Oh, really!' said Daisy. 'Why do you still care about Alexander? You're such a bother, Hazel.'

'I care because he's good, and nice, and ... sometimes I think he might care about me too,' I said boldly. 'And you can't stop me, Daisy, because I'm *your* bother, and you wouldn't know what to do without me.'

Daisy sighed again. 'It's true,' she said at last. 'I would not want to be without you, no matter how many idiot boys you fall in love with. Now, Hazel, can we *please* go and bathe in the sea?'

I looked outside. A very small spark of sunshine was gilding the edge of a cloud far down on the horizon. And, despite all the horror of the murder, and the shock of its solution, I suddenly felt warm for the first time since we had arrived here in Saltings.

I was with Daisy. We were on holiday. And tomorrow – why, tomorrow was my fifteenth birthday.

'There, see?' said Daisy. 'You look more cheerful already. Didn't I tell you you'd get to like the seaside in the end?'

# THE HOUND OF WESTON SCHOOL

Written by Alexander Arcady
(Junior Pinkertons Co-President).
Weston Boys' School, Sunday 6th December 1936.

(Written in invisible ink, and delivered to Deepdean
School for Girls after Hazel and Daisy had departed
for Egypt in December 1936. Only opened and
decoded by Hazel Wong in January 1937, after she
returned to Deepdean for the spring term.)

Dear Hazel,

You asked in your letter last month whether George and I had solved our problem with the dog, and I guess I never replied. I'm awfully sorry. It's just that the problem with the dog kept changing, until it became less about the dog after all, and a lot more about – well, you'll see.

I keep thinking about you waiting for this letter, though, and feeling guilty. I'm hurrying to finish it, because I want to catch you before you leave for Cairo – and before we leave too. George and I are going to be on the SS *Hatshepsut* on the thirteenth, see, the same ship you're travelling on. I hope you don't mind. Now that I think of it, it seems awfully bold of us, but I thought – I mean, I guess we're all friends, aren't we? We're travelling with one of Harold's college pals, Joe Young. He's a bit of a fool, if I'm honest, which is why we picked him. That was George's idea, so we can do what we want without him getting in the way. Not that I think anything's going to happen! Except it often does with you and Daisy around.

It's awfully hard to know what to say in this letter, somehow. George says I should put it all down, and I guess he's right – it's easier to write what I feel than say it out loud. I know I can jaw away for hours, but I don't always say much when I'm talking. I think I've been in England too long to be able to simply come out with it any more.

The fact is, Hazel, I think you're ~~absolutely completely~~ ~~Hazel, you're just~~ ~~Ever since the summer I~~

I've bottled it again. I'll just tell you about the dog, and then maybe the rest will follow.

We came back to Weston after the summer hols feeling pretty spiffing. We'd solved the seaside murder with you, of course, and then we went back to London to stay with George's father. George was reading a lot of books about history and politics, so we spent most days walking round and round London baking in the heat while George told me about the Dreyfus Affair and the Spanish Revolution. I was just longing to get back to the house and keep re-reading *The Hound of the Baskervilles* – somehow Sherlock Holmes always reminds me of you and Daisy. I guess it's that nickname she calls you. Though I don't think you really are the Watson, whatever she says.

Then I went on to Wilkie Collins, though when George saw me reading *The Moonstone* he said, 'I hope you're not going to start asking me to hypnotize you!' and grumbled about only the bit-part mystics in detective novels having brown skin. He's right, of course, and it made me feel like a poor sort of detective for not having seen it as clearly as he did. Reading is just another sort of detection, after all.

This is all relevant, I promise, because of what happened when we got back to Weston in September.

Being a fifth year isn't all it's cracked up to be, Hazel, and that's a fact. You've got the younger years slogging for you, of course – it's jolly nice not to have to worry about tidying up after yourself, or at least that's what I expected before it began to happen. But as soon as it did, I realized that it's also unbearably awkward. It was like George telling me off about Wilkie Collins again – I felt I should have realized sooner how utterly unfair slogging is, and it made me wish I was a better person.

And then there are all the rules you've really got to follow, because all the young fellows are looking up to you now, and the masters are watching you and expecting great things from you, university entrance and so on, so there's heaps more prep.

So George and I didn't notice at first that something wasn't quite right at Weston.

It's not as though there was anything big, not at first. Or at least – not the kind of thing we're taught to see as big. Not wars, or kings, or even jewel thieves or spies. (Our first mystery, of course, was a spying one, and you and Daisy always seem to trail murders wherever you go. I guess that influenced the way we were thinking.)

But this started small, and we didn't even realize it was all related until later. One week Mr Gambino forgot to give us prep, and the next week he gave us double. Our breakfast was late several times, and our porridge tasted burnt. Our friend Bob Featherstonehaugh was missing a pair of pyjama trousers from his washing, but Bob always has his mind somewhere else – and I couldn't find one of my undershirts, but I thought I must have just left it in London. A first year screamed out one evening that he had seen an enormous rat, but he was told to stop making up silly stories. Weston usually has mice in the classrooms but never rats, so everyone knew he must be a fantasist.

And then *it* happened.

I've told you before, Hazel, about the cross-country races we're forced to go on, as part of our blasted officers' training programme. Between Weston School and the village is wild moorland, with great craggy rocks and hilly scrambles and trees that menace the horizon, and during the races we have to weave up and down and in and out of tufty bits of grass that grab our ankles and rabbit holes that trip us and scree that takes our legs out from under us for miles and miles.

The first years usually cry during the first race of the term, and quite often they get lost, so us older boys have to go find them. (There's a rumour that years ago a boy fell into a marshy bit and suffocated, but I think that's bosh, just a story to scare everyone.)

As I've said, George and I use the races to hold Junior Pinkertons meetings – we sprint the first mile, then rush down a certain hill when no one's looking and duck into the cave at the base of it. It's dry and warm inside – at least, it is if you sit to one side – and it has a handy hollow log that we perch on, to hold our meetings, as well as store our Detective Box inside.

So that was where we were headed, anyway, that afternoon – it had been fearfully long since our last meeting and we were feeling guilty. George was ahead of me, as always, already ducking down the hill in the rain. I was looking around to make sure we weren't being watched – when I heard a great yell from the trees away to my right.

George says I'm too tender-hearted, and maybe I am – but I don't think that's such a bad thing. And, as you'll see, it's lucky I did decide to pull up and veer towards the yell.

When I burst through the trees into the clearing I found it was one of the third years, Bly Minor, doing the yelling. He was lying crooked on the ground and screaming as though his heart would burst. His left hand was cradled in his right, and I saw blood shining on it.

Somehow the agonized sound Bly Minor was making (just like a dying cow) and the blood on him made me think about those Wild West books I used to read when I was a kid and we first met. Remember, Hazel? I was such an idiot then. Anyway, my first ridiculous thought was that he'd been shot.

I swung round to see the assailant, expecting – a masked horseman on a black stallion, I guess. But then I came to myself and remembered I was in England, on a drizzly fall afternoon, with nothing bigger than a pheasant and some approaching fourth years in sight for miles.

'IT BIT ME!' hollered Bly Minor. So that put paid to the gun idea.

By this time the fourth years – and George, looking annoyed – had arrived on the scene, pushing through the trees to stand next to me.

'What bit you?' I asked, kneeling beside him and taking his hand in mine. I turned it about and saw that it was marked with a curving row of small, neat punctures, deep enough to draw blood.

'A WOLF!'

The fourth years, who were standing in a ragged line behind me, laughed.

'Shut up, pipsqueak,' sneered one, who was called Squeers. 'Missing Mummy, are you? Making up wolves? You fell over and cut your hand on a rock.'

'I did not!' whined Bly Minor. 'It was alive! It leaped on me, I tell you! It would have gone for my throat if I hadn't stopped it!'

'Be quiet,' I said to Squeers and the other fourth years, as sternly as I could manage (George will tell you this wasn't very stern – I'm trying, but I can't get the hang of it). 'It wasn't a rock.'

'You saw the thing that bit you?' asked George. I looked at him and saw he was staring a little past Bly Minor at the disturbed mud on the ground behind him.

'What, don't tell me you two believe him!' laughed Squeers's friend, a boy called Cartwright. 'Just what I'd expect from the Yank and the—'

And he called George one of those names which no decent person would use and that I've promised him *never* to repeat.

'FOURTH-YEAR SCUM!' George bellowed, drawing himself up as tall as he could – which as you know is tall, Hazel. 'WHAT ARE YOU DOING STANDING HERE? RUN! RUN! RUN! GET OUT OF MY SIGHT BEFORE I PUT YOU IN DETENTION FOR A MONTH!'

The fourth years, Squeers, Cartwright and the rest, startled and fled, leaving George and me alone with Bly Minor. The rain was falling more heavily now, running

167

down our faces and sticking our shirts to our backs. The blood on Bly Minor's hand was washing away in pink tear tracks.

'That's them dealt with,' said George, panting a little. 'Bly Minor, get up. You're not dead, stop crying. Is there anything you want to say?'

'It was a wolf,' said Bly Minor stubbornly, still cradling his hand.

'It wasn't a wolf. You're quite all right. Go to San and tell them when you get there that Mukherjee and Arcady sent you. Go on, go!'

'I thought he'd been shot at first,' I admitted, as soon as we were alone in the clearing.

'Idiot!' said George affectionately. 'He wasn't shot. He was bitten, though.'

'I know,' I said. 'Toothmarks. Little ones. I thought a fox?'

'Hmm. Look at this,' said George, gesturing at the ground. 'I know we've obscured it with all our messing around, but you can see where Bly Minor was running. He was going in a straight line until – here – something made him swerve. He jinked and stumbled and fell, here, where we found him.'

I looked. There, in the wet earth, was a set of tracks that weren't plimsolls at all.

'Paws!' I said. 'So it is a fox!'

George was down on the ground now, his eyes narrowed and his nose almost in the mud. I joined him reluctantly. 'No. These paws aren't the right shape to be a fox. They're too rounded.'

'A cat?' I suggested, imagining a panther stalking the woods around Weston.

'These prints,' said George, taking a deep breath, 'are not a cat, or a fox. They are none other than the footprints of a tiny hound.'

I laughed at him. I couldn't help it, Hazel. He might have been making a *Hound of the Baskervilles* joke, but kneeling there I don't think he'd ever looked less like Sherlock Holmes. George is usually so well put together, but that afternoon in the rain his hair had lost its careful brilliantine slick and his knees were filthy.

'Oh, come on, I couldn't pass up the opportunity to say it,' he went on, grinning at me. 'Even if I couldn't make it exactly work. If only the footprints had been a bit more enormous! And it's perfectly true: the thing that attacked Bly Minor was none other than a small black dog with rather long fluffy hair and a pointed snout.'

'How do you know?' I asked. This seemed a bit rich to me.

'First of all, my dear Alex, the distinct placement of the paw pads and the nails mark it out as being obviously canine. Second, you can see some long dark hairs caught on this low branch – hairs not consistent with either a fox or a cat. And third – I saw a small black dog shoot out of the clearing and run past me down the hill as I was coming after you just now. I suspect it was going into our cave.'

'GEORGE!' I exclaimed, thumping him on the arm. 'Why didn't you say earlier?'

'It wasn't the time,' said George, shrugging unrepentantly. 'Besides, you know most of Holmes's best deductions were really through tricks like that. So, shall we go hunt for the dangerous creature who savaged Bly Minor's hand?'

George might have said it was a small dog, but I was still kind of nervous. Bly Minor's hand had been bitten, after all – it didn't seem in a particularly good mood.

We went out of the clearing into the real heaviness of the rain, and scrambled down the hill to our cave – to find frightful chaos. I stood stock-still with horror.

Sharp teeth had gnawed on the wood of our log, prised out the Detective Box, and played havoc with its contents. The tin itself was punctured in a kind of Morse code of bite marks, my notebooks were torn to shreds and George's crime books had chunks taken out of them.

I exclaimed over the remains. George, though, went spying about in the dark recesses of the cave and I heard a series of anxious squeaks, like the air being let out of a balloon in bursts. The noise went spiralling upwards into shrill yelps – and at last an extremely hairy black creature leaped out of the shadows and hurled itself at us.

'Hey!' said George, stepping back smartly, but I was not so quick. A moment later it was on me, its needle teeth nipping at my fingers and my cheek.

'Ow!' I cried, falling backwards in a whirl of black hair and hot breath, and then I felt paws on my neck and a small tongue lick my nose.

I heard George begin to laugh. 'A ferocious hound!' he said. 'Shall I get him off you, Alex?'

The dog yipped as it was picked up, but then wiggled about in George's arms, chewing at his hands.

'Who do you belong to?' George asked it. 'What are you doing here?' As it wriggled I saw that its fur was baby-soft, its eyes were large and its paws, though still small, were ridiculously out of proportion to its skinny legs.

'He's only a puppy!' I said. My hand was stinging and bleeding a little where the puppy had bitten it with its little teeth, and I understood how Bly Minor had got his injuries.

'But he won't always be. Look at those paws! He's going to be huge.'

Then George began to smile to himself.

'What?' I asked.

'Well,' said George, 'this puppy clearly has a keen interest in crime – look at the way he's devoured our notes! Why don't we call him Baskerville?'

While Baskerville whisked about in front of us, growling at his own tail, we sat on what was left of our log, deciding what to do next.

'It's quite obvious what's happened,' said George. 'Someone's been keeping this puppy in this cave, since we used it last. See, there's a bowl, and a bone for him to chew, a rope he must have been tied up with, and a pile of rags for him to sleep in. He obviously gnawed through the rope, found our detective files in the log and chewed those up too, and then got bored and went to find his master – but found Bly Minor instead.'

I was still very upset about our Detective Box – and worried. I'd spent hours on those notes, and for them to be gone like that – it wasn't sporting at all. 'And what if whoever left Baskerville here read them before they were chewed?' I asked. 'What if someone else knows about the Pinkertons?'

'Most likely it's just someone from the village,' said George. 'They can't tell us Weston boys apart. Don't worry, Alex, we're safe.'

'Even so,' I said bitterly. 'I'll just have to write everything up again, I guess.'

I got up and kicked at the nest of cloth that Baskerville had been sleeping in. Then I exclaimed in shock. 'George!' I said. 'Look here – it's not someone from the village at all. This isn't a blanket. It's – it's my undershirt, and Bob's pyjama trousers. The clothes that went missing!'

I could see the Weston laundry labels on them both.

'Whoever's keeping this puppy is from our school,' said George. 'It fits now I come to think about it – that rat the first year thought he saw. Puppies look a bit like rats when they're really tiny, you know. What if that was *him*, and his owner moved him for fear he'd be discovered again?'

'Then it does matter about our detective notes!' I said. 'If they're from Weston – they'll know who we are, and what our notes mean. We have to find out who it is, and make sure they're not going to spill the beans on us.'

'And,' said George, 'I want to know why someone has a contraband dog.'

After that, George and I were dedicated to discovering the owner of the hound of Weston School.

We decided to leave Baskerville in the cave where we had found him – it was sheltered and dry, and of course we did not want to move him away from the person who was giving him food, since we knew we would not always be able to escape from school to look after him. But we thought there was no harm in feeding Baskerville a little extra while we worked on the problem. I didn't know exactly what food puppies ate, and I said so to George.

'We hardly have a choice,' said George. 'It'll have to be food from our plates – which is barely fit for boys!'

It's true that the food at Weston is filthy, Hazel, real slop – most days we have to play a guessing game of what the meat is – and there's never enough of it. But sometimes you can get into the kitchens and charm some extras from the maids, if they like you and you say you're growing, and so that's what George and I set out to do after dinner that evening.

George went striding into the kitchens, head held high in the way he does, knowing he's being looked at, and I ambled after him, grinning at everyone and cheerfully saying hi to them. That makes them all look away sharpish, so they're not caught by my chattering. On our way in we passed the laundry baskets, full of dirty things – and I saw then how easy it would be for anyone at Weston, masters, boys or servants, to snatch up a bundle of them to keep a puppy warm.

We were both hoping to find Beryl – she's the ~~prettiest~~ most friendly maid, always good to talk to – but it was Kate who was hovering over the pots and pans.

Kate was new last year, and is still very quiet. She has big dark eyes, brown skin, dark frizzy hair that she keeps pulled tight back in a bun and a Welsh accent. I've heard the other maids teasing her for it. George is very protective of her, though he denies it when I say so to him.

Kate looked up, startled, when she heard us. But then her eyes shone when she caught sight of George, and we hardly had to say a thing before she was plying us with biscuits and cakes, which we slipped into our school bags to take to Baskerville the first chance we could. She had a series of scratches on her right hand, and for a moment my heart raced – could they be from Baskerville, just like Bly Minor's injuries? – but when George pointed them out she shrugged and said, 'I tried to stroke Bumpkin when he was in a mood, *you* know.'

Sprawled in the corner of the kitchen, Bumpkin the cat made a crosspatch noise and rolled over, showing his padded belly and flexing his sharp claws. Kate smiled fondly at him. 'He's a good cat, really,' she said, which isn't true, Hazel – Bumpkin is a horror and none of the rest of us will go near him.

Kate told us that she'd swapped evenings off with Beryl, who was out walking on the moors with her young man, Hanrahan, and soon the conversation led to the moors in general. 'It's bad enough when you boys are going for runs in this weather,' said Kate. 'Now the masters are getting a craze for it too. Mr Gambino's been going out almost daily – the number of times I've had to clean mud off his trousers and patch them up this term!'

I glanced at George and saw him looking meaningfully at me – and when the bell rang for prep we used that as an excuse to rush off. '*Gambino!*' said George to me as we hurried. 'His trousers torn and covered in mud! You don't think it could be a master who's hiding Baskerville?'

'I don't know!' I gasped. But it was a horrid thought, Hazel. If a master had found our notes, especially Gambino, who had a mean streak . . . I knew my shorthand was hard to read, but all the same it wouldn't be impossible to trace them back to us. And there were some things – well, not only things about the masters themselves, but things that I'd noted down about the cases we'd solved with you two, Hazel. I was on edge.

And that was why I was the one to spot the map and newspaper cutting on Mr Gambino's desk during lessons the next morning.

I ought to say more about Gambino before I go on, Hazel. He's our debating master. He's sort of dull and sort of grey, and he wears little glasses that reflect the light and never show his emotions, but, all the same, when he gets riled up he can be awfully cruel. I don't like him, and we all have to tread carefully around him.

So I was tense as I went up to his desk to hand in my essay (*Is it Man's natural state to live a 'nasty, brutish and short' life, or do we need Society?*). I saw that Mr Gambino was leaning over some bits of paper, making sharp expressive marks on them. One was an Ordnance

Survey map of Weston and its surrounding moorland countryside (I recognized the peaks and troughs of it – George and I have been studying maps to help train ourselves to be better detectives, and the Weston map was one of the only ones we could get without drawing attention to ourselves), and the other was an article torn out of the *Gazette* from a few months ago. I saw the date – August – and the words *treasure* and *lost* and *moors* before Mr Gambino flicked his hand over the papers and sent them spinning under his dull old textbook.

And then I saw that his hand had sticking plasters on it.

I thought about Bly Minor and his bitten hand. I thought about what Kate had said about Gambino's trousers. I thought about the story of *The Hound of the Baskervilles*, and the way some hounds are used to catch on to a particular smell – sometimes a person, sometimes an object – and hunt for it anywhere.

And I wanted to know more about this treasure.

At lunch time George and I went to the library. Mr Holtz the librarian was there alone, a pair of muddy boots drying on the radiator and comfortable slippers on his feet, shuffling books about on his trolley. He looked pleased when he saw us come in. The library's usually quiet – after what happened a couple of years ago, there are still plenty of rumours about it going around, and not many boys come in. I feel bad for Mr Holtz when I think about that.

'Mr Holtz,' I said, 'do you keep the *Gazette*?'

'I have the past three weeks' copies,' said Mr Holtz. 'Which one would you like?'

'We were hoping for older editions,' said George. 'From over the summer. For . . . research, for an essay.'

Mr Holtz waved his hands. 'Gone, I'm afraid,' he said. 'I give them to the maids to put scraps and ashes from the grates in. What were you looking for in particular?'

'Results from the Olympics,' I said, for it was the first thing that sprang to mind when I thought of this past summer.

'Interested in sport, are you?' asked Mr Holtz. 'Moved on from those mysteries of yours?'

'J-Jesse Owens, sir,' I managed to stutter out – which was truthful enough; he was awfully impressive and he won us four golds, Hazel, even if Hitler was horrible about it afterwards. But what had Holtz meant by 'those mysteries of yours'? Was he – was he trying to hint at something? My legs felt like jello, and when Holtz went to get us a photo book of sportsmen and began to talk through it I just let him jaw on until the bell for the end of lunch went.

'Was that a hint? What if he's the one who hid Baskerville – and found our notes?' I said to George, when we finally escaped just after the bell.

'Hmm,' said George. 'I don't know about that, but I *do* think he's lonely, Alex. He was desperate to talk. He *might* even be lonely enough to keep a secret puppy. And you must have noticed the mud on his boots. He's been out walking beyond the school grounds too! That's two for our suspect list. Rotten luck about the *Gazette*s, though. Where do we turn now?'

The answer to that was our friend Bob.

Now Bob, as you'll know from the affair of the letters I wrote to you about last year, is a terrible gossip. You can hardly stop him blabbing – no secret is safe with him, and he goes digging out stories like – well, like a dog after a bone. We thought that if anyone at Weston knew anything about treasure, it would be Bob. So when we interrupted him chattering away about the contraband fireworks he was hoarding under his bed for Bonfire Night, and mentioned treasure to him, he came up with the goods at once.

'You didn't hear?' he cried. 'It's absolutely ripping. Thieves held up a post train from London during the summer hols – right here in Weston. They made off with bags of gold bullion, and they escaped over the moors before the police could catch them!'

'Wouldn't bags of gold bullion be heavy?' asked George. 'How did they get away?'

Bob looked uncomfortable at that, and said, 'Er, was it bullion? It might have been coins.'

'Featherstonehaugh, you're an ass!' said an older boy, Spackman, coming past and hearing our conversation. 'It was pound notes, and they caught all the thieves, anyway. There was one bag unaccounted for but that'll have rotted by now.'

George and I exchanged a glance very quickly. Could this be Mr Gambino's treasure?

Bob turned red and muttered something we couldn't catch. The group of fourth years who had come upon Bly Minor the day before came swaggering by us and jeered at him.

'HEY!' shouted George. 'Respect your elders, you worms!'

'Shan't!' said Squeers, sticking out his tongue.

'Make us!' said Cartwright.

'GET OUT OF IT OR I SHALL GIVE YOU ALL DETENTION!' roared Spackman, and they scattered at that.

'Kids have no respect these days!' said Bob once they had gone. 'We were never like that, were we?'

'You were worse,' said Spackman, who is in the year above, and a prefect now. But I know that's not true, Hazel. We might have been callow and foolish – and I wince at some of the things I did and said – but we were never cruel, not like that. This crop of fourth years is quite different, and quite awful.

I watched out of the window as they went hurtling across the courtyard, shouting something at Kate as she went toiling by with a bucket and mop. Kate stepped backwards, raising her laden arms as though she'd been struck. I felt sick at heart at that, for I remembered the dreadful word they'd called George, and I suspected they were saying the same sort of thing to Kate. But what could I do?

Rugby was that afternoon, and we decided to use that as an excuse for a Junior Pinkertons meeting, and to see Baskerville. You see, if you pretend to be knocked down and injured in a scrum the games master will tell you to go for a run to buck up, and if you're looking wobbly he'll send you with a friend. Of course, you're supposed to stay at the edge of the pitch, and if he notices you're gone you might get a caning when you get back, but we're used to that by now.

I filled my games kit pockets with the cakes and biscuits from Kate (now rather the worse for wear) and George did too. At the first scrum George fell over, clutching his ankle and howling, and ten minutes later we were scrambling down the hill to our cave.

Baskerville greeted us by hurling himself up at us, crying with joy, and while he played round our ankles and shared the rest of the cake and biscuits with us (for

we were hungry too by then), George and I made a list
of suspects in the case.

# SUSPECTS

*Mr Gambino* – the most suspicious person in this case.
Was seen researching the moors, and had an article about
the robbery over the summer. Kate the maid told us that
his trousers are often muddy and torn – it sounds as
though he has been searching the moors as well! Has he
purchased a dog to help follow the scent of the robbers to
the missing money?

*Mr Holtz* – we noticed his boots were covered with mud
from the moors, when as a librarian he would have no
reason to leave school grounds. He also seems lonely, and
he seemed to hint at knowing about the Junior Pinkertons.
Did he buy Baskerville to help keep him company – and
discover our detective notes in the cave?

*Bob Featherstonehaugh* – unlikely, for it is very hard
for boys to get out of school every day, and Baskerville

looks well fed, but we did find his pyjama bottoms in the cave so we can't rule him out. We're unable to think of a good reason for him to decide to hide a secret puppy near to school grounds, though, unless he wants to trace the missing money – but if he did, he'd probably have told us by now!

*Squeers and his gang* – just as unlikely as Bob, really, though they were there when Bly Minor was bitten, and they are horrid enough to have bought a dog and trained it to attack people!

'So, what do we do now?' I asked, when we had finished.

'Well,' said George, 'we should probably get back soon, before we're missed, but why don't we take Baskerville for a walk first and see what he'll do? We can find out if he's being trained to hunt for money, or bite people, or anything else.'

This seemed like a good idea, Hazel, but the reality was that Baskerville was not showing much sign of being trained at all. He led us over several hillocks, round and round some trees and into every boggy patch he could find, until he looked less and less like a dog and more and more like a swamp creature. And all he seemed to care about was eating disgusting things he found under bushes.

It was starting to get properly dark. We were beginning to despair as we stood on top of a small windy hill and watched Baskerville chew a rock, when George said, 'Hi, Alex, look! It's Gambino – *and* Holtz! You hide with Baskerville, I'll distract them.'

I looked, and he was right. Mr Gambino and Mr Holtz were struggling up the hill towards us, Holtz following Gambino and Gambino turning away from him, a grim expression on his face. We were rather hidden by the trees, and so they hadn't seen us yet. I crouched down, holding onto Baskerville (who squeaked in annoyance and then curled up against me, getting mud all over my Aertex shirt) and George halloaed them.

'Mukherjee!' I heard Holtz say. 'What a surprise. What are you doing out?'

'Rugby,' said George. 'Well, running, while the others play rugby. I fell, you see.'

'Good, good,' said Holtz. 'I thought I'd get out for a walk too, and I met Mr Gambino.'

'A nice surprise,' said Gambino, not sounding as though he thought it was nice at all.

'He's quite knowledgeable about the area,' Holtz went on. 'He's been telling me about its ancient history – it's quite fascinating! In fact, there is apparently a bur—'

'Yes, never mind that,' said Gambino, gritting his teeth. 'Surely you should be almost finished with your exercise, Mukherjee? Back to school, if you please, in time for dinner.'

'Yes, sir,' said George – and then, of course, he had to go. I heard him walk away down the hill. My heart was going, Hazel, I don't mind telling you. I didn't know what I was going to do if the masters discovered me – and they were so close now. I could feel Baskerville twitching on my lap – what if he barked, and gave me away? What if he recognized his master?

But a second later I was glad I'd stayed.

Mr Holtz was chatting on about ancient sites and prehistory. Mr Gambino stayed quiet, until at last he burst out, 'Don't you think you should be getting back as well? You're on dinner duty this evening, after all.'

'I suppose I am,' said Mr Holtz, and I could hear the hurt in his voice. 'All right then – I shall see you later.'

Off he trotted, back down the hill, and Gambino was left alone. And, as soon as he was, he began to pace. So close to me that I trembled, he shuffled about and kicked his feet into the dirt and even got out some sort of tool from his pocket (I could hear him jabbing about with it – it sounded metallic and pointed). 'It must be near here!' he was muttering. 'But where?'

This was making Baskerville more and more excited – and at last I couldn't hold him quiet any more. I slipped the rope from round his neck, and he bolted out of cover, straight at Gambino, who yelped in surprise.

'What the devil is this!' I heard him say. 'Who are you? Get away from me or you'll regret it!'

I went cold at that. *Regret it?* I heard another yelp, from Baskerville this time, and I realized Gambino had hold of him.

And I don't know what came over me at that moment, Hazel, except it was almost dark by then, and I could hardly see the hands in front of my face. I burst up from the undergrowth and hurled myself at where I thought Gambino was. My white Aertex shirt and shorts were covered in mud, and I was a darker figure than I might otherwise have been. Gambino yelled in surprise, and dropped Baskerville – who came racing back towards me, barking madly. I couldn't trust myself to call out to him in case Gambino recognized my voice, but I hissed and clapped invitingly, and I felt him scurrying around at my feet. Then I rushed him all the way back to the cave, not stopping once to look back.

As soon as I had calmed him down, I tethered Baskerville back up to the log. I could not think what else to do – my mind was racing. We had been thinking that Gambino was the most likely person to have been keeping Baskerville, to help him hunt for the treasure. I had been expecting them to recognize each other – but instead Gambino had seemed surprised at his appearance, and even prepared to hurt him. And, more than that, Gambino had been messing about with a treasure-hunting instrument, instead of using Baskerville's nose. So did Baskerville belong to Holtz, then? Or had we been entirely wrong?

And as I was wondering that, I heard a noise outside the cave. I froze, and Baskerville went wild, spinning in circles and howling with delight. Whoever was outside was someone he knew.

But the person who ducked into the cave and came face to face with me was not Gambino, or Holtz, or Bob, or Squeers.

It was Kate the maid.

We both yelled at each other. She shrieked – well, so did I – and Baskerville started to bark.

'Please!' cried Kate, holding up her arms. 'Don't hurt me!'

I didn't know what she meant, until I stopped feeling so terrified and realized that although I could see her, still half outside in the gloom of the evening, she couldn't really see me apart from a dark shape in the dark cave. And – well – I guess I'm really tall these days. I felt guilty.

'Kate!' I said. 'It's me, er, I mean, it's Alexander.'

Kate took a gasping breath, hand on her heart now, and said, 'Oh, sweet Jesus, what are you doing here? I mean, listen, I didn't mean that, honestly, Mr Alexander. I, oh— I mean, whose dog is that?'

Now, I'm not so good as George at sniffing out when people are fibbing, but anyone could have seen that Kate wasn't telling the truth – and besides, Baskerville had got over his nerves at the unexpected yells and was lunging at her lovingly, making pitiful excited whimpers.

'He's *your* dog,' I said. 'Isn't he?'

'Look, that's not – it isn't . . .' Kate trailed off, and then turned her huge eyes on me and said, 'Gwyllgi was *supposed* to be a secret. How did you find him?'

'Oh, we – er, sometimes *I* come to sit in this cave,' I said, only just managing not to give away the Junior Pinkertons.

'Ah, were those papers yours?' asked Kate. 'I thought they must have been someone's diary. I'm sorry about them. He ripped them to shreds. I didn't read them, I promise. I thought the best thing to do was leave them be.'

I was flooded with relief. That was one question solved, at least.

'But why *do* you have Baskerville – I mean, Gwil-whatever?' I asked. 'You were keeping him at school, weren't you, until he got too big? That's why you burned the porridge – because you were busy looking after him! But why hide him? And why have him in the first place? We're not allowed dogs; no one is.'

'I—' Kate began. 'I – well—'

And then there were rustlings outside the mouth of the cave, and George stuck his head round the side of it and cried, 'Hurry up! Get out of the cave! Twining's coming and he's on the warpath! It's ages after we ought to have been back inside. He's seen me, so he knows you must be nearby!'

Kate and I looked at each other in horror. I knew what she was thinking, that he mustn't discover Baskerville – I mean, Gwyllgi (it's Welsh apparently, Hazel).

'You stay here!' I whispered to Kate. 'I'll go out – I won't get in as much trouble.'

I trooped out of the cave, my cheeks red – to find Headmaster Twining standing at the top of the ridge in his coat and hat, looking absolutely raging.

'GET BACK TO SCHOOL, ARCADY!' he bellowed at me. 'YOU TOO, MUKHERJEE! DETENTION FOR A WEEK!'

George and I stumbled up the path in front of him. 'He was coming back from the village and caught me as I was slipping through the gates,' muttered George to me. 'He asked where you were and I didn't manage to bluff it well enough. He knew you must be out too. Worse luck! Did you put Baskerville back?'

'Yes!' I whispered back. 'But I met Kate in the cave. She was there to feed him – *she's* the one who put him there in the first place!'

George's eyes grew wide. 'No! Really? Golly. *Kate* – now there's someone we weren't expecting! Good of you not to rat her out.'

'I couldn't,' I said uncomfortably. 'She'd get in awful trouble.'

'Quite right,' said George. 'I wonder why she did it? She's an animal-lover, of course – we should have seen that and thought of her for it – but it still doesn't explain why she kept him secret. It's a terrible risk to run!'

'STOP TALKING!' barked Headmaster Twining behind us, and we stopped. He herded us both back to the school gates – several boys saw us filing in and jeered at us. By dinner time (which we missed, as punishment) several different rumours were all around the school: that we had been treasure hunting (that one was uncomfortably close to home), that we had been trying to run away (in our games kit! Unlikely) and even that we had been plotting Headmaster Twining's downfall. Bob told us so when he came up to our dorm afterwards with some bread rolls in his handkerchief.

We took them and ate them gratefully, ignoring his questions as best we could. I found that my face was burning with embarrassment – I hate it when people misunderstand things, and I hate being in trouble.

'You lump,' said George once we were alone again. 'Stop looking so miserable!'

'I can't help it!' I protested. 'And anyway, you said it yourself on the way back to school: we haven't really solved the mystery! We know who Baskerville – I mean, Gwylli – belongs to, but we don't know why.'

'*Gwyllgi*,' said George. 'It's a sort of Welsh hellhound. And we don't know *yet*, that's all. There's lots more to understand all round – we don't know what on earth Mr Gambino is doing, or why Mr Holtz is wandering around after him. The case isn't over! And we need to work out how to help Kate. She's doing something illegal under school rules, and if she's caught, she'll lose her job.'

'She wouldn't!' I said, horrified.

'She very well might,' said George. 'Think about it. She's not just keeping a secret puppy, which is already forbidden – no pets at Weston, no exceptions, right? She's also sneaking food and clothing that doesn't belong to her out of school. That's stealing! And, in case you haven't noticed, Alex, looking like me or Kate makes people apt to think the worst of you. They'd have her out in a second.'

'But what do we do about it?'

'Talk to Kate for one. And come up with a plan – one that will keep Kate and Gwyllgi safe and end all this creeping about. So, what will it be?'

I was stumped at that, and sick at heart, and still awfully ashamed at being caught. I lay on my bed and thought – and I'm pretty sure I didn't sleep at all, although I was terribly alarmed by the sound of the morning bell the next day.

What I didn't know then was that this was only the beginning of the real trouble.

We were allowed to have breakfast the next day, but it really was torture, for Kate was serving. It seemed that everywhere I looked I managed to catch her large brown eyes – and I caught too the looks that some of the other boys were giving her. Whispers and awful ripples of laughter travelled down the dining tables from that horrid group of rough fourth years. Squeers even called out something as Kate passed him that I won't repeat to you, Hazel, because it's simply too foul. Not that I think you're too delicate or something, I don't mean that, just – it wasn't nice and I don't want you to have to remember it too. Mr Jesperson, taking breakfast, bellowed at us all to be quiet, as though we were all being equally naughty – and as though he hadn't heard Squeers, though I know he had. And I saw from Squeers's face that he wasn't ashamed of himself at all.

On our way to Latin later, George and I were crossing the courtyard when we saw a figure hovering beside the entrance to the kitchens, waiting for us. It was Kate, but before we could go over to her to talk at last, Squeers and Cartwright and their friends came bursting out of one of the classrooms, whooping and jeering. They made straight for Kate and darted around her like bats, their gowns flapping (I've never exactly told you this, Hazel, but we're made to wear these ridiculous short black cloaks as part of our uniforms. I know you complain about your uniform, but really I'd prefer it to ours. It's just too silly).

I'm ashamed to say I faltered, but George took one look and went charging into their midst, waving his bag about militarily. He managed to drive them away, though they hovered around the fountain in the middle of the courtyard, sneering at us until the bell went for lessons.

'Are you all right?' George asked Kate when they were gone.

'Perfectly,' said Kate, but I heard her sniff, and saw her swipe a hand across her face.

'They've been doing this to you all term!' I heard myself saying, and I was so upset now that I forgot not to stare at her.

'What of it?' asked Kate fiercely. 'They did it last term too. I can handle myself! And I know I can't look for help from any of *you*.'

She made a gesture with her chin that seemed to take in the whole square shape of Weston.

I suddenly realized something I ought to have seen before.

'That's why you got Gwyllgi!' said George, understanding too. 'To protect you!'

'And I can't even have him in school grounds,' said Kate. 'It was a silly idea. I shouldn't have bothered.'

With that cutting into us both, she turned on her heel and marched away into the darkness of the kitchens.

What were we to do? We knew the answer to the question of why he was there at last. But although the mystery was solved, the problem was not fixed. And I felt hopeless, Hazel, for I knew that if we told the masters the truth about why Kate had got him, and how Squeers and his friends were bullying her, she would simply lose her job for owning a contraband dog. Despite their disgusting behaviour, the fourth years would face no consequences. It was not right at all, and though I do understand, Hazel, that sometimes the world isn't right, I don't have to *like* it. I couldn't simply stand by, not any more. That was too cowardly. We had to do *something*. But what?

I think George was feeling as disconsolate as I was, and we drifted through the school after lunch, somehow ending up (as we always do) in the library.

Mr Holtz brightened up considerably when he saw us. His boots were muddy again, I saw, and he had several books about Iron Age burial customs out on his desk.

While I chattered to him – I can't think what I said now; I hardly even knew then – George went looking through the records, and then strode off into the dustiest stacks, returning a few minutes later with a heavy green book called *Welsh Myths and Legends*.

'What's that for?' I asked quietly.

'An idea,' said George. 'Hold on while I read.'

I held on, and watched him bend his head over the pages, brow creased with thought.

At last he sighed, and looked up. 'Read this, will you, Alex?' he asked. 'And when you've done that – remind me of the plot of *The Hound of the Baskervilles*.'

And that afternoon we realized that there *was* something we could do.

We told Kate, of course – she was in on it as much as we were. George was very insistent about that. 'He's her dog!' he said. 'And, Alex, think how Hazel and Daisy would react if they were here and we tried to do something without them.'

I did think, and I took out your latest letter and looked at it, and it made me feel lighter.

While Bob was out of the dorm one day we raided his tuck box, and the next time we were allowed into town after our detentions were over we made a foray into the craft section of the general store and came out with several heavy parcels that we stuffed inside our coats, glad it was getting so cold.

We went into the music room's supply closet too, and the chemistry labs, and when we could we crept out to the cave and helped Kate train Gwyllgi. We were very careful not to frighten him, and he caught on quickly – soon he was quite fearless. He also was getting bigger and bigger, and his growls and barks were now quite menacing. He looked like no breed of dog that I had ever seen, or a mix of at least ten sorts, which made me feel even more fond of him.

One day I sat down and, using all my journalistic skills, wrote a careful note that I slipped under the fourth-year dorm's door.

And then George and I waited for the next cross-country race.

We were in luck that day – heavy dark clouds came lower and lower to the earth all morning, and by the time the gates of Weston School were thrown open and the starting gun fired, they seemed to be dragging against the ground, a heavy swill of rain covering the hills. Any sensible person would have called the race off, but the English aren't sensible (you know that as well as I do, Hazel), and so we were shoved out of the doors, turning blue in our Aertex shirts and shorts, and sent on our way.

As usual, George and I sped up as much as we could to get ahead of the pack, then swung sideways and down the hill to our cave – where Kate was waiting for us. It was her half-day, and we'd agreed with her that we'd meet there. Gwyllgi was chewing contentedly on some sort of bone, so absorbed he barely noticed the additions we were making to him and to ourselves.

This was the sticky bit. We had to wait until half past four, the very end of the race, when the sun had gone down (lost somewhere in the gloom) and the lamps of Weston were being lit. I kept on checking my wristwatch, jittery with energy, and Gwyllgi caught my nerves and began to squeak and bounce between us until Kate said, 'Gwyllgi, shush!'

At last I heard the clock in the village strike the half hour away down behind us. Kate took a deep breath, and nodded at us, her hands tight on Gwyllgi's collar.

There were voices outside. 'Hello?' called Squeers's voice. 'We're here. So, where are you? What's this information that's going to get that maid fired?'

George lifted the trumpet we'd pinched from the music room to his lips, and gave it a blast. Gwyllgi, predictably, howled with shock. Kate said, 'GWYLLGI, GO!' and he burst out of the cave, the paper horns we had fashioned for him bouncing on his head. We had covered them with phosphorescent paint from the chemistry labs, and put more dabs of it on his cheeks, and the effect was very menacing. Once he was a safe distance away I scrambled forward and struck the match that I had in my hands, touching it to the paper of Bob's contraband fireworks. They went off with a red flash and a demonic puff of smoke, and I could imagine the view from outside the cave: a sudden burst of hellfire, and in front of it, Gwyllgi: a glowing, mad-eyed creature, his fangs wide and slavering, bellowing with excitement. He had become quite fond of performing. It was half the trick from *The Hound of the Baskervilles*, of course, and half from the legends of the Welsh Wild Hunt. Kate and George and I had all draped ourselves in dark cloth, and we rushed out after Gwyllgi at this point, all screaming furiously and waving our arms. Kate was shouting in Welsh.

I had been afraid it might look and sound hokey, but it clearly had its desired effect. Squeers and Cartwright and their friends screamed and scattered, and Gwyllgi pounced after them, growling and panting and snapping at their heels.

'CROSS THE MAID AGAIN AND WE'LL SET WORSE ON YOU!' Kate roared after them. 'BE WARNED!'

George and I chased Squeers and Cartwright for a few minutes more and then abandoned the pursuit. When we got back to the cave, Kate was standing quite alone, panting, her arms still held above her head.

'Well done!' cried George. 'Very believable.'

'I feel a bit like a witch,' said Kate, her eyes bright and ferocious and her hair wildly bursting out of its usual bun. 'You won't say anything to anyone?'

'Honour bright,' I said fervently. I have to say I was a little afraid of Kate too at that moment.

Gwyllgi was bouncing about our feet, barking at us, his cardboard horns beginning to droop, and Kate bent down, patted him and fed him a biscuit. 'Good boy!' she told him.

Then there was a yell from above us. We all three froze.

'Hey!' called a voice that I knew very well. It was Mr Gambino. 'Hey, who's there?'

We all three looked at each other. 'Quick!' George whispered. We threw off our cloaks, took off Gwyllgi's horns and rubbed the paint off his cheeks, and then Kate dropped to the ground, holding her foot.

Over the hill came Gambino, with Holtz behind him. They both had sticks in their hands, and torches, and looked extremely displeased to see us.

'The fourth years told us that magical beings came out of the hill and tried to murder them,' said Holtz. 'You don't know anything about that, do you?'

'We don't know what you mean!' I said earnestly.

'We were running,' George went on, 'and then we heard something barking. We came down the hill to find Kate here. She's hurt herself – and this dog seems to have found her. Otherwise we'd have missed her!'

'It's true!' Kate called out. 'I tripped down the hill and got stuck – I don't know what I'd have done without that dog calling them over! He came out of nowhere, but he seems quite friendly. My apologies, Mr Gambino, for keeping the boys – but they're helping me.'

'Indeed,' said Mr Gambino. He did not sound entirely convinced. 'Indeed! Well, where did the dog come from? I've seen it before, I'm sure. Hi, what's it got there?'

At that moment Gwyllgi came bounding towards Mr Gambino, dragging the bit of bone he'd been worrying at before. At least, I thought it was a bone.

Mr Gambino froze. So did Mr Holtz. Then they both made a lunge towards Gwyllgi.

Gwyllgi yelped and sat back on his haunches, staring nervously at the two men and letting the object fall out of his mouth.

Mr Gambino picked it up reverently. 'Good grief,' he whispered. 'It isn't. It can't be. It IS!'

'It is!' sighed Mr Holtz, waving his torch on it. 'A piece of what looks like an Iron Age dagger! This came from this cave? Yes?'

'Maybe?' I said.

'We've found it!' cried Mr Gambino. 'The burial mound! Oh, boys, boys – this is a miracle!'

And he and Mr Holtz began dancing about and hugging each other – which is very strange to see your masters doing, Hazel, and more than a little embarrassing.

And that is the story of how Gwyllgi the dog discovered an ancient burial chamber in the back of our detective cave, and saved our bacon in a time of great stress.

It turned out that what Gambino was looking for was not the missing banknotes from the summer's robbery at all, but treasure from one of the mounds that surround Weston. That's what Holtz had been trying to tell us about before Gambino stopped him – he'd decided to help Gambino in his hunt. The cuts on Gambino's hand were from treasure hunting – and I'm pretty sure Holtz was just being friendly about the mysteries. Though I do wonder . . . He is very smart, Hazel. It seems to be a good thing that they're friends now – Gambino isn't quite as mean, and Holtz isn't quite as lonely.

Anyway, Holtz and Gambino were so pleased with Gwyllgi that they petitioned Headmaster Twining to let him stay in the kitchens – and there he's been for the last month, still growing, and reaching such an enormous size so quickly that the fourth years haven't dared to go near Kate again. And I've finally found the courage to yell at the younger years if I catch them treating anyone meanly or making jokes – it's worth it to remind them that *some* people won't tolerate them saying those horrible things.

So that is the end of that, and the end of this letter, Hazel – but although I've got to the end of it at last, I'm no closer to saying what I want to say to you. Maybe I'm the kind of person who's better at speaking face to face, after all. I think I must be. When I sit down to write, the sentences just kind of get away from me, and I'm too busy telling the story to think properly.

But I do have to come out with it, and I will. Hazel, ever since the case of the body on the beach that we solved together, I – well, I've realized how stupid I've been. I think you're absolutely spiffing, and I ought to have noticed it immediately, only I didn't. I'm not very good with girls (George says that's ridiculous, and girls are only people, but . . . well, George would say that, I don't believe he's ever been nervous in his life), and I'm no good at all with saying really important things like this, even though I'm usually as honest as anything.

I really like you, Hazel, and I hope that you might – maybe – like me too. Or you might only want to be friends, and I'd understand that, I really would, but – I guess I have to try.

If you like me too, send a reply back as quick as you can. We're coming to Egypt to see you and – well – I can't wait. But I'll try not to bother you if you'd rather I didn't. So, I mean, it's up to you. I'll try to say this when we meet, but if I don't – I hope you'll have this letter, so you'll know how I feel.

Love to you – just you,

Alex x

# THE CASE OF THE SECOND SCREAM

Being an account of

The Vanished Heiress,
an investigation by the Wells and Wong
Detective Society.

Written by Hazel Wong
(Detective Society Co-President),
aged 15½.

Begun Thursday 9th April 1936. Written up
Monday 12th April 1937.

# 1

Daisy and I were sitting on her gravestone last night, arguing about how many cases we've solved together so far.

I said fifteen: ten murders and five others; and I thought I was right until Daisy sat up straight and snapped, 'Nonsense! You are not being *rigorous*, Watson! You've forgotten the one onboard the ship back from Hong Kong – Mrs Van Dine, remember? Really, I ought not to allow you to keep our records when you *clearly* can't be trusted with them. Do I have to do everything myself?'

I pointed my chin meaningfully at the gravestone, and Daisy said 'Humph!' and turned pink. '*That* was quite different,' she went on. 'And anyway, me being officially dead is working, isn't it? Uncle Felix was delighted with how quietly we sorted out that business with the foreign minister. It's been the most wonderful spring – I'm only sad it's all over now. I wonder if Lappet will scream when

I pop up in her History lesson again next week. What a bother that I've been ordered back to Deepdean, but at least I shall come back from the dead in style. I'll be just like Je—'

'*No*,' I said firmly. 'Don't say it.'

'Ugh, Hazel, you're so boring,' said Daisy, rolling her eyes. She had wanted to appear in Fallingford church on Easter morning, and we all had to persuade her that it might be a little much. But she was due to come back to Deepdean with me next week, so everyone would know that she had not really died in Egypt – although, of course, we could not be quite truthful about what Daisy had been doing for the past three months. (The story we had decided upon was that she took a bump to the head when she fell from the SS *Hatshepsut* and lost her memory, and had to convalesce in hospital for several months before it returned.)

If I am honest, Daisy's jokes about returning from the dead still make me itchy. Even though it's been more than three months since she came back from Egypt, I have never stopped feeling superstitious about it. Living through the whole spring term at Deepdean without her gave me a going-down-in-a-lift sensation all the time, and these holidays I have woken myself up most nights just to make sure I can still hear her breathing in the bed next to mine. Daisy's favourite place, of course, has become the little memorial gravestone we put up to her last Christmas, when we thought she was – gone – but when she drags me there I always make sure I am sitting facing away from it, so I don't have to see it and remember.

'But anyway, it *is* sixteen,' she went on firmly. 'Why didn't you ever write that case down, Hazel? You ought to have!'

'I don't know!' I said, and I don't. Perhaps I was still too upset about what had happened during our Hong Kong mystery. I remember I spent most of the journey back to England trying and failing to write *that* case up. I went to look through my old casebooks after we spoke, and all I can find after my Jade Pin Crimes account are the barest scribbled notes, a torn page from the onboard activities list, and a plan of the ship with cabins and names marked up in my younger handwriting.

So, because Daisy has asked me to, and because it is her sixteenth birthday tomorrow (of course she has pointed this out and said, 'Amina's bought me a necklace and written me a beautifully long letter; I can tell from the parcel. What have *you* got me, Hazel?'), here at last is the account of the mystery of the vanished heiress.

# 2

It all began just before midnight on Thursday 9th April 1936, when Daisy sat up in our cabin on the SS *Strathclyde* with a gasp and said, 'Something's happened, Hazel.'

'How do you know?' I asked blearily – for I had been lying on my bed, my insides churning until I felt like a stormy sea pinned at the edges by lighthouses of distress. I thought I was awake, but I suspect I was really in a sort of miserable half-sleep where everything felt enormous. As I have said many times before, I do not do well on most boats.

'I can hear feet,' said Daisy. 'Running. Listen!'

I sat up, gulping, and listened – and, as usual, Daisy was right.

'What are you doing?' I asked, for Daisy was upright, pulling her coat over her nightdress, and jamming her feet into boots.

'Investigating!' said Daisy. 'It might be interesting. It might be murder! Oh, Hazel, Hazel, come on, come on—'

Which is how I found myself, my coat buttoned up wrong and rubbing against the thin stuff of my nightdress, both shivering and sweating, rushing up the starboard side of the ship after Daisy, along with several other people. The *Strathclyde*'s first-class deck had all the cabins arranged in a long loop, with even numbers on the port side and odd numbers on the starboard. The heavy door of each cabin opened out onto a wide promenade space, blocked off from the foaming sea below by a waist-high railing.

We came round the bow of the ship and arrived at what was clearly the source of all the fuss: cabin 114. Its door had been forced open, and a pink-faced round old man with a white moustache was standing in front of it, his evening dress disarranged and his bald head bare. Clinging to him was a middle-aged woman in a beaded gown and a shawl, her eyes red and anxious.

I recognized them both – they were Mr Jacob Van Dine and his daughter, Miss Miriam Van Dine. They sat two tables away from ours in the first-class dining room (which was on the deck below our cabins, with the lounge, the bar and the library) along with Mr Van Dine's wife, Bernadette, and their son, Holden. Mrs Bernadette Van Dine (according to Daisy, who as usual

211

knew everything about everyone) was quite fabulously wealthy. She was the daughter of a man who'd made money in the California gold rush, and then invested in the Ford Motor Company. But Mrs Van Dine had got tired of being so rich. She had given half her wealth away to charities, and was spending most of the rest of it on building a collection of Asian art with the help of her daughter Miriam. She had been in Hong Kong purchasing a wildly expensive pair of vases, and some other pieces, but had decided to return home early (via an exhibition in London) when her husband's health, never good, took a turn for the worse. I looked at him now and saw that his face was ruddy and he was panting brokenly.

'She should be here!' Mr Van Dine was saying between gasps. 'She told me at the end of dinner that she was coming back up to her cabin to read. She's gone! Someone – I'm sure someone's hurt her! Search the ship!'

'Papa, it'll be all right!' said Miss Van Dine. 'Come on, sit down – remember your heart! Have you taken the medicine I left out for you?'

Another man came surging along the deck, almost knocking into us as he went. This was Holden Van Dine, and if I had not guessed who was missing before, I did now. 'I've searched the ship, and she's nowhere to be seen,' he said furiously. 'Where is she?'

'I heard a scream!' a woman cried out next to us. 'I know I did, just half an hour ago! It must have been *her*! Someone's done something to poor Mrs Van Dine!'

I was intrigued. This did look very much like the beginning of a mystery.

'Holden!' whimpered Miss Van Dine. 'This is terrible! What shall we do?'

'She's not here, sir,' said another man, striding down the deck from the other direction towards us. Daisy's face brightened at once – it was Mr Protheroe, a police detective travelling with us on the SS *Strathclyde*. Of course, Daisy had managed to get us seated on his table, and away from the bother of having to pretend to be a silly girl uninterested in detection she spent most evenings grilling him mercilessly about fingerprint analysis and bloodstains. On the first night Mr Protheroe had enjoyed answering her questions. By the tenth he looked distinctly nervous whenever he saw Daisy approaching. His face now took on the same grim expression I was used to when he caught sight of us.

'You shouldn't be here, girls,' he said. 'Something's happened.'

'What is it?' asked Daisy brightly.

'Mrs Bernadette Van Dine is missing,' said Mr Protheroe. 'She doesn't appear to have returned to her cabin after dinner as she said she would. Her family are concerned. I'm sure it will be found to be nothing, but—'

'But I heard a scream!' the same woman insisted. 'A terrible scream outside my cabin!'

And at her words Mr Protheroe glanced away from the row of cabins – straight out at the dark churning sea.

Daisy was needling me furiously with her fingers, eyes glinting in the moonlight.

'Ow!' I said. 'Daisy, stop it!'

'A case, Watson!' she breathed in my ear. 'A proper case! And *don't* say you're too ill to take it on. This is fearfully important – I told you how rich Mrs Van Dine is, and how she's been spending her money. I should think there were plenty of people on this ship with an interest in getting rid of her.'

The ship rolled under me, and I stared at the horizon and swallowed down an uncomfortable and unladylike burp. The light on the water only made it seem blacker and more dangerous than ever. I imagined tumbling off the deck into it. Would the fall take long? Would I have time to take a breath and scream before the waves crashed into me?

Mr Protheroe was speaking, waving at the crew. 'You, man, and you, to me,' he said loudly, and then in a lower voice, 'You, Jameson, get Mrs Chandha and bring her and the Van Dines into the lounge for questioning.

And you, Tse, take some men round the cabins and ask if anyone heard anything. We have to move quickly on this. Mrs – Davidson, is it? Please follow me at once, so I can get your full statement about this scream.'

The men he pointed at looked uncertain for a moment, but Mr Protheroe had a persuasive voice, and the sort of stature that detectives had in books and at the pictures. He was hard to not obey.

'What are we waiting for?' hissed Daisy. 'Watson, lounge, now!'

# 3

The ship rolled again, and the lamps in the lounge flickered, the crystal glasses on the sideboard tinkling gently together.

Daisy and I were crowded together in the velvety dark of the space beneath the grand piano's covering, peering out between its fringes. Daisy was perched on someone's discarded dinner jacket, and I was sitting uncomfortably back on my heels, toes aching and casebook in my hand. Mrs Davidson's evidence had been short and to the point. She had heard a scream outside her cabin, number 117 on the starboard side, at 11 p.m. She had been too afraid to go out to see who it was, and had only followed other people out on deck in the commotion when Mrs Van Dine had been discovered to be missing from her cabin, just after 11:30.

Mrs Davidson was thanked and dismissed. Now I saw Mr Protheroe's feet in their shiny black dress shoes go pacing past us towards the Van Dines, who had come in and were huddled on a low sofa. 'Please do remain calm,' he said rather sternly. 'It's very possible Mrs Van Dine has simply wandered into another part of the ship. The men are looking – we may yet find her. Mr Van Dine, would you like to begin, as you raised the alarm? When did you notice your wife was missing?'

'We were at dinner together,' said Mr Van Dine. 'Bernie ate her dessert – never lost her appetite, even during the storm last week; she's some girl – and then told me she wanted to go up to her cabin and read. I kissed her goodbye, watched her walk out of the dining room, finished up my drink and then went to play a few last games of cards in the bar. I arrived there at five to eleven, and stayed there until it closed at eleven thirty. Then I went back to my cabin. I tried to look in on my wife – we have adjoining cabins, and I'm in 116 – to wish her goodnight. But both the connecting door and her outer door were still locked, and the light switched off. Now, Bernie never goes to sleep without saying goodnight, not in over forty years of marriage! So I knew something was off, and when the crew helped me open the outer door I could see straight away that her things hadn't shifted from the way she had left them before dinner. I'm certain she never arrived at all – someone must have waylaid her in order to cause her harm!'

'Can anyone confirm you were in the bar?' asked Mr Protheroe.

'The men I was playing cards with,' said Mr Van Dine. 'I was winning. And the barman made sure I wasn't going anywhere – he makes his drinks strong!'

'Very good,' said Mr Protheroe. 'Mr Holden, what about you? When did you last see your mother?'

'I didn't do a thing to her, if that's what you're trying to say!' said Holden hotly. 'I left the table before her, anyway. She and I – we had a dust-up.'

'What about?' asked Mr Protheroe.

I heard Miss Van Dine giggle, and stifle it. It was an odd sound, almost shrimp-like, for a woman who was so grown-up.

'My latest invention,' said Holden sulkily. 'A really smart new mousetrap. Shut up, sis. It works! I've spent years perfecting it, and I know it'll go great guns so long as I can raise some capital to make it. I said so to Mama, but she wasn't listening, as usual. Told me I was wasting my time! Like she can talk. She's wasting all her money – *our* money, it should be – on rescuing old soldiers' horses and stray cats, and buying ugly vases. I don't see why she can't give some of it to me! I was so mad at her I got up and left, right when the waitress was bringing dessert. I knocked into that waiter guy – you know, the one who serves wine – on the way out. I went into my cabin for a while, then I stood out on deck, trying to get my head straight. I'm on the starboard side, 115, the other side of the ship from Mama and Papa, so I wouldn't have seen Mama go past me – I tell you I didn't hear anything until you guys started making a scene.'

I breathed in quickly. Was Holden lying? How could he be in the cabin next to Mrs Davidson's but not have heard the scream she did – unless he helped cause it?

'Anyway,' Holden went on, 'weren't you saying that she might just be in some other part of the ship?'

'Of course she might,' said Mr Protheroe, clearly not convinced at all by the idea. 'Now, you, if you please, Miss Miriam. Can you confirm any of this?'

'Oh – well – it's true that Mama and Holden argued, and he stormed off just like he says he did at about ten thirty. Then the rest of us—'

'The rest of you?'

'Yes, Mama, Papa, me and that art dealer woman, Mrs Chandha – the rest of us just sat there awkwardly for a while. Then Mrs Chandha got up and left – embarrassed, I think – but she did invite Mama to come to her cabin later. They'd been talking about a sculpture, something that Mrs Chandha wanted to sell. I was interested in the piece, but Mama told me she thought it wasn't worth it. Maybe that's where Mama's got to, and this is all a misunderstanding? Mama left, then I made sure Papa was all right and left too. I stopped by my cabin just before eleven, to pick up a magazine for my friend Elaine, and went on to Elaine's cabin. We were still together when the alarm was raised.'

'And you didn't hear anything? Anything that might help?'

'No, I'm sure I didn't. I'm sorry!'

'Thank you,' said Mr Protheroe. 'This has been useful. You may go back to your cabins – I'll call you again if I need you.'

'Most suspicious!' whispered Daisy. 'Really, they all have motives for wanting to get rid of her. If she is dead, then they stand to gain – and just from their statements we can see why each of them might have wanted money. Mr Van Dine gambles, Holden wants money for that invention of his and Miriam wants to be able to buy that sculpture from Mrs Chandha.'

I thought that, as usual, Daisy was leaping to the most dramatic conclusions possible. We still did not even know that a crime had even taken place – although there was that scream Mrs Davidson had heard. I kept coming back to that . . .

The Van Dines trailed out, Mr Van Dine supported between Miss Van Dine and Holden, and a new pair of shoes, fashionable and silver, entered beneath an electric-blue saree.

'Ah, Mrs Chandha,' said Mr Protheroe. 'Do come in. I hoped you might be able to shed some light on this disappearance.'

'I don't think I can,' said Mrs Chandha, sitting down decisively. 'I don't have much to say about it! It's been a difficult few weeks sitting with the Van Dines. They're always arguing! I worry about Mr Van Dine's heart – I trained as a doctor, and I can tell a heart patient anywhere. Tonight was the son's turn. He's invented some ridiculous animal trap, and he stormed off in a huff after his mother laughed at him and refused to fund it. I decided to leave myself, but before I did I invited Mrs Van Dine to come to my cabin and look at a sculpture I'm selling. I hoped she might be interested in it, but she never came to see it, though I think the daughter wanted to. They can never agree on the direction of that collection – they have very different tastes, and it clearly caused problems. Mrs Van Dine won't listen to anyone with a different viewpoint – like a lot of collectors, she mistakes preference for objective value. While I waited for her I sat and read *The Mysterious Affair at Styles* – I can't get enough of Mrs Christie – and that's where I was when the alarm was raised.'

'Mrs Van Dine has just purchased a valuable pair of vases, I believe,' said Mr Protheroe. 'That was why she was in Hong Kong. You don't happen to know anything about them?'

'I know how important they are,' said Mrs Chandha. 'The most beautiful set of *famille rose* double gourd vases, Ch'ien-lung period. It's unusual to find such a

221

lovely pair. Alone they wouldn't be worth half as much. What wouldn't I give to own them – but I wouldn't *harm* her for them! What a ridiculous idea.'

'Thank you,' said Mr Protheroe. 'That will be all, I think. Please let me know if anything else occurs to you.'

Mrs Chandha left, and Mr Protheroe got to his feet and swung his arms, sighing. Mr Jameson came in again – I recognized him by the tear in his dress trousers, just below the knee – and said, 'Anything, sir?'

'The daughter and the father have alibis, the son and Chandha don't,' said Mr Protheroe. 'Though the son's our man, I'd guess. A fairly obvious lie in his statement. Go and knock on the cabins around his – find out if anyone else apart from Mrs Davidson heard anything. He's saying he didn't hear that scream, which is pretty damning evidence. Though if I'm right, and he's pushed his mother off the ship in a fit of rage, it'll be hard to prove it.'

I was shocked. As far as I could see, there were plenty more possible solutions, and quite a few more avenues of investigation.

'This is really dreadful, Hazel! He's not being rigorous at all!' whispered Daisy, and I squeezed her arm in agreement. 'All right. As soon as this clodhopper – and I must say, Mr Protheroe has disappointed me greatly – has left the room, what are our next steps?'

'Checking alibis first,' I breathed. 'Which is – the bar, Miss Van Dine's friend Elaine, people on the starboard-side deck to see if they saw or heard Mrs Van Dine and – well, wherever Mrs Chandha's cabin is.'

'Indeed,' said Daisy. 'I want to know more about those vases, and the statue Mrs Chandha is apparently selling – and I also want to talk to the wine steward Holden mentioned.'

'Harry Guo,' I said. 'What? He's nice. He picked up my casebook when I dropped it last week.'

'You don't *know* he's nice, Hazel; he might only be pretending. All right, him. And the waitress who looks after the Van Dines' table too, whoever that is. We want to get every account we can, because I am convinced that the Van Dines aren't telling the whole story.'

# 4

The ship pitched as we descended the stairs past tourist class to the crew area, the carpet under our feet thinning and the paintwork cheapening until we reached bare boards and gloomy grey walls. We had to wait, hiding in a doorway, until a maid came out of the door to the crew cabins, and then duck inside before it closed again. Once we were through I awkwardly stood watch outside the empty personnel office while Daisy crept inside to pilfer a copy of the crew's cabin arrangements. I never get more comfortable with this part of being a detective. The lights down here were low, and I had to squint to consult our map as we pattered through the long corridors. Just like our first-class cabins, the crew cabins were arranged in a loop of the ship, with even numbers on the port side and odd numbers on the starboard.

'Harry Guo's in 357,' I said. '369, 367 – oh!'

Daisy hissed. We had seen it at the same time: a small nervous figure hurrying towards us, and turning to knock on what looked very much like cabin 357. She had not noticed us in her haste – we were keeping close to the wall, and were half obscured by a large pile of washing that someone had left outside cabin 363. I seized Daisy's hand, and pulled her down low behind it.

'That's the waitress from the Van Dines' table!' I whispered, wrinkling my nose at the scent of sea and stale sweat rising from the clothes. 'What's she doing here?'

'An excellent question, Watson!' said Daisy. 'Let us observe the scene.'

'Who is it?' called a voice. 'I'm changing!'

'Harry?' said the little waitress. 'It's me, Sally.'

The door to cabin 357 was pulled open and Harry Guo stepped out into the corridor. I raised my free hand to my face in embarrassment – he was shirtless and looked entirely unlike the slick-haired bow-tied waiter I knew from dinner service.

'Mrs Van Dine's missing,' said Sally urgently.

Harry Guo reached out his hand and seized hers.

'No!' he said. 'What – how did you hear?'

'Is Anwar there?' asked Sally, peering round Harry's shoulder.

'No, don't worry. His shift doesn't end until two. I'm alone. I've only just got down here myself.'

Sally breathed out. 'All right. Mr Tse's going round all the cabins asking if we know anything. They want to pin it on one of us, I'm sure of it! He was brutal to me until Mary spoke up and told him I'd been in my cabin with her since I came back from dinner – and I came back as soon as I'd finished serving the puddings.'

'Still not feeling well?' asked Harry sympathetically.

Sally shook her head. 'There is one thing,' she went on. 'I didn't want to say it to Mr Tse's, but – it's not quite true, what Mary said. I thought I might feel better if I got some air, so I went on deck outside our cabin for a few minutes. I was out there at eleven – and I *swear* I heard a scream above the noise of the waves.'

Daisy nudged me frantically, and I scribbled down *Sally heard splash 11 p.m.* in my casebook. I squinted at the plan in my hands, and saw a small, neat square with *Sally Lennon/Mary Gallagher* written in it. Cabin 312 – but that was on the port side, on the other side from where we were now, and from Mrs Davidson's cabin. I was puzzled.

Sally was still talking. 'So you see, I had to come find you,' she said. 'I don't know what they'll do – they know, don't they, about . . . what you told me? Why you were in prison?'

Her voice had dropped, and Daisy and I had to strain our ears to hear. Harry's response, when it came, was softer still.

'They know,' he murmured. 'I had to tell them. But I haven't put a foot wrong on this ship, and they know that too! I've been a model employee. I haven't been near a paintbrush for three years. I don't even go to the entertainment deck! Funny thing, though, how the past follows you, no matter what you try to do. Serving the Van Dines – in another life, I'd have already lifted those vases Mrs Van Dine can't stop talking about and made impressions of them to copy.'

'You wouldn't!'

'Of course I wouldn't *now*. And especially not since – you know what I told you. I'm not the only person with black market art connections on this ship. I don't think I've been recognized, but when I served that table I knew at once . . . I was going to say something to Mrs Van Dine about it, but I suppose now I won't have the chance.'

Daisy elbowed me. I was so interested I almost forgot the rolling in my stomach, which was feeling worse and worse the nearer we came to the sea itself. Prison? Paintbrushes? And someone – or several people – at Mrs Van Dine's table that Harry Guo remembered from his quite obviously criminal past.

'Do be careful, Harry! I must go, in case they catch me, but – I'm afraid of Protheroe.'

'I know he'd love to blame it on me,' said Harry, 'but I swear, Sal, I didn't do it.' And he stepped back inside his cabin and shut the door.

Sally Lennon rushed away, and Daisy and I were left alone.

'Write it down, Watson, write it all down! A waiter with a criminal past as an *art forger* serving a table with not one but two women involved in the art-collecting world – and a second scream, this time heard on the *other* side of the ship! Look at the plan – the odd numbers are all on the starboard side, and the evens on the port. Mrs Davidson in 117 is on the starboard side – and very close to Holden Van Dine in 115 and Miriam Van Dine in 113, incidentally. She's the person who reported the scream that's got Mr Protheroe thinking Mrs Van Dine fell overboard – but now we've heard from Sally Lennon in 312 that there was a *second* scream at around the same time, on the *port* side of the ship. How do we account for both?'

'I don't know yet,' I said. 'But I do know that Harry Guo doesn't have an alibi. Didn't you hear him say he's been alone since the end of dinner?'

'Excellent point, Hazel,' said Daisy slightly reluctantly, as always when she has to praise me. 'So then—'

'We ought to keep narrowing down our suspect list,' I said. 'Mrs Chandha and Holden Van Dine's alibis can't be checked, but Mr Van Dine and Miriam's can. Our next steps ought to be to visit the bar and Elaine.'

I think this was really when I began to be bold around Daisy. Our adventures in Hong Kong still had a hold of me, and my years of being polite to Daisy were over, although she had not yet quite realized it.

'All right,' said Daisy, wrinkling up her nose. 'I shall go to the bar, you visit this Elaine person, and we shall meet back in front of Mrs Van Dine's cabin in twenty minutes to discuss our findings.'

'Perfect,' I said sweetly. 'See you soon!'

# 5

Elaine Kingston, in cabin 122, was frustratingly vague about Miriam's visit. I woke her up – she had not known what was happening, and I was able to pretend to have been told by Mr Protheroe to notify the other guests – and she fluttered and gasped in shock.

'Poor dear Miriam!' she said. 'She's a lovely girl – we've struck up such a friendship since we met over quoits last week. She was so friendly and ordinary when she introduced herself – I'd never have guessed how wealthy the Van Dines are! Why, she was with me this evening – she came by at about eleven with the magazine she'd promised me, and we sat and chatted until about half past.'

'What time exactly?' I asked, and Elaine looked at me oddly and said, 'Goodness, what am I, a clocktower?'

I had to leave, rather annoyed – and I found Daisy lurking near cabin 114 looking even more sulky.

'Mr Van Dine really was in the bar,' she said. 'Ten fifty-five to eleven thirty, when it closed. The barman remembered him, and remembered him coming in. It wasn't a busy evening.'

'Well then, we can rule him out!' I said, trying to be encouraging.

'I hate ruling people out,' said Daisy. 'I always hope they'll all be guilty.'

Knowing this was not strictly true, but that Daisy would not appreciate me saying it, I held my tongue.

'*And* the barman called me a little girl and told me I shouldn't be there. *Little girl!* I'm – I'm fifteen next week! Just you wait until I'm twenty. I'll show him.'

'So,' I said, trying to move things along, 'Miriam did visit Elaine, even though she's not quite sure when. We have to keep her on the suspect list. But we can cross out Mr Van Dine altogether.'

'Indeed,' said Daisy. 'What's next?'

'Bed,' I said. 'Daisy, it's half past one in the morning! There's nothing more we can find out tonight.'

'Ha,' said Daisy. 'Nonsense, Hazel. YOU may go to bed, but I have no intention of doing such a . . . a namby-pamby thing. Someone needs to watch this cabin for any developments. BED! Ha!'

I sighed. 'All right,' I said. 'If you're staying up, I'll stay up too. But I'm going to get the pillow and blanket from my bed so I'm comfortable.'

'Comfort!' hissed Daisy. 'Who needs comfort!'

'Me,' I said.

And I did mean to stay up, I really did. Only I closed my eyes just after 3 a.m. and woke up at six on Friday morning, cold and stiff and leaning against a rigidly upright Daisy as the ship sailed through thinning mist and the deckhands clattered buckets and mops, washing the boards round us.

'You snored,' said Daisy without looking at me.

'I did not!' I said.

'Believe what you want,' said Daisy with a shrug that I felt through my blanket. 'Anyway, no one's been into Mrs Van Dine's cabin while you were asleep. Make of that what you will.'

## SUSPECT LIST

~~Mr Jacob Van Dine~~ – the missing woman's husband, cabin 116. Last saw his wife leaving dinner to go and read in her cabin. Says he went to the bar at 10:55 to play cards and was there until 11:30. Found his wife's cabin locked and empty shortly after that. He is behaving as though he's devastated at his wife's disappearance — but is this all for show? Might she have disapproved of his gambling? RULED OUT! His alibi checks out — he couldn't have hurt his wife.

## Mr Holden Van Dine – the missing

woman's son, cabin 115. Argued with his mother about money for a new invention of his at dinner and left the table at 10:30 as Sally Lennon was serving pudding, knocking into Harry Guo on his way out. According to his story, he went into his cabin for a while and then stood alone on deck outside it until the alarm was raised. Is this true? How can we prove it? Why didn't he hear the scream Mrs Davidson in number 117 did, as their cabins are so close? And did Holden think that by getting rid of his mother he could get the money she refused to give him while she was alive?

## Miss Miriam Van Dine – the missing

woman's daughter, cabin 113. Left dinner just after her mother — according to her, she went to her cabin briefly and then on to her friend Elaine's cabin

(122) to lend her a magazine. She was there from eleven until eleven thirty. We know that she and her mother disagreed about which art pieces to buy — could Miriam want to take control of her mother's collection by killing her?

Mrs Priya Chandha — the other person on the Van Dines' table, cabin 162. An art dealer who trained as a doctor, she is selling a sculpture that she was trying to get Mrs Van Dine interested in. She invited Mrs Van Dine to her cabin to see it after dinner, but says that Mrs Van Dine never arrived. She waited there, reading an Agatha Christie, until the alarm was raised. She said she'd love to own the vases Mrs Van Dine bought — could this be a motive for her?

Harry Guo — wine steward at dinner, cabin 357. Served the Van Dines' table. Has a dark past — he seems to have been an art forger — but he swears that he's left that life behind. Is this true? And who is the person in the art 'black market' he has apparently recognized and was going to talk to Mrs Van Dine about? He has no alibi for the time of the disappearance — he was alone in his cabin!

# 6

The next development in the case happened at breakfast on Friday morning. Mr Protheroe came in late, looking even more tired and out of sorts than I felt. He buttered his bacon and dipped his toast in his tea and it seemed only natural for me to ask, 'Are you all right?'

'Difficult case,' said Mr Protheroe shortly.

'So no leads?' asked Daisy in a tone I knew she thought was sympathetic.

'Hardly. Though it's quite obvious what's happened now – I initially suspected the son, but we've had a new lead. I searched Mrs Van Dine's cabin and found that one of those vases of hers is missing. Then I had my men search the cabins on the lower decks again, and found just what I expected: it was in Harry Guo's cabin.'

I gasped.

'I happen to know that Harry has a criminal past. He was a forger – and although he told the management of the ship he'd mended his ways to get a job, these criminal types can't ever really change their stripes. It's clear that he crept into Mrs Van Dine's cabin after dinner to steal it to sell on the black market, and when Mrs Van Dine surprised him he wrestled her overboard. He's in the brig now, waiting to be offloaded at the next port. I hope he's charged with murder.'

'But what fingerprints did you find on it?' asked Daisy. 'Are you sure it was Mr Guo?'

'Guo was wearing gloves, of course – he had several uniform pairs in his cabin. That means nothing. Mrs Van Dine, Miss Van Dine and Mrs Chandha's prints were on the vase, but both Miss Van Dine and Mrs Chandha can account for that. Miss Van Dine helped her mother with her collection, and Mrs Chandha came to Mrs Van Dine's cabin yesterday afternoon to view the vases. No, it's clear it was Guo. I shall look forward to getting some sleep now it's all cleared up— Hello, what's this?'

This was Mr Tse, Mr Protheroe's second, who was hurrying through the dining room, weaving in and out of the tables. I saw Sally Lennon, plates of omelettes and congee piled up in her arms, watching his progress nervously.

'Sir, sir!' gasped Mr Tse, as soon as he was close enough to our table. 'Sir, something's happened to Guo!'

'What do you mean?' barked Protheroe.

'He – er – he's taken poison. Something in his water this morning. The doctor's testing it, but he thinks that it's – er – dogoxin?'

'Digoxin!' snapped Daisy, before she could help herself. 'Oh, do excuse me – it's just that my grandfather takes it for his heart.'

I know perfectly well that Daisy's grandfather is dead, and she had read it in one of her medical textbooks. But my own heart was racing horribly. Was Harry all right? Was he dead? Who had done this to him – or had he done it to himself? I knew that the story Mr Protheroe was telling did not add up.

'He's not dead, is he?' asked Mr Protheroe, speaking for me. 'Good god, man, he can't die before we charge him! The Van Dines will have a fit!'

'Not dead yet, sir, but it's touch and go.'

'Well, tell the doctor to keep at it. This man must live to face his trial!'

And Mr Protheroe jumped up, threw his napkin down onto his plate and rushed out of the dining room with Mr Tse hurrying behind him.

'Harry's been framed!' I cried.

'Of course he has,' snapped Daisy. 'It ought to be clear to anyone to see – if only Mr Protheroe wasn't the most infernal idiot. The police always are! How could anyone believe Harry was behind this? First of all, art forgers don't *steal* art without having a copy to replace it with. Second, any forger worth their salt would know that the vases are only valuable together. That's what Mrs Chandha said, isn't it? No, the only reason someone would steal one of the vases is to frame Harry. And, third, Mr Protheroe claimed that the scream was on the starboard side, but now he's assuming that Harry pushed Mrs Van Dine over the port railing. And this morning Harry's been poisoned, probably by the person who framed him!'

'Are we sure he didn't take it himself, though? We do know that there *was* a second scream and a splash on the port side, even if Mr Protheroe doesn't.'

'Of course not!' cried Daisy. 'What, when all three of our remaining suspects had knowledge of the effects of digoxin?'

'How do you know that?' I asked.

'Oh, Hazel, it's perfectly clear. Mr Van Dine has a bad heart, and I'm willing to bet that medicine Miriam mentioned him taking is digoxin. So that's both Miriam and Holden. And then there's Mrs Chandha. She trained as a doctor, so she'd know exactly what digoxin does and how to administer it. Harry Guo, on the other hand, is young and healthy, so unlikely to be taking it, and poor enough not to have easy access to such a thing. So it's one of those three. We must *think*! Are you finished with your breakfast? Come on, then, let's go.'

I was not quite – but Daisy was on the warpath, so I stuffed my last bite of toast into my mouth, pocketed a buttered roll and followed her out onto the port-side deck.

The sun was bright that morning, now that the mist had cleared, and the waves glittered below us. I squinted and tried not to look at them. Suddenly my swallowed toast was threatening to reappear.

Daisy paced along, lost in thought, but my eyes were drawn to a knot of deckhands crowding round one particular spot at the edge of the deck. They were all staring downwards expectantly, and at that moment there was a cheer from someone below, and a cry of 'Success!' in Cantonese. Everyone cheered, and then the deckhands began to pull a length of rope up. I stopped to watch.

Up came another deckhand, the end of the rope round his waist. He held aloft in his arms some sort of spiky metal cage, inside of which a fish flopped.

'Daisy!' I said in excitement. 'Come here!' And to the deckhands, 'What's that?'

'Dunno, miss,' said one, turning to me politely. 'It was stuck in the anchor chain. Must've got in there since we checked everything last night.'

'DAISY! Come look at this! May I have it, please?'

'If you like, miss,' said the deckhand, looking at me very oddly.

'Good heavens, Hazel, what's wrong?' asked Daisy, her cheeks pink and the wind whipping her hair in her face. 'Why do you have an instrument of torture?'

'It's a mousetrap,' I said. 'And I know who pushed Mrs Van Dine off the ship.'

# 7

We found Mr Protheroe in the sick bay, standing angrily over a weak, but very much alive, Harry Guo.

'You can't get away so easily, man!' Mr Protheroe snapped as we arrived. 'You shall face the full might of English law!'

'Excuse me,' I said.

Mr Protheroe ignored me.

'EXCUSE ME,' said Daisy, louder. 'MR PROTHEROE, WE HAVE SOME IMPORTANT INFORMATION FOR YOU.'

Mr Protheroe turned to her, his hand raised a little as though he was trying to brush away a fly.

'Girls, why don't you go and play quoits on deck instead of messing about with – good grief, what is that thing? It looks positively murderous.'

'It's a mousetrap,' said Daisy. 'Mr Protheroe, IF you don't mind, my friend Hazel has something to say to you.'

'Mr Protheroe, I know what you think, but Harry Guo didn't hurt Mrs Van Dine or steal her vase,' I said, trying to breathe calmly and not rush over myself. 'He didn't have access to the digoxin he took, and he would *never* have stolen only one vase – he would know that they're more valuable together, and he's a forger, not a thief.'

'Oh, I'm sure he had his reasons,' said Mr Protheroe. 'He's a cunning fellow, and a wrong'un through and through.'

'He isn't!' I said crossly. 'He's innocent. But he does know who did it, only I think he's been afraid to say anything in case you didn't believe him.'

'Does he indeed? Really, what nonsense, girls.'

'Do be quiet and listen!' snapped Daisy. 'This is important! Look at the object my friend has in her hand, if you please. It is a mousetrap, as we've said. It was found this morning caught in the anchor chain on the port side – the anchor chain, by the way, beneath Holden Van Dine's cabin.'

'This is his!' I said, nodding. 'Ask him, I'm sure he'll confirm it. And it proves his story is true! He really did go and stand on deck outside his cabin and brood after dinner, and that's where he was when Mrs Van Dine was pushed overboard. You see, two different groups of people heard screams at eleven p.m. on two different sides of the ship – Mrs Davidson on the starboard side, *and Sally Lennon on the port side.* Ask her and she'll tell you! What Mrs Davidson heard, though, was the yell of Holden Van Dine throwing his mousetrap overboard in a fit of rage, while what Sally heard was Mrs Van Dine being pushed into the sea. So we know that Holden was on the wrong side of the ship when his mother went into the water. He does have an alibi, after all.'

'And once Holden is ruled out, of course it's quite obvious who did push Mrs Van Dine in,' said Daisy.

'Mrs Chandha!' said Mr Protheroe. 'Er, I mean – not that I think there's anything to all of this, girls.'

'Not at all!' said Daisy. 'Mrs Chandha, like Harry Guo, knows the value of those vases as a pair. She'd never have stolen just one, even to frame him – it wouldn't have occurred to her. Yes, her prints were on the stolen vase, but that's only because she handled it yesterday afternoon. And, yes, she had the *knowledge* to poison Harry, but not the opportunity. Because the only person in this case who we know has a bad heart—'

'– is Mr Jacob Van Dine,' I finished. 'And as we've heard, the person who cares for him and makes sure he takes his medication is his daughter, Miriam. Miriam could easily have gone down to visit Harry and put the digoxin in his water this morning. She was also the only person who could have taken the vase out of Mrs Van Dine's cabin after Mrs Chandha came to look at it yesterday afternoon and planted it in Harry's cabin before dinner, where he wouldn't find it before his cabin was searched – we ought to have seen that there was really no time for anyone to take the vase and put it in Harry's cabin after the crime!

'We know that Miriam and Mrs Van Dine have been disagreeing on art purchases, and arguing about the direction of the collection – Mrs Chandha said so. Now, on its own that's not enough to hurt anyone – but we heard from Harry Guo that there's someone on the Van Dines' table who he's worked with on the black market, and he was going to mention it to Mrs Van Dine. I'm willing to bet that person is Miriam. If she's been selling art forgeries, and was afraid that Harry might reveal that to her mother, both the crimes make sense – bump off her mother before she could find out, and frame and murder Harry before he could say anything!

'And although Miriam seems to have an alibi for the time of the splash, it's important to take into account how close to Mrs Van Dine's cabin her friend Elaine's cabin is. Mrs Van Dine is in 114, and Elaine is in 122. Miriam could easily have shoved her mother into the water and then gone in to see Elaine, arriving only a minute after eleven p.m. Elaine is very vague with time, and she'd never remember that extra minute. Miriam said that she went first to her own cabin to pick up the magazine, and then on to Elaine's, but Holden never mentioned seeing her, despite pacing the deck outside their cabins throughout that time. I think it's more likely that she had the magazine in her bag during dinner. She followed her mother upstairs when she left the dining room, shoved her into the sea, took out the magazine from her bag and went in to see Elaine. I think this was a carefully premeditated crime – and if it wasn't for the evidence of the mousetrap, we might never have solved it.'

'You – this is fantasy!' said Mr Protheroe. 'How can you back up any of it?'

'I think Harry might be able to help,' I said. 'Harry, it was Miriam Van Dine you recognized, wasn't it?'

Harry sat up in bed painfully. 'Yes,' he said. 'She bought several of my forgeries four years ago. She used her mother's standing to pass them off as genuine and sell them on at a profit. I think she was afraid, when she saw me, that I'd tell Mrs Van Dine everything – so she must have tried to get rid of both of us, so she could keep her below-board art business running.'

'Well, you *would* say that,' Mr Protheroe muttered.

And I am not sure quite what would have happened if Holden Van Dine had not run into the sick bay just then, shouting, 'There it is! My mousetrap! They told me you had it! I knew I shouldn't have thrown it overboard. I regretted it as soon as it happened. Kid, hey, hand it over, that thing's going to make me money!'

I saw Mr Protheroe realizing he was beaten. He sagged, rubbed his hand over his face, and said, 'Mr Van Dine? I think I may need to speak to your sister.'

'Quite right too!' said Daisy triumphantly. 'Come on, Hazel, I think we ought to be there, don't you?'

And that is nearly all of this story told, apart from one last, very odd thing: that afternoon, when Harry Guo had been released and Miriam Van Dine was locked up in the brig with Mr Tse standing guard outside, the SS *Strathclyde* was contacted by a fishing vessel. A woman in evening dress had been picked up in their nets on Thursday night, at around 11:15 p.m. – she had been so unwell that she had not been able to speak until Friday morning, when she announced that she was Mrs Bernadette Van Dine, and she had been pushed overboard by her own daughter.

'I told you we were right,' said Daisy to Mr Protheroe smugly.

# 8

I let Daisy look at all of this, and she was mostly pleased with it (though she remembers the denouement differently, and is convinced that she was the one to realize the importance of the mousetrap).

'Weren't we good, even then?' she said to me.

'We *had* already solved six murders by then,' I pointed out.

'Really, sometimes I don't know how we managed it,' said Daisy. 'You were so green then, Watson. I had to coach you almost constantly.'

'Daisy!' I cried. 'Don't be rude. You got plenty of things wrong too.'

'Shush, Watson, we don't talk about that. Anyway, I'm perfect now.'

'You are not,' I said. 'And nor am I, and that's what makes us good at detecting.'

'Humph,' said Daisy. 'We really are very different, you and me. Ugh, I don't half wish I didn't have to go back to Deepdean next week.'

She really is in a mood about it, although she is pretending not to be. I am pretending not to be hurt by that, for it was so lonely to be there without her this last term. I raced towards the hols like a train rushing through a tunnel, and the thought of having to do another term so alone is dreadful. I know she wants me to say that she does not have to come back, but it isn't up to me – her work for Uncle Felix and Aunt Lucy is over.

And then, just as Daisy's maid Hetty was packing our last things ready to go back to Deepdean this morning, Chapman the butler brought in a telegram. I had rather hoped it would be from Alexander, but I was disappointed.

'For you, Miss Daisy,' he said. 'An early birthday message.'

Daisy reached over and took it listlessly.

She read it once.

She read it again.

I felt a change come over her, and braced myself without knowing what for.

Daisy put the telegram down and took a deep breath. She was suddenly beaming.

'George and Lavinia have run away to the Spanish Civil War,' she said.

248

'WHAT!' I cried, diving for the telegram. It felt flimsy in my hand, the paper fluttering with my breath, but there was no mistaking what it said.

**TELEGRAM**

HAPPY BIRTHDAY DAISY STOP GONE TO SPAIN STOP DOWN WITH FASCISM STOP DON'T FOLLOW US G & L

'Did you know about this?' I cried.

'I might as well ask you the same question. George's best friend is *your* boyfriend, after all.'

I felt myself blush. 'Alexander never told me anything! Are – are they allowed?'

'Almost certainly *not*,' said Daisy happily. 'I should think this'll spark an international incident. George's father is a knight, and Lavinia's is terribly rich and cross.'

'And . . .' I said slowly, for I could feel Daisy building to something.

'And I should *think* that they might get in touch with the government, who might quietly get in touch with

Uncle Felix and Aunt Lucy to ask them to get George and Lavinia back,' said Daisy. 'And if I was Uncle Felix . . .'

'Oh NO,' I said. 'Daisy, we are not going to Spain. It's a *war*! It'll be dangerous! And we have to go back to school this afternoon!'

'Hazel Wong,' said Daisy. 'Did I or did I not promise you a life of adventure?'

'Yes,' I said.

'And have we ever had an adventure that wasn't terribly dangerous?'

'No,' I said begrudgingly.

'Exactly,' said Daisy. 'Oh, Hazel, come on! It'll be brilliant fun! And besides, this is a far more elegant way to raise me from the dead. People turn up in all sorts of surprising ways during a war. I shall let Amina know so she's not worried.'

And that is why I am writing this on a jolting train on our way to the Spanish Civil War to find our friends – which, I suspect, will be another story for my casebook.

# May Wong and the Deadly Flat

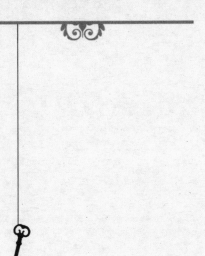

Written by May Wong, aged almost ten
Saturday 9th September 1939

I am May Wong and *no one* ever listens to me. If they had, I would still be in Hong Kong with my mother and Teddy instead of stuck in England with a war on, and I wouldn't have to be speaking English and going to a stupid freezing-cold school with horrible European girls who stare at me. (I haven't actually gone to Deepdean yet – my sister Rose and I are being put on the train tomorrow – but I *know* they'll stare.)

Of course, *Rose* is excited about school. Rose loves books and she wants to please everyone. Which is why it was so unlucky that the day the murder happened *she* was the one playing on the stairs.

It's sort of Rose's fault that I'm here at all. I wasn't supposed to be for two more years except that Rose was starting at Deepdean School (which is where Big Sister Hazel went, and her friend Daisy, and so where we have to go too). Father wanted to travel with Rose, and decided that I should come along with them, so that I could practise my English and see that England is a nice place to be. Which it isn't. We've been staying with Daisy's uncle, Mr Mountfitchet, in his flat all summer. I was supposed to go home to Hong Kong with Father as soon as Rose went to Deepdean – but then war broke out, and everything went wrong.

I thought at first when we got to England that being at war would be an exciting adventure. There are sandbags in all the parks and air-raid warning signs on the walls of buildings. Father tried to distract me from seeing them, as though I was still a baby and not almost ten years old. (Well, nine years and four months, which is almost ten). Of course I saw them, and so did Rose. She pretended not to, because she's trying so hard to keep everyone happy, but I don't care about that.

We've all been fitted for gas masks that smell of rubber and squeeze my face like a hand, and people go by in the street with yards and yards of heavy black fabric sticking out of bags. And then last Sunday morning the grown-ups (which includes Big Sister Hazel now, and Daisy) all went into Mr Mountfitchet's study and put the wireless on and played it very low so we wouldn't hear.

I climbed up on top of the table in the dressing room next door and put my ear against the vent, so of course I heard. First the man on the radio did a long speech that I couldn't really understand, saying that no one was safe but everyone had to be calm, and then Mrs Mountfitchet said in a very stiff voice, 'So it's war.'

Then there was a babble of voices, everyone talking at once, which resolved into –

'You can't risk the children on the journey home,' said Mr Mountfitchet.

'Rose will be all right at Deepdean, at least,' said Big Sister.

'But little May . . .' said my father.

And that was when I was betrayed.

'Should stay here with Rose,' said Mr Mountfitchet. 'Deepdean will accommodate. We can telephone them, but I can't see any issues. It'll be flooded with evacuees, anyway. If you feel you must go back—'

'No question about it,' said Father. I was sure he'd say that he needed me with him. But – 'I have to go back to my family. If you're sure the little ones will be safe?'

That's why I hate Father now, and Mr Mountfitchet. *I'm* Father's family, and so is Rose, and he shouldn't be allowed to choose Teddy and my mother over us. (Hazel's big enough to look after herself – and she's going to university at Oxford next month, or at least she's supposed to.)

I was so angry then that I ran away to our room and kicked the wall. I couldn't even pretend to be surprised when Rose and I were called into the study and told the news hours later – but of course no one bothered to notice that I wasn't shocked.

So England is at war and I can't go back home.

I've always wanted to fight, and do brave things, and be a hero, and at first I hoped that I would be able to help the grown-ups win this war so I could get on the ship home as quick as possible.

I put my head out through the blackout blinds that first night to see if I could spot enemy soldiers coming to kill us. I wanted to kill them first. But then Bridget, who's the Mountfitchets' maid, came in and found me. She got very upset that I was breaking blackout, and told me to go to bed at once.

'But the soldiers might be coming!' I said. 'I want to fight them!'

'I'll fight any soldiers who try to come in here; don't you worry,' said Bridget. I did believe her. Bridget isn't the usual sort of maid, any more than the Mountfitchets are the usual sort of English people. I think, even though no one will say it in front of me, that they might be *spies*. But what I realized that night is that no matter how unusual Bridget and the Mountfitchets are, they won't let me help them. No one lets children do anything brave – and especially no one lets *me*.

So this is why, even though I thought the war would be an adventure, it's not. The only properly interesting thing to happen is the murder. And that's why I'm writing all this down, so I have something to prove that there *was* a murder in the flat above this one, a murder that I solved. I've made at least one grown-up sorry for what they did, even if I can't do anything to the ones I am really angry at.

Again, the grown-ups didn't tell us that anyone was dead, they just whispered about it behind closed doors. I knew what had happened, though, because on Wednesday afternoon I heard the grocer talking about it with the maid from the third-floor flat. The grocer was on his rounds (in England, grocers are the people who deliver food every day – he comes just after 2 p.m., and I always go outside to play so I can listen to him gossiping with the maid), and the maid told him that Mr Murchison from the second-floor flat had been found dead in his bed that morning.

He was found by the charwoman who comes in a few times a week to clean for him. Mr and Mrs Mountfitchet live in the first-floor flat, and Mr Murchison lived in the one directly above. He was an old professor who went to the British Library to read every day. He was supposed to be very rich, only he didn't look it when I saw him. That was all I knew about him.

Except that now I knew he was dead.

'Couldn't bear it,' said the maid, and the grocer nodded. 'Not another one, *you* know. It's terribly hard. Poor man!'

'Britain's in a tight spot,' said the grocer. 'Invasion soon, I heard. Now, I'd better go, or I'll be late.'

I realized what the grown-ups thought – that Mr Murchison was upset about the war, because he'd already had to fight in one years ago, and so he had . . . *killed himself.* Which was a stupid thing to think, but then again grown-ups *are* stupid, even the good ones.

And I was even more sure they were wrong when Rose had new nightmares on Wednesday night.

Rose has been worrying about the war all summer. Rose wants everyone to be safe. Her English is better than mine, so she's been reading the papers. She told me all about Hitler rolling through Europe like a ball going down a hill, and all the awful things that happened while everyone got ready to fight him. There was an English submarine that sank in June with everyone still on board, and Rose couldn't sleep for three nights because of it. I imagined all those people at the bottom of the sea, tapping and tapping to get out, and I told Rose so and she SCREAMED.

Rose has been even more worried since Sunday morning, now we know the war is an actual fact. But when she had bad dreams on Wednesday, I knew they weren't the same as usual. Rose lay in her bed and cried and cried, and when she finally went to sleep I heard her say, 'I'm sorry! I'm so sorry!'

I knew that Rose had nothing to be sorry for, because SHE didn't cause the war and it isn't OUR fault we're in England during it (it's Father's), so I went over to her bed and put my arms round her and squeezed. She woke up with a jump and a shriek and I said, 'Ling Ling, what's wrong?'

'Nothing,' said Rose. 'Go away.'

'Won't,' I said. (We were speaking Cantonese, which is what we speak when Father can't hear us. We're supposed to be practising our English, but I don't like it.) 'What's wrong?'

'*Nothing*,' said Rose, and she began to cry again.

I poked her in the arm. 'Tell me tell me tell me tell me,' I said.

'I can't! It – it's all MY FAULT!' sobbed Rose, and then the whole story poured out of her.

It went like this.

On Tuesday at lunch time the Mountfitchets and Father were out, and Big Sister was supposed to take us to buy uniforms (mostly me, because I don't have anything. I'd hoped that Deepdean would say no to me arriving two years early, but they didn't. I'm going to be part of a new form for younger girls, and I hate it!). But Rose wouldn't come, no matter how excited she was about Deepdean.

'I won't!' she said. 'There might be bombs!'

Big Sister Hazel explained again that there were no bombs – not yet, at least. I didn't trust her about that, and nor did Rose, and we could tell Rose wouldn't be swayed. So Big Sister said, 'Well, I know your size, Ling Ling! I suppose you can stay here. You promise to be good?'

'I promise,' said Rose.

'If I'd asked to stay, you wouldn't have let me!' I said, as we walked down the street outside, me bumping into grown-ups and their gas masks with every step.

'If you'd asked to stay, you'd have had some sort of plan,' said Hazel. 'Rose isn't like that.'

This was rude, but true. So to take revenge I asked her about the Mountfitchets being spies all the way to the department store, and she shushed me and blushed and looked very suspicious. For someone who knows so many spies she's very bad at being sneaky.

So I had a boring afternoon fidgeting in fitting rooms (and then a less boring tea with Hazel and Daisy at the Ritz), but what was happening to Rose wasn't boring at all.

After we had gone Rose sat on the stairs outside the Mountfitchets' flat. The building they live in has four flats piled one on top of each other (they don't even have a building to themselves! England is so strange!) with stairs in the lobby going up to each one, and a lift to get you there even faster. (Although Rose and I don't take lifts if we can help it, because of the thing that happened to our brother Teddy in Hong Kong.)

Rose was playing with her paper dolls. She has a book full of brightly coloured outfits, and she spends hours cutting out little shirts and knickers and hats. It's boring; Rose is boring. But what's not boring is what she saw.

She hadn't been there long when Mr Murchison went past her, off to the British Library, the way he always did. Rose says he looked the way he always did too: ordinary and dull in his tweed suit that was baggy at the elbows. She hardly looked up.

Until half an hour later, when the door to Mr Murchison's flat opened again and a man came down the stairs. Rose knew that it was Mr Murchison's flat he came out of (I asked her!) because his door squeaks, and she heard the squeak twice that day: once when Mr Murchison left, and then again. She was looking up when he came round the corner of the stairs and saw her.

She said he was tall (or was he just standing up, while she was sitting? She wasn't sure), and European, with brown hair. He was wearing a nice new blue pinstriped suit with pink lining, but it was a bit creased and dusty, and there was dust on his brown shoes. He was wearing leather driving gloves. Rose really only cares about clothes, and you can tell that because it was all she could tell me. She thought he was younger than Mr Mountfitchet, but again she wasn't sure. She hadn't seen him go up into Mr Murchison's flat, but she didn't think much of that – Rose never does. She's not suspicious like I am, and like Big Sister Hazel is. I want to be like Hazel when I'm older, a detective, and I will, just you wait and see. I've already helped her solve two cases.

He smiled at her and said, 'Hello, young lady! Do you speak English?'

Rose nodded at him. She can get shy sometimes.

'Well, I've just been into my father's flat. I've left a surprise for him. But don't tell anyone you saw me, all right? I'll give you a shilling.'

Rose took the shilling, all pleased, and waved to him as he went on down the stairs. I remember us coming back, and seeing her looking pink and happy. Rose loves helping people, and she loves the thought of surprises. She didn't say anything – but she waited to hear what Mr Murchison would say about his present.

And then the next morning, Mr Murchison was dead.

I remember Rose went pale when I told her. I remember that she hung about Bridget as she was cooking lunch, pestering her with questions.

'Do you think he suffered?' she asked. 'How old was he? Will his son come to take his things away?'

'Possibly,' said Bridget, who is very honest. 'Seventy, at least. And he doesn't have a son, or a daughter, so I should think his things will be sold along with his flat.'

And at that Rose turned as white as a sheet and ran away to her room.

That was what Rose told me, and it made me feel wide awake and giddy with excitement. I bothered her with questions.

'Are you sure it was yesterday afternoon? What time? Why didn't you see him going in? Would you know him again? Are you sure he wasn't a ghost?'

The last question made Rose cry more because, like Big Sister Hazel, she's afraid of ghosts. I think that's funny. It's true that some of them have big burning mouths and some of them have needles for hair and some of them have breath so disgusting that they can make themselves faint (at home I listen to the maids when they're talking, so I know), but if I saw a ghost I'd hurt it before it could hurt me. I'm not worried.

'It *was* that day,' she said between sobs. 'I know because I was wearing my pink dress with the high collar. I don't know what time it was. You'd been gone for about an hour, I think?'

I know that dress – I have one the same. We have the same dresses made for us in different sizes, which I hate – Hazel doesn't have to wear them, and nor does Teddy, so it's not fair we are always dressed like twins. We look too similar already, apart from the fact that Rose is prettier.

'And I don't know why I didn't see him earlier – I was there all afternoon, really I was, and he didn't go up. Perhaps he'd arrived before I went out to sit on the steps, though? And perhaps I heard him wrong, and he didn't say *son*. He might have been a servant, I suppose?'

That was silly and I knew it wasn't right. Rose speaks good English. If she thought he'd said he was Mr Murchison's son, then that's what he said – she wouldn't have got that wrong. And he might have been a servant, but servants didn't usually wear suits like the one Rose had described, at least not in England. In Hong Kong they wear smart black and white tunic suits, like penguins, but England is different.

What we did know is that he had been in Mr Murchison's flat on the day before he was found dead, and he had told Rose that he had left Mr Murchison a present. I didn't believe that. What I did believe was that the man had something – or a lot – to do with Mr Murchison's death.

Grown-ups are always telling children to keep quiet about things (or just to keep quiet), and I've noticed that it's never for a good reason. They do it so their secrets don't get out. They do it because they think children can be used, but they can't, and it's not right of them to try. I didn't like that this man had tried to use my sister as part of whatever trick he was playing on the world, and I decided then that I was going to work out the truth and tell everyone I could about it.

And then we'd see whether people would listen to what I had to say.

I got up the next morning and pulled on my clothes from the day before. While Rose was washing behind her ears and doing her hair nicely I went looking for something to use to help me solve the problem. I've seen Big Sister Hazel using notebooks when she's being a detective, but I couldn't find a notebook so I went into the kitchen and stole some waste paper that Bridget was using for shopping lists and to write codes on. Then I picked up an old pencil from next to the Mountfitchets' crosswords. I tied my hair back with a bit of string and I was ready.

I wrote down the important questions, which were:

HOW DID MR MURCHISON DIE?
WHO WAS THE MAN ROSE SAW?
DID HE KILL MR MURCHISON? WHY?
HOW DID HE GET INTO THE FLAT?
WAS HE A GHOST?

And then I went to find someone to interview.

As usual the grown-ups were pretending to be busy. Mr Mountfitchet was in his dressing room, putting cufflinks in his shirt sleeves.

'Hello!' I said. 'I think someone killed Mr Murchison.'

I've found that if I say exactly the thing I mean, grown-ups generally think I'm just being amusing. They also try to distract me by telling me answers to questions I didn't ask, which can be very useful.

'No one killed Mr Murchison, littlest Wong,' said Mr Mountfitchet, fiddling with his right wrist. 'Not everything is murder. I suppose I shouldn't be surprised that you're going the way of your oldest sister. There must be crime-solving in the Wong blood. Look, I'm sorry to have to be firm, but this isn't a case for small girls. It isn't a case at all, d'you hear me? Your father will have my hide if I don't warn you off. I tell you that I was on the scene and it's quite clear what happened. I read the note myself.'

'What did it say?' I asked. 'Also, I'm not the littlest, Teddy is.'

'Good lord, she's even worse than her sister,' said Mr Mountfitchet to his cufflink. Then to me: 'Forget I said that! Go away!'

I went away, satisfied. I'd found out that there was a note, which is why the maid had told the grocer that Mr Murchison had killed himself. But what if it wasn't Mr Murchison who had left it? What if it was . . . the man Rose had seen?

I thought about who to speak to next. I almost went to find Mrs Mountfitchet, but then I remembered that sometimes she actually listens to what I say. Also, I think she's cleverer than me, and I hate that. Then I thought about Father, but I remembered that I was still angry at him for leaving us. So I went to find Big Sister Hazel.

Hazel was still asleep in her room so I jumped on top of her. She made a grunting noise and sat up and said, 'DAISY? WHAT?'

'It's not Daisy; it's ME,' I told her. 'Hello, Big Sister, did you know that Mr Murchison killed himself? How did he do it? Was it awful? Tell me, tell me!'

'Get off, Monkey!' grumbled Hazel. 'You're disgusting. Have you brushed your teeth yet?'

'Don't need to!' I said. 'And you're not my amah; you can't say things like that.'

'You don't have an amah any more,' said Hazel. 'You're in England, May – you have to look after yourself. I'm not going to tell you anything about Mr Murchison; it's not for you to hear about.'

'You would be investigating it if there wasn't a war!' I said. 'You and Daisy would!'

'May! Listen. It's not a mystery. He – he poisoned himself. There was poison in the glass of milk beside his bed. There was a note in his study desk drawer that explained everything. DON'T tell Father I told you that.'

'Thanks, Big Sister!' I said, jumping off her. 'I'm going to investigate!'

'May, NO!' shouted Hazel. 'I told you, you're NOT a detective!'

'I helped you solve a murder when I was only six!' I said crossly. 'And now I'm nearly ten—'

'You're nine!'

'I AM NEARLY TEN and I don't see why I can't solve another one. Just you wait and see!'

Hazel might have been a good detective when she was younger, but now she's a grown-up she's begun to act like one. These days she believes things other grown-ups tell her without asking questions, and that's all wrong if you want to solve crimes. Why would Mr Murchison write a note but leave it in his desk drawer? Why not put it beside his bed with the glass of poison? It didn't make sense to me at all. I wrote down NOTE IN STUDY DRAWER SUSPICIOUS and circled it to make it look more important.

I had one more person to interview.

I went into the living room to bother Bridget while she was laying the fires. This is a thing that happens in England even in the summer, because England is horribly cold and as grey as a charcoal pencil.

'I think Mr Murchison's son killed him,' I said to Bridget's behind as she bent over.

'Do be quiet, you,' said Bridget without turning round. 'I told Rose yesterday that he hadn't any children at all.'

'His butler, then,' I said.

Bridget turned round, wiping the dust off her fingers. 'No butler, either,' she said. 'He'd only got a charwoman who came in Mondays, Wednesdays and Fridays once he'd gone off to the British Library Reading Room. So she wasn't there on Tuesday. What'll you do now, eh? You're out of suspects.'

A bell rang away in another room. 'Ah, that's the butcher, right on time,' said Bridget, getting up. 'Come on, missy, help me get the delivery in.'

I trailed reluctantly after her to the kitchen, trying to think how I could get out of this. But I realized when we got there that it might be useful, after all.

Bridget went to the back of the kitchen and swung open a wooden door. Behind it was something I hadn't seen before: a rope and pulleys. She tugged on the rope and after a minute up came a flat wooden board, a pile of wrapped meat on it.

'What's that?' I asked.

'Dinner,' said Bridget. 'And the service lift. Haven't you seen it before?'

'No!' I said. 'Does it go to all the flats?'

'It does,' said Bridget. 'There's a door in the basement, next to the air-raid shelter. The delivery man comes in through the service entrance, loads the food onto the board and rings the bell, and then we open the door and pull up the lift. But it's not for you to ride on! You might get stuck. D'you hear?'

'Yes, Bridget,' I said, as though I've ever listened to any grown-up telling me not to do anything.

'I know how the man got up into Mr Murchison's flat,' I said to Rose.

Rose looked horrified. I was cross with her, and then I remembered that I hadn't exactly told her I was going to investigate.

'He's not a ghost,' I said. 'Promise you. He was real and I think he killed Mr Murchison!'

Rose burst into tears. 'I should have said something!' she wailed. 'I should have known he was lying!'

'No you shouldn't!' I said. '*He* shouldn't have said anything to you at all. He was being stupid, and he deserves to be caught. And we're going to catch him! But first you have to help me prove how he got in. Come on!'

I led her (still pink-faced with tears) into the kitchen and showed her the service lift. 'We just have to get in it,' I said. 'You can go first.'

Rose took a wavering step towards it – I'm very good at making her do things usually – and then she stopped with a shriek. 'NO!' she cried, shaking her head. 'I'm not going in there! I won't!'

I sighed. 'All right,' I said. 'You don't have to. I will.'

This is proof that I love Rose even though she's annoying. Because of what happened to Teddy I still have nightmares where I'm trapped in a lift, being squeezed tighter and tighter until I pop. But I knew if I was going to be a detective I'd have to do awful things, and that included getting in the service lift, even though it was dark and small and smelled horrible, like English food. I was going to be brave. There's a war on, after all, so anyone might die, any time, and there's no point being scared of anything.

We decided (I decided, and Rose nodded) that before I got in we had to test the weight the lift could carry, so we piled in pots and pans from the kitchen. Bridget shouted, 'WHAT ARE YOU TWO DOING?' from the living room, and I shouted, 'PLAYING AIR-RAID SHELTERS,' and she ignored us after that. The lift held the weight of at least a dozen heavy pots and pans, so it was no good delaying any longer.

I took a deep breath and climbed in. It smelled worse than ever, and it was so dark. It echoed too, up and down, and I could feel air above me and below. I hated it.

Rose stuck her head in after me. 'Are you all right?' she asked.

'YES,' I snapped, lying. 'Now you have to raise me up. Go on, turn that pulley.'

'Hold on,' said Rose, and she began to wind the rope. She sent me down a bit first, and I yelled at her and Rose almost cried again, but then I started to rise. I

273

squeezed my eyes shut tight and clenched my fists and imagined fighting people. That always calms me down.

Up and up I went, the wooden board creeping upwards and my breathing getting tighter and tighter, and then a little pinpoint of light appeared above me and stretched out into a sliver, and I saw I was looking at a closed wooden door just like the one in the kitchen below. I tugged on the rope, and Rose stopped winching me up.

I put out my hand and pushed at the door and it opened. I crawled out into a kitchen that was shaped exactly like the Mountfitchets' kitchen but looked entirely different. The tiles were different patterns, and the cupboards were painted the wrong colour. It made me feel strange.

I stood up and stamped and shook myself to get off the feeling of being in the lift. Then I wondered whether I'd been heard by someone in the flat. So I shouted as loud as I could. But no one came.

I went through to the pantry, and opened the refrigerator, looking for suspicious things. The milk was in its proper place but it looked curdled. I sniffed it and it smelled odd – more than off. I remembered what Big Sister had said, and I worked out that this must have been what the murderer had poisoned. I decided not to drink any of it.

I moved through all the rooms, humming to keep myself brave. I found the bedroom, and if I'd been

Rose I'd have been afraid, but I wasn't – and anyway, they'd stripped the sheets off the bed and it sat bare and sad.

'Poor bed,' I said to it. I wondered how Mr Murchison had looked when he'd died.

I went rooting in the bedside table (there was a crusty ring on its top, where the milk glass had been), and found some bits of paper and pens and a diary that was full of entries in spiky old-man handwriting. It's hard to read English when people don't print their letters properly but I saw *get suit patched* and *dentist* and *refute Julian of Norwich????* and it was obvious even though I didn't know all the words that this was Mr Murchison's reminders list to himself. Rose keeps one because she is efficient. This list sounded extremely boring and grown-up. Was this evidence that he didn't kill himself? I wrote down BORING LISTS, and then after a pause PAPER NEXT TO HIS BED – SO WHY NOTE IN STUDY?

I thought this was an important question. I had seen the study, on the other side of the flat, and I went back to it now. There was good creamy paper on Mr Murchison's tall desk in a tidy stack, its pen in its holder and the chair pushed in like a school desk at the end of a lesson. I pulled it back and climbed up to investigate, tucking my feet under me and putting my notepaper down my front for safekeeping. The desk had a green leather top that was satisfying to put my hands against.

I imagined being Mr Murchison, sitting exactly where I was kneeling and writing his final note on a piece of this nice paper. Still being Mr Murchison, I put down the pen and reached out for the blotter, which I could see resting in its proper place. I pretended to roll the blotter over the paper, the way you do when you've finished a letter, to help the ink dry – and then I got an idea in my head and turned it round so I could look at it properly.

Mr Murchison was tidy, and as I'd expected he replaced the paper in his blotter regularly. I could only see the ghosts of a few words, from the last thing he'd written.

*Come on Saturday. It would be delightful to se*

I wanted to yell with excitement, so I did. I'd found proof that Mr Murchison hadn't written a suicide note at this desk. The last thing he'd written was a letter about someone visiting on Saturday – Mr Murchison had been found dead on Wednesday morning, and today was still only Thursday. *He hadn't been expecting to die.*

I was sure that the man Rose had seen leaving Mr Murchison's flat on Tuesday afternoon was the killer. I thought he had got into the flat from the basement, using the service lift, and he'd left a suicide note in Mr Murchison's desk in the study – I remembered that Hazel had told me it was in a drawer. That would make sense if the murderer had planted it: he'd left it somewhere Mr Murchison wouldn't see it when he got back from the British Library late on Tuesday evening, but also somewhere it'd definitely be found by the police when they searched the flat. Then, I thought, he'd put poison in the milk in Mr Murchison's fridge, knowing he'd drink it on his way to bed.

I had discovered a definite, actual murder – and a definite, actual murderer.

But how could I work out who he was?

I got back into the lift in the kitchen and tugged on the rope as a signal to Rose, and she lowered me down. It seemed to take even longer than before, but at last her scared face came into view, hair first then eyes and nose and mouth. I crouched down so I could see her as quickly as possible and said, 'Rose, I did it! It was murder, and I can prove it!'

Rose gasped, and the lift shook.

'Don't do that! Let me out first!'

'So – I really did kill him?' whispered Rose.

'Don't be stupid!' I said. 'The man you saw killed him. But that wasn't your fault. How were you to know? You're nice.'

'I'm *too* nice,' said Rose miserably.

'Yes,' I agreed. 'But I love you anyway. Now, are you going to help me catch the murderer or not?'

'How? We've only got three days before we go off to Deepdean,' said Rose. 'Should we tell Big Sister what's happened?'

'NO,' I said. 'She missed it, didn't she? She and Daisy and the Mountfitchets. They're terrible detectives and we're much better than them. And we're *not* telling Father. He's leaving us here in this awful country while he goes home without us. He doesn't deserve to know *anything*, not until we've found the murderer and arrested him.'

I crawled out of the lift so we could talk about how to catch the murderer, and Rose sighed.

'Oh, look at your clothes!' she said. 'Your dress is all crinkled, and your shoes are all dirty!'

I made a face at her. Rose cares too much about clothes. But I looked down at myself and saw that it was true.

'Did the murderer look like me?' I asked.

'Oh goodness!' said Rose. 'Yes! His shoes were dirty, and his suit was dusty and creased.'

'You sound like Big Sister,' I grumbled. 'But that's a clue, isn't it? That proves that the murderer must have come up in the lift, even though he didn't go down that way!'

'Ooh!' said Rose. 'Yes!'

'Oh!' I said, very excited because I'd worked something else out. 'And I'll bet I know why he had to use the stairs!

When I was on the lift, I needed you to raise and lower it for me, didn't I?'

Rose looked blankly at me.

'You can't operate the rope and pulley system yourself when you're crouched on the platform. And that means that someone must have raised the lift for him, like you did for me. But they weren't there when he needed to come down again, so he had to use the stairs. So we don't just have one murderer – we have two! Now we just have to work out *why* he couldn't go back down the way he came. What happened to his friend?'

After I'd changed, and got Rose to stop crying, we went down into the basement.

If I didn't know by now that grown-ups lie, the basement would prove it to me. On Sunday, when Rose and I were finally sat down and told that the war was happening (hours too late), they said that if there were an air raid, we could go down into the basement and be safe there, even if a bomb hit the building. Since I am not stupid, it took me no time at all to realize that if a bomb hit this building and we were down at the bottom of it we would be crushed like bugs. Probably the only thing left of us would be a few speckles of blood and some nail parings. And I know the grown-ups know that, because they can't wait to pack us off to stupid Deepdean where we'll be 'safe' – which means that where we are now *isn't* safe.

So grown-ups lie, and the basement is a death trap – but it was also very probably connected to a crime. I turned on the little electric light and peered around in the shadowy corners, looking for suspicious things.

I found plenty of dirt, and folded-up blankets that people have put down here for when the air raids happen, and cart tracks from the butcher and baker and grocer, and footprints – but I wasn't sure which of them were suspicious. They all looked the same, really – just big heavy prints, so much bigger than Rose's and my slippered feet.

'I FOUND SOMETHING!' said Rose with a shriek. 'Oh no, it's just a blanket.'

'Here's the opening to the lift,' I said, peering in. 'There's the door, and the winch to move it upwards – and here's a handprint on the door! No, it's a GLOVE print! Ooh, remember the man you saw was wearing gloves!'

'Isn't it dirty down here?' said Rose, coming to stand next to me. She seemed to have got over her fear a little now that it was obvious there weren't any murderers waiting to pounce on us. 'What if it was just the grocer who left that print?'

'Well, it wasn't!' I said, cross with her. 'The grocer and the butcher and the baker all have horrible thick old worn gloves, see *here*, and *here*, but these prints have been made by nice new leather. You should be able to tell the difference! *This* is the murderer!'

'But what could have happened to his friend?' asked Rose.

I still didn't know, and I told her so. 'We ought to go and look outside,' I said to Rose to distract myself from the crossness I was feeling at not being sure. 'There might be more clues!'

I marched her up the little ramp out of the basement to the service entrance. It was at the back of the building, the other side to the big marble entrance for rich people at the front. That entrance reminds me of the Big House – *our* house – a bit, only much, much uglier and smaller.

Bridget and the maid from the third-floor flat were there in their uniforms, sitting on a bench and talking, and standing opposite them was a woman who looked familiar, only I couldn't work out from where. I stared at her, and she said, 'Hello, Miss Wong.'

Then I realized – it was Mr Murchison's charwoman, who had discovered the body. I wasn't used to seeing her not in her usual uniform.

'Why are you here?' I asked. 'Mr Murchison's dead.' I was suspicious of her, then. A cleaner would easily be able to get into the basement to send the murderer up to Mr Murchison's flat.

'May!' said Bridget. 'Rude! She's just stopped by to tidy the flat before the viewings start.'

'Viewing Mr Murchison's body?' I was hopeful that it might have been brought back, because I wanted to see it. I thought it might help with our investigation.

'Viewing the *flat*,' said Bridget. 'This is London; people are vultures. A place like this will be snapped up.'

I turned on the charwoman. 'Mr Murchison was murdered,' I said, wanting to see if she'd flinch. 'Did you see the person who did it?' Guilty people always show it on their faces, that's what I thought – and even though she couldn't be the man Rose had seen, she might be the one who'd winched him up.

But she just blinked at me, said, 'Don't be silly, dear,' and turned away back to Bridget and the third-floor maid. I wanted to hit her, so instead I pinched Rose hard enough to make her whimper.

'May!' said Bridget to me warningly without even turning round.

'D'you know,' said the third-floor maid, 'that reminds me. Yesterday my sister heard from her friend's cousin's husband that they found a Nazi spy in the drains. The drains!'

'No, it was the Serpentine, my Tuesday lady said so,' said the charwoman. 'And it was *two* spies. They're everywhere, you know! There was two tins of Bovril delivered to her house instead of our usual Horlicks so I threw them away in case they were bombs. We really have to be on the alert. Report *any* suspicious activity.'

'Hmm,' said Bridget. 'Yes. But is that really true about the Serpentine? *Where* did you hear it again?'

I decided to leave them to it. We hadn't worked anything out, and now we were being ignored. I was upset. I had thought I'd be good at detection, but I was just as useless as Rose. How were we supposed to solve this crime? We couldn't go anywhere, or do anything, or get anyone to listen to us properly.

I marched back into the building and out into the marbly front hall. I sat on the stairs with my forehead against the cold metal-smelling railings and felt horrible. Rose sat down next to me. Rose can be annoying, but she knows when I need to be left alone. After a while she went to get her doll book and began to cut out skirts on the step up from mine. I was gnawing on the last of the chewy ginger my mother had packed in my trunk for seasickness. There was no point saving it since I wasn't going to be allowed home.

We sat there while the charwoman went thumping up the stairs past us, the door to Mr Murchison's flat squealing, and down again with another squeak half an hour later. We sat there while Mr Mountfitchet went past, and then the lady from the ground-floor flat with a heavy bundle done up in patterned paper. Then a couple came in through the big main doors, looking about them and smiling at each other. Behind them came a man with light hair and a moustache, carrying a clipboard. I remembered what Bridget had said, and realized the couple must be here to view Mr Murchison's flat – and the man with the clipboard must be the estate agent.

I heard a clatter and turned to see Rose's pale face, her dolls' clothes spilling across the stairs.

'Mei!' she hissed to me in Cantonese, so I knew it was important. 'That man. I've never seen *him* before, I'm sure. But his suit – blue pinstripes, with that lining – that was what the murderer was wearing!'

I had to do something.

The grown-ups hadn't noticed us yet. I pushed myself up on my hands and crawled backwards like a crab up the stairs away from them, nodding for Rose to follow me. She did, more politely than me of course. Rose always looks nice.

I heard their steps across the foyer, then a pause. I hoped that they would take the lift, but then a man's voice said, 'Would you mind if we took the stairs? I never do trust lifts.'

Next to me Rose was making a gentle whimpering noise, her face pinched with horror. Her dolls' clothes were still scattered all over the stairs, and I rushed to pick them up. I was bending them but I was hurrying so I didn't care. (I never care but especially not then.)

We scuttled up, and up and up, the grown-ups' feet always tapping behind us, just round the bend of the stairs. It felt like being in one of my nightmares.

At last, though, we got all the way up to the third floor, higher than Mr Murchison's flat, and heard the squeal as the door opened and shut below us.

We were safe.

I collapsed onto the marble steps in relief. 'They didn't see us!' I whispered.

'I hate this,' said Rose, tears in her eyes. 'This is awful, Mei!'

'Be quiet! Are you *sure* about the suit?' I asked.

'Yes! I remember the way it was cut – it fits this man better. He's different, and the shoes he's wearing are different, black not brown, but the suit's the same. I *remember.*'

It was such a stupid idea – two men sharing a suit – that I wanted to ignore her. But I knew I couldn't.

'All right,' I said. 'We can't just go downstairs. We have to investigate.'

Rose gave a shaky sigh and said, 'If we're caught, Father will kill us.'

'We won't be caught,' I said. 'We're already up above them. We can stay and listen in.'

What I learned that afternoon is that investigation is actually fairly boring most of the time. It's not all creeping through flats that don't belong to you and spotting murderers. It's also sitting until your bum gets frozen into the shape of the stair and your legs ache.

Rose, of course, sat next to me perfectly, cutting out more dolls' clothes.

'They're going to tease you about that at Deepdean,' I said. 'Dolls are for babies.'

'But it's fashion!' said Rose.

I sighed. Rose is no fun.

After a while we heard the couple come out of Mr Murchison's flat. I leaned forward so that my face was pressed against the stair rails and listened.

'—nice,' said the man's voice.

'A little outdated but—' said the woman, and then some other things I didn't catch. I still sometimes miss bits when people I don't know talk in English.

'—did you say it was?' said the man, his voice rising up in a question.

'—thousand—' said another man's voice – the man in the murderer's suit.

Both the other man's and the woman's voices raised in amazement. 'But really! We've seen much bigger places for half that!' he said indignantly. 'I was led to believe that—'

'—thought this was a serious proposition!' agreed the woman. 'And in wartime too! Bobby, come along.'

And off they went into the lift.

We sat on the stairs all that afternoon, and listened to the estate agent trot up and down the stairs, and the same thing happen two more times, with two more couples, who seemed equally upset when they learned how expensive the flat was. Next to me Rose even began to calm down. The estate agent hadn't noticed we were there, and he didn't seem to be doing anything more dangerous than showing boring grown-ups round the flat. I was tired and annoyed and frustrated, because this investigation was not going the way I expected, and I still didn't know how I was supposed to solve it.

I took a deep breath and thought about what I knew.

Mr Murchison had been murdered, and the man who had killed him had been wearing the same suit as the estate agent who was now showing off Mr Murchison's flat. The man who had killed him had help to take the service lift up, but then he had to walk down using the stairs afterwards. So had the estate agent been the person helping him? And if so, why? It must be to do with the flat, I thought. Did they want to sell it? The estate agent seemed to be trying to do exactly the opposite, which was interesting. Was there something *in* the flat? Was it treasure? We knew Mr Murchison had been rich. But then if it was treasure, why didn't the murderer just steal it, instead of killing Mr Murchison?

I was still thinking furiously about this when Bridget came out on the stairs to call us for tea.

'Where have you two been?' she asked when we reached the kitchen. Rose looked at me big-eyed.

'Solving a mystery,' I said – and of course Bridget said, 'Sure you have,' and put down our plates in front of us.

I glared at her while I struggled with my knife and fork – English food comes in stupid lumps you can't get your mouth around without chopping it up; they're not polite enough to cut it up for the people who have to eat it – and I thought and I thought. We only had three days before we went to Deepdean, and I didn't know how to solve this case.

I stayed up late peering round the edges of the blackout curtains to look for enemy soldiers again, but I still couldn't see any. Rose apologized in her sleep. I heard Father come in when the lights were off and he thought we must both be sleeping, but I stuck my head further round the curtain and growled and he went away again without even reminding me that I was breaking blackout. I still wasn't talking to him.

Next morning, Friday, I realized that because Bridget had been packing our school trunks, the only clothes left out were my Deepdean uniform and the pink dress that matches Rose's. My other dress was in the wash. I hate looking like Rose but I refuse to look like I go to that stupid school a moment before I have to, so I put on the pink dress.

It itched and all through that morning I got crosser and crosser. After lunchtime I was so angry – at Father and at Mr Mountfitchet and at Bridget and at Rose, even, for being so pathetic that she let a murder happen (which isn't fair but it was how I felt) – that I went storming downstairs and out of the back of the building to hit the wall. I wanted to run and run like I would at home, but this is London and there's nowhere to do that; it's all grey and close and as itchy as my dress.

I was digging my fingers angrily into the stuff between the bricks and getting them scratched and dirty under the nails when I heard a cart pull through the archway and heavy footsteps approaching. They faltered, and I turned round because I wanted to know why – and there was our grocer, the one who I had seen talking to the maid on Wednesday afternoon, with a bag on his shoulder, looking at me. It was only a second, and then he pulled his face into a grin and said, 'Hello, young lady!' but I knew what I had seen – an expression like I was the most frightening thing he'd ever caught sight of.

When I was a baby I used to think that people could hear my thoughts, and sometimes I still imagine it's true. Maybe he'd heard me thinking about the case. But that was silly. All he'd been able to see was me, in my pink dress, a person who isn't interesting at all at home, but in London seems to make everyone stare. But it wasn't my face he'd been looking at.

It was – it was my dress.

And then I had it. There was only one person in London who'd be afraid to see a little Chinese girl in a pink dress.

I looked up at Mr Murchison's murderer, and I *yelled*.

I have a very loud voice. I'm always being told off for it, but I have to be loud because otherwise no one pays attention to me.

Mr Murchison's murderer put out his hand, in a horrible dirty glove, to shut me up, and I screamed harder. I looked down at his shoes – and they were brown and dirty, the shoes that Rose had described the murderer wearing. I knew I was right.

Out ran Bridget, with Rose just behind her.

'HELP!' I screamed. 'I'M BEING KIDNAPPED!'

This was a lie obviously, and such a bad one that even I felt guilty about it – I hate joking about kidnapping, especially near Rose, but I had to do *something*. Bridget leaped forward and somehow – she moved too quickly for my eyes to follow it – suddenly the murderer was in a headlock under her arm. I want to know how she does that. It looks useful.

'I wouldn't!' the murderer was shouting. 'I never!'

Then Rose looked at his shoes too (because I was pointing at them) and screamed, 'HE KILLED MR MURCHISON!' Then she fainted.

Muttering terrible things under her breath, Bridget dragged the murderer up against the wall and tied him to the drainpipe with a bit of rope that she had in her pocket. She was very strong, I realized. I was impressed.

'Explain!' she said to me.

'He didn't actually kidnap me,' I admitted. 'But Rose is right. He's a murderer and he killed Mr Murchison and he's working with the estate agent and they want –' I paused while I thought about it again – 'I *think* they want the flat. Mr Murchison's flat. The estate agent is telling everyone who comes to look at it that it's thousands and thousands of pounds more than anyone seems to be expecting, so that everyone just leaves. I'll bet they're spies! And – and they want to spy on you and the Mountfitchets!'

'You're talking absolute nonsense,' said Bridget, shaking her head.

'I'm NOT!' I said crossly. 'It's all true but you just don't LISTEN. I've been saying for DAYS that someone killed Mr Murchison, and it was HIM! He put poison in his milk and he left a note in his study, at his writing desk – but he wrote it somewhere else, which is why there's no sign of it on the blotter. It all fits and if I was TALLER, you'd LISTEN TO ME!'

'It's hard not to listen to you,' said Bridget drily.

'HE IS A MURDERER!' I shouted.

'Hmm,' said Bridget. 'Sure he is. And you're the Queen of Sheba.'

Then she froze, her hands patting through the murderer's pockets. 'What's THIS, then?' she said sharply, and held up a handkerchief.

'It's a handkerchief,' said Rose helpfully. She had come round – or she hadn't really fainted at all. 'It's pretty.'

'It's very pretty,' said Bridget, untying him. 'But this embroidery – it's a code. And not one I've seen before, either. Get up, you! You're coming with me.'

This she said to the murderer, who stood up – and then tried to escape. He bolted away towards his cart while Rose screamed – and Bridget leaped, kicked out her leg and felled him neatly.

'I told you!' I said. 'He's a MURDERER!'

'There's certainly some funny business here,' said Bridget. 'You two, come with me.'

Up we went to the Mountfitchets' flat, Bridget dragging the man behind her. Mrs Mountfitchet was sitting making notes on a bit of card. She looked up as we came in.

'Good grief!' she said. 'What have you done to the grocer?'

'He's a MURDERER,' I said.

'Hush, you,' said Bridget. 'Lucy, this man has a code on him. Embroidered. Look at it, will you?'

Mrs Mountfitchet looked and frowned, holding it very close to her eyes and then far away again.

'I've seen something like this before,' she said. 'It isn't one of ours.'

'That's what I thought,' said Bridget, and they looked at each other as though they wanted to say something but not in front of children.

That was when I realized that the murderer really *might* be an enemy soldier, the kind that I'd been looking for every night. It's a funny feeling knowing that you guessed something right. I wondered whether I might be good at detecting, after all.

Mrs Mountfitchet and Bridget were still holding the murderer in our living room when Mr Mountfitchet came in.

'Good grief!' he said when he saw us all.

'THIS IS THE MURDERER!' I said to him.

'Our grocer,' said Mrs Mountfitchet (ignoring me, as usual), 'has enemy codes on his person. Why weren't we informed that there might be a threat from certain quarters?'

'Really, Lucy, I—' Mr Mountfitchet began. Then he shook his head. 'Distracted,' he said. 'Too much going on in the world at large. Are you sure?'

'Take a look,' said Mrs Mountfitchet grimly, and Mr Mountfitchet pored over the handkerchief.

It still looked just like a handkerchief to me, and I was impatient because although the murderer had been captured, the man who had helped him was still walking about selling flats to people.

'He's not alone!' I said, but no one listened to me.

'It's true!' said Rose. 'They were sharing a suit!'

Of course the grown-ups ignored her too. It sounded like something the dolls from her book would do. And perhaps they'd have gone on ignoring us, no matter how loudly we spoke, until we were at Deepdean and couldn't do anything – if we hadn't heard the sound of something smashing in the flat above us.

'IT'S MR MURCHISON'S GHOST!' screamed Rose – and that was so silly that the grown-ups, apart from Mrs Mountfitchet, who was watching the murderer, ran out onto the landing and up the stairs.

The door to Mr Murchison's flat was open, and inside was the estate agent, standing next to Mr Murchison's desk, which now had a hole it its side, and holding a funny little device, all wires.

'I'm fitting a new telephone line,' he said weakly, rubbing his moustache – and that was when I realized that although grown-ups don't listen to children when they say something absolutely true, they notice when other grown-ups say something obviously false. And that was quite enough to get Mr and Mrs Mountfitchet to investigate.

After that things moved very quickly. Grown-ups CAN move quickly when they want to, which makes it even more frustrating when they don't. The estate agent was tied up too, and Bridget was dispatched to find where he worked.

He really was an estate agent, it turned out, and the grocer really was a grocer. Only they were also working for The Other Side, which means Hitler. I heard this by standing next to the vent again and eavesdropping, and I'm glad I did, because the grown-ups never would have told us this face to face.

The grocer had worked out who Mr and Mrs Mountfitchet were by talking to the maid from the third-floor flat – who was a terrible gossip, as I should have realized from overhearing her talk to the charwoman and Bridget. He thought he could learn even more useful official secrets by getting access to the flat above theirs and using listening devices to spy on them. So he talked to his estate-agent friend, and together they decided to get rid of Mr Murchison and then use his flat to listen in on the Mountfitchets.

On the day before Mr Murchison was found dead, the grocer had arrived at his regular time, with the estate agent hidden inside his cart. He'd wheeled the cart through the service entrance and down the little ramp into the basement, and then put all the shopping for each flat into the service lift and sent it up to them as usual. Then – well, I can't be sure what happened then, because the grown-ups won't tell me. But because of what happened when I tried to make Rose go into the lift, I have a suspicion. I think that the estate agent was supposed to go up to the flat and poison the milk and come down again via the stairs. The grocer could have gone off on the rest of his rounds as normal, after all, and if anyone saw the estate agent he could lie and say that Mr Murchison had asked him to value the flat. But it all went wrong because, as Rose and I heard while he was showing people around the flat, the estate agent doesn't like lifts any more than we do. He must have panicked when he was faced with that horrid little dark space and refused to go in.

So the plan had to change. The estate agent and the grocer swapped clothes, as quickly as possible, and the grocer was winched up in the lift to the second floor, wearing the nice estate-agent suit but his own shoes. (Rose says she should have worked it out, for no one wears a blue suit and brown shoes together.)

The grocer climbed out into Mr Murchison's flat, planted the note (he must have written it beforehand to be quicker) and put poison in Mr Murchison's milk so Mr Murchison would die later that day or the next morning once he was long gone. Meanwhile, the estate agent carried on with his friend's rounds, to make sure that no one noticed their deliveries arriving late and asked difficult questions. Everyone knows when the grocer arrives each day, after all. But he made mistakes – and that was the reason for the Bovril being delivered instead of Horlicks.

And, of course, the grocer ran into trouble too when he had to take the stairs back down. If he'd been seen by anyone in the flats, they might have recognized him – it really was a silly plan now that he was pretending to be the estate agent. I'm sure he must have been delighted when the only person he saw was Rose. He didn't realize what bad luck it was for him, and even worse luck that he tried to pay her off and tell her a lie instead of simply ignoring her.

I'd have done much better. If I'd made up a plan like that, I wouldn't have let it be ruined by my friend who was afraid of small spaces, and two little girls.

But grown-ups never do think about children catching them out.

So I was proud of myself, even though the grown-ups didn't give me proper credit. Only Big Sister Hazel even came to talk to me about it on Friday evening, on her way out to somewhere exciting and grown-up with Daisy.

'I'm sorry, Mei,' she said, sitting down next to me on the sofa where I was sulking. Daisy nodded to her and went to wait in the hall. 'I should have listened to you.'

'Yes you should!' I said. 'Because I'm an excellent detective!'

'No you—' Hazel began, and then she sighed and said, 'I suppose you are.'

'I've helped solve THREE murders now!' I said. 'You should take me seriously!'

I knew she wouldn't, though. Big Sisters never can.

'It won't be so bad at Deepdean, you know,' said Hazel after a pause. 'You'll like it in the end. I did.'

'Humph!' I said. 'But you like English things! I'm not like you, and I don't want to go. Why can't Father take me home with him? It's because he doesn't love me as much as Teddy.'

I felt angry tears in my eyes at that, and I scrubbed them away.

'Mei! Don't be silly!'

'I'm not being. He loves you because you're the oldest and he loves Rose because she's the sweetest and he loves Teddy because he's a boy.'

'And he loves you because you're the fiercest,' said Hazel. 'He wants you to stay safe, and he knows you're brave enough to handle this. You're not afraid of anything, and I don't believe you'll let a *school* frighten you. Can I tell you something, if you promise not to say it to anyone?'

I considered. 'Only if it's not something bad,' I said.

Hazel laughed. 'It's not bad at all,' she said. 'But I think you might have to look after Rose a bit. She's like

I was – she can't wait to go and live in a storybook. But school isn't like books, and English people aren't always as nice as they look. *You* know that already, but Rose has to learn. So will you watch her for me?'

'Yes. But you have to promise to come and get me if it's awful,' I said.

'Promise,' said Hazel. 'But only if it's really awful. If it's only *mostly*, try to bear it.'

'All right. But I'm still angry at Father. He'd better come and get me as soon as the war's over.'

Hazel looked worried, and then tried to pretend she wasn't. She really is turning into a grown-up.

'The war might not be over for a while, Mei,' she said. 'Things might get quite difficult before they get better.'

'So we *will* be invaded?' I asked.

'Not if I can help it,' said Hazel with a determined look on her face. 'I'm not going to Oxford, no matter what Father says. I'm going to stay here and help Daisy and Uncle Felix and Aunt Lucy. I think I can really make a difference.'

'Can I stay too?' I asked. 'Please, Big Sister, don't make me go to school! I could be really useful!'

'Absolutely not,' said Hazel. 'Mei, you're still too little. You have to wait until you're older. For the moment, the best place for you is Deepdean. Leave everything else up to us.'

Which is when I made a decision.

The war might be an exciting adventure after all, but I still want it to end so I can leave England and go home. And that means I can't just sit around waiting to get older. I have to help *now* – and that means doing what Big Sister Hazel is doing, and Mr and Mrs Mountfitchet and Bridget, whether or not they ask me to.

I'm not just going to be a detective. I'm going to be a spy.

I'm going to uncover more people like Mr Murchison's murderers, and I'm going to do it so well that Hitler is frightened away and everything goes back to the way it used to be. Then I can get back to Mother and Teddy and Father.

I'm going to make everyone listen to what I have to say.

# May's Guide to England

I've learned that the English language is full of a lot of confusing words. Big Sister Hazel has been putting together these stories, and she's asked me to write some explanations for you of the most difficult ones. She thinks I don't know that she wants me to improve my English while I do it. The joke's on her, because the only reason I'm learning English now is so that I can be the best spy in the world. Hah.

- **Aertex** — a sort of cotton used for shirts.

- **Air-raid shelter** — a place in your house or garden where you go to hide from bombs.

- **Automaton** — another word for robot.

- **Amah** — in Hong Kong it means a nanny or nursemaid.

- **Bigamy** — when you marry more than one person at the same time. In England this is bad.

- **Blackout curtain** – big heavy curtains everyone puts up to stop light from their houses being seen by German planes.

- **Bosh** – nonsense.

- **Bounder** – a bad, dishonourable man.

- **Brilliantine** – stuff men put on their hair to make it shiny and slicked-down.

- **Brig** – a ship's prison.

- **Bunbreak** – according to Hazel, this is a Deepdean word that means a time when you stop lessons to eat biscuits or cake.

- **Charwoman** – another word for cleaner.

- **Clodhopper** – a fool with big feet!

- **Congee** – in Hong Kong, a delicious breakfast food of rice porridge. I call it *juk*, but Rose tells me that the word 'congee' comes from India.

- **Evacuees** – people, particularly children, who have to leave their homes in a city and go live in the country so as to be safe from air-raids and bombs. In a way, Rose and I are being evacuated to Deepdean.

- **Fascism** – a horrid, cruel sort of political belief that hates difference and crushes opposition. Hitler is a fascist.

- **Halloa** – a shout or exclamation.

- **Jaw** – to chat or talk.

- **Jilt** – to abandon someone you were in love with.

- **Kate Greenaway dresses** – fancy dresses that Rose would think were pretty. I don't. They're named after the illustrator, Kate Greenaway.

- **Master** – the Weston word for teacher.

- **Minor** – I thought this meant small, but Hazel told me that when you're at a boys' school it means younger. So Rose and I would both be Wong Minor if we were boys.

- **Mistress** – the Deepdean word for teacher.

- **Monocle** – an eyeglass that is only for one of your eyes.

- **Namby-pamby** – silly and weak.

- **Nazi** – someone who supports Hitler, the horrid German leader we are at war with. Not all Germans are Nazis, though.

- **Quoits** — a game where you try to throw a ring over an upright peg. It's very popular on ships. I think it's boring.

- **Registry office** — a place people go to get married if they don't want to do it in a church.

- **Reticule** — another word for handbag.

- **Saree** — a long draped piece of clothing that Indian women wear.

- **Satin** — a silky fabric.

- **Scree** — a mass of loose stones on the side of a hill.

- **Shilling** — English money. It's worth twelve pence. There are twenty shillings in a pound.

- **Shrimp** — a Deepdean word for the littlest girls.

- **Slogging** — a Weston word for doing work for someone else, tidying up after them and so on.

- **Tulle** — another type of fabric, a sort of gauzy netting.

- **Wireless** — something you listen to the radio on.

# HIEROGLYPHIC ALPHABET

# MORSE CODE

Morse code was invented in 1836 by a man named Samuel Morse. He was trying to show how messages could be sent as sounds along telegraph wires, which had never been done before.

There are only two types of signal in Morse code: a short one and a long one.

A short signal (it's called a dit, but you can just say 'dot'), is shown by a dot like this: .

A long signal (which is actually called a dah!) is shown by a dash like this: –

The most famous Morse signal is SOS, which stands for 'Save Our Souls'. It's what you send when you want to call for help. An S is three dots in a row, and an O is three dashes in a row. So SOS in Morse code is: ... / – – – / ... (I've used a / to separate the letters in the codes.)

Daisy and I used Morse code on our Orient Express case. We did it by tapping sharply for each dot, and scraping our nails along the wall for a dash. It worked very well!

See if you can use the table below to figure out the Morse code in Uncle Felix's notes in 'The Case of the Missing Treasure' like Hazel did!

| Letter | Morse |
|--------|-------|
| A | · – |
| B | – · · · |
| C | – · – · |
| D | – · · |
| E | · |
| F | · · – · |
| G | – – · |
| H | · · · · |
| I | · · |
| J | · – – – |
| K | – · – |
| L | · – · · |
| M | – – |
| N | – · |
| O | – – – |
| P | · – – · |
| Q | – – · – |
| R | · – · |
| S | · · · |
| T | – |
| U | · · – |
| V | · · · – |
| W | · – – |
| X | – · · – |
| Y | – · – – |
| Z | – – · · |

# Author's Note

**The Case of the Uninvited Guest (January 1936)**

People don't usually believe me when I try to explain how long publishing takes – I think the creation of this story is a great (if slightly extreme) example. I first published *Mistletoe and Murder* in late 2015, and got my first requests for a short story that explained what exactly *did* happen at Uncle Felix and Aunt Lucy's mysterious wedding almost immediately. I've been fielding them ever since – it's by far the most popular short story request I get – and for years I've been promising you all that you'd find out what happened . . . one day.

I got married myself in a tiny registry office ceremony in 2016, and for our first wedding anniversary in 2017 I decided to finally write the story of Felix and Lucy's wedding as a gift for my husband. And in 2021 'The Case of the Uninvited Guest' is finally publishing, just in time for . . . our fifth wedding anniversary. See? One day.

Although we had absolutely no uninvited guests at our wedding, nor did any of the plot points in this story happen to us, the setting of this mystery (and a lot of the details, from the room to Aunt Lucy's blue and red outfit to the flowers Daisy and Hazel carry) is taken from my memories of that day. I changed the name of our registry office and moved it to London, to better fit the Mountfitchets, so unfortunately you can't visit the St Pancras Registry Office. Headington Grammar also does not exist, of course, though its name is similar to a real school.

This is one of my favourite stories from the collection, because it's so personal to me. I hope you agree that it's been worth waiting for!

Oh, and one more thing: unlike Felix and Lucy's cake, ours was chocolate. I think Hazel would have approved.

**The Case of the Missing Treasure (May 1936)**

This story started life as a tiny standalone book, first published in March 2019 as a sort of prequel to the book *Death in the Spotlight*. We decided to include it in this anthology to make sure that all fans could have equal access to it – plus it's a really fun story that I'm still very proud of.

When I was growing up, my mother worked at the Ashmolean Museum in Oxford, and as an adult I spent some time working in the British Museum, at the British Museum Press. I love both museums, especially the ancient Egyptian collections in each – but as I've learned more about the history of museum collection I've also come to feel the same deep unease that George does about what these objects are doing in the UK, so removed from their historical context and cultural heritage.

This is also, of course, the first time that Egypt is mentioned in my books – when I wrote it I was already planning Daisy and Hazel's Egyptian adventure, the book that became *Death Sets Sail*. So you can see it as the first step on the road to the end of this series! The Unlucky Mummy is real, by the way – though the curse on it is (probably) not . . . Please don't climb into any mummy cases to find out.


## The Case of the Drowned Pearl (July 1936)

This story was originally written for World Book Day 2020, a celebration of books and reading in the UK and Ireland. If you live in those countries, you may already have a pocket-sized copy of this story – but I know many of my fans don't, and so, just as with 'The Case of the Missing Treasure', we decided to include it in this anthology to make sure that everyone has equal access to it.

It's the only short story I've written so far starring Daisy and Hazel that involves a murder, and it was inspired by my experiences visiting British beaches as someone born in the USA. If you (like me and Hazel) expect a beach to be hot and sandy, with warm light-blue water, the reality of sharp pebbles and shockingly cold dark waves is at first less than pleasant. Although I'm fonder of the experience now than I was at first, I still refuse to swim.

The beach in this story, by the way, was based on Worthing beach. I was also inspired by Gertrude Ederle, the first woman and sixth person to swim the English Channel in 1926 (in a time that beat every one of those five men!), and the Indian soldiers treated at the Brighton Pavilion during and after World War One.

## The Hound of Weston School (December 1936)

Eagle-eyed readers will have spotted Hazel's question to Alexander about 'your problem with the dog' in *Death Sets Sail* – and this is the story of that case! It's Alex and George's version of *The Hound of the Baskervilles* (my favourite Sherlock Holmes story), and I wrote it during the first lockdown in the UK, two weeks before we got our own fluffy black dog, Howl. In the first draft of this story I called the dog 'Howl' in two places, so you can see what I was thinking about during the writing process. Howl himself is now a fully grown cockapoo and (unlike the dog in the story, who I'm imagining to be a surprising mix of many breeds including wolfhound, mastiff and greyhound) has turned out to be a soft-hearted lapdog who, when left ungroomed, greatly resembles a mop with eyes. But in appearance the puppy version of this dog is very much based on him.

One (hopefully obvious) thing to say about dog care: if you have a dog, please do not keep it in a cave, feed it cake, or let fireworks off anywhere near it, even after the kind of careful noise training given in this story. These are all bad ideas (although it *is* a good idea to get your dog used to loud noises early in life – speak to a trainer about how to do this safely)! Children in adventure stories like *The Famous Five* have the kind of cheerful, loose attitude to pet ownership that George and Alexander display in this story, which is why I've included it (plus the cave was absolutely necessary to the plot), but in 2021 we know a lot better. Be kind to your pets!

**The Case of the Second Scream (April 1937)**

A few very committed fans may recognize the bare bones of this case. I first plotted it out in 2017 around the publication of Daisy and Hazel's Hong Kong adventure, *A Spoonful of Murder*, and it had a brief first life as an interactive online quiz. When I came to write the stories for this anthology, I decided to flesh out my plan and turn it into a fully fledged story – and this is the result. Please note that I know next to nothing about cruise ships, and any correct information in this story is due to my eagle-eyed and very helpful readers. The SS *Strathclyde* was the name of a real ship that sank in 1870, by the way – but obviously that never happened in Daisy and Hazel's version of reality.

Whether or not you did play along with the original mystery, though, you'll find a lot of new information in this story, because I decided to use this case as an excuse to tell another story that you've all been eager to know: what happens just after the end of *Death Sets Sail*.

We're heading to the Second World War for the next series (read on for more about that!), but what about the three years between the events of *Death Sets Sail* and May Wong's first case? This story gives a *little* bit of the answer, and I hope at the end of it you'll be able to imagine a bit more of the rest. The Spanish Civil War, by the way, took place between 1936 and 1939. Although it was, of course, fought in Spain by Spanish forces, anti-fascist young people from all over Europe heard about what was going on and travelled to the war to help the Republicans (as in, people who wanted the country to be a democratic republic) fight against General Franco's fascist army. This is a very basic explanation, so if you're interested at all I suggest you find out more!

I think that George and Lavinia, with their Communist sympathies, would absolutely have been drawn into the struggle – I'm imagining that their experience of the war would be very similar to events in a book that I adored when I was younger, and which I have been thinking of throughout this series: *Hons and Rebels* by Jessica Mitford. Older readers (I'd say twelve and older) may also enjoy it – but be warned: it's a true story and there is, sadly, no happy ending to it. George and Lavinia, on the other hand, will both appear in *The Ministry of Unladylike Activity* series, as will Alexander and fan favourite Amina.

### May Wong and the Deadly Flat (September 1939)

I created this story to connect the world of *Murder Most Unladylike* with the world of *The Ministry of Unladylike Activity*. We first met Hazel's littlest sister May Wong in *A Spoonful of Murder*, and she helped detect the case in *Death Sets Sail*, but here for the first time she's the lead detective, properly starting out her crime-solving career (with a little help from her other sister, Rose).

The story is set during the very first few days of the Second World War, in September 1939. I planned and wrote it at the end of the first UK Covid lockdown, in May and June 2020, and I couldn't help seeing some eerie similarities between the two historical moments. Shortages of everyday goods, nationwide public addresses, and (especially for someone May's age) a sense of trapped waiting with the added suspicion that no one in control really knows how to deal with the situation. It's no surprise that I decided to have May be stuck in the UK, unable to travel home to the (apparent) safety of Hong Kong, or that almost the whole story takes place inside Uncle Felix and Aunt Lucy's block of flats.

In the *Ministry of Unladylike Activity*, May will have to share her spotlight with two fellow detectives, but here, for one case only, she gets to be the star. I hope you enjoy this story, and May's character (it's no secret that she's one of my favourites) – and I hope it's made you even more excited for *Ministry*. May and her new friends will be back soon!

# Acknowledgements

I wrote this book during a very strange time in all our lives. I don't know that anyone had a positive and productive 2020 or 2021. I certainly didn't. I would definitely compare it, creatively, to floating in outer space while simultaneously swimming through mud. I frankly cannot believe this book exists, although I'm pleased that it does.

I lost my father in January 2021, after a long illness, just as we were finishing work on the text of *Once Upon a Crime*. That felt, creatively, like being repeatedly hit by a pole (while floating in outer space, while swimming through mud). My father was the reason I began writing *Murder Most Unladylike* – he first became ill just before I started the very first draft in 2010 – and there's a certain symmetry about the fact that he made it all the way to the publication of *Death Sets Sail*, the final murder mystery in the series, in summer 2020. I certainly never expected to have so much time with him, though of course I wish he'd seen me write ten more series.

I feel so lucky that I was able to be with him and my mother during his last days, and also very proud to finally work out why I've been writing all of these books: so that my mother could listen to them on audio every night to help her get back to sleep. Mum, I hope you like this new addition to your collection. I also feel incredibly lucky to be supported through this whole thing by my brilliant, loving husband, David – the only person I believe when he tells me everything is going to be OK.

In March 2021 I also lost another small but significant member of my *Murder Most Unladylike* support network – my beloved pet bearded dragon, Watson. She has been there to cast her beady eye over my writing process from the very first book onwards, and these days my study feels very empty without her. The universe, I think, really wanted me to know that I've come to the end of an era.

And now, my thank yous.

Thank you to my readers, whose thoughtful feedback made these stories smarter, more insightful and more realistic: Anne Miller, Aishwarya Subramanian, Wei Ming Kam, Joel Rochester, Pippa Lacey, Caroline Thrasher, Kieran Gray, L. J. Moss, James Harkin and Kathie Booth Stevens.

Thanks to Team Bunbreak, scattered by the pandemic but still as wonderful as ever: Natalie Doherty, Ruth Bennett, Harriet Venn, Chloe Parkinson, Michael Bedo, Sonia Razvi (whose amazing work on these books is now officially over, but whose contribution has meant so much over the years!), Steph Barrett, Wendy Shakespeare, Kat Baker, Jan Bielecki, Jennie Roman, Julia Bruce, Petra

Bryce, Pippa Shaw, Francesca Dow and everyone else at Puffin who has worked so hard to make this series what it is. Thanks, too, to the audio team under Roy McMillan, and to the brilliant Katie Leung, who has read Hazel's voice for so many books.

Nina Tara brings Hazel and Daisy (and now May!) to life on all of my covers – I'm so grateful for the beautiful work she's put in over the years.

Thank you to my agent, Gemma Cooper, who saw something in my first draft of *Murder Most Unladylike* all those years ago, and who has continued to be my biggest support and champion.

And, finally, thank you to *you*, reader, whoever and wherever you are. I am so immensely proud and thrilled to have had you with me for so many books. What an adventure we've been on together! And now I can't wait for the next one.

# A COMPLETE HISTORY OF

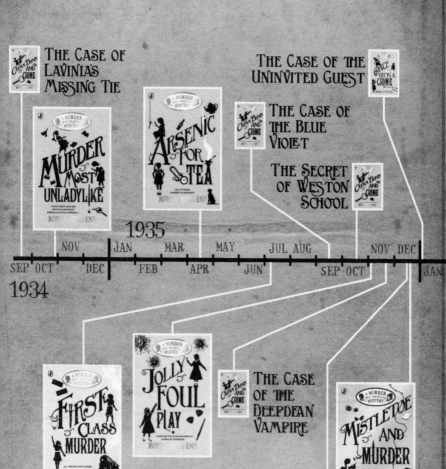

THE CASE OF LAVINIA'S MISSING TIE

THE CASE OF THE UNINVITED GUEST

THE CASE OF THE BLUE VIOLET

MURDER MOST UNLADYLIKE

ARSENIC FOR TEA

THE SECRET OF WESTON SCHOOL

1935

NOV | JAN | MAR | MAY | JUL AUG | NOV DEC

SEP OCT | DEC | FEB | APR | JUN | SEP OCT | JAN

1934

FIRST CLASS MURDER

JOLLY FOUL PLAY

THE CASE OF THE DEEPDEAN VAMPIRE

MISTLETOE AND MURDER

THE MYSTERY OF THE MISSING BUNBREAK

# CASES SOLVED BY THE DETECTIVE SOCIETY

THE CASE OF THE MISSING TREASURE

THE CASE OF THE SECOND SCREAM

1936     1937     1939

FEB   APR   JUN   JUL   SEP   DEC   FEB   SEP

MAR   MAY   AUG   OCT   NOV   JAN   MAR

THE CASE OF THE DROWNED PEARL

DEATH SETS SAIL

MAY WONG AND THE DEADLY FLAT

THE HOUND OF WESTON SCHOOL

Hello Detectives,

I hope you enjoyed *Once Upon a Crime*! This anthology brings together all of the remaining stories about Daisy and Hazel and their friends, and finishes up the Murder Most Unladylike series.

But don't worry, this is not the last you'll read about Daisy and Hazel's world! At the moment I'm writing a brand-new series called the *Ministry of Unladylike Activity*. It's set during the Second World War, and stars May Wong (who you've just met properly in 'May Wong and the Deadly Flat'), as well as two totally new characters. They're going to be just as important as May (which she won't like much at first!) – and in fact, one of them is going to be the series' main narrator . . .

The first book, *The Ministry of Unladylike Activity*, takes place in the autumn of 1940. In the UK, the Blitz is entering its most terrifying phase, meaning that a lot of children are being evacuated out of cities into the countryside. And some of those evacuees are spies in disguise . . .

May and friends are on a deadly secret Ministry mission to infiltrate a country house and find out crucial information about one of its inhabitants. They're expecting danger – but they're not expecting a murder. Now someone is dead, and our detectives have to crack the case . . . before the killer strikes again!

Expect twists, turns, puzzles, scares and a brilliant new group of crime-solving friends. I can't wait to introduce you to my new detectives and their first mystery – see you in 2022!

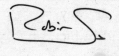